T0319123

HOME REPAIR AND ROMANCE

Keagan's ladder leaned against the roof of the front porch. When he saw her, he called, "The paint's already dry up here. If you bring me the shutters you painted, I'll put them up at the two windows."

She gave him a thumbs-up and almost ran to the barn. He'd asked her, not one of the others, to help him. She hurried to grab a pair of shutters. When she got back, he'd come down for them and jammed a screwdriver and screws in his jeans pocket. Then he scurried up to the porch roof and stood on that to work. Karli squirmed. The porch roof slanted downward and didn't look safe to her.

"Be careful," she said.

He gave her a look. "I've been balancing on a ladder to paint the peaks all day. I think I'll survive this."

She went to get the shutters for the second window and climbed a few rungs to hand them to him. Once he'd finished installing them, he started down. He'd reached the ground when Karli noticed someone's paint brush lying on the roof. She scrambled up the ladder to reach it and then carefully retraced her steps. Before she reached the bottom, though, two strong hands lifted her and set her on the ground. Keagan's touch sent heat through her fleece hoodie.

She turned and found herself toe to toe with him. His solid chest was eye level. She looked up at his strong jawline, his lips. She sucked in her breath and tilted her head, staring up into his cobalt-blue eyes. She could smell his scent—clean and manly. His gaze burned with intensity. Her lips parted. One more inch and she'd be pressing against him...

Special Delivery

A Mill Pond romance

Judi Lynn

LYRICAL PRESS
Kensington Publishing Corp.
www.kensingtonbooks.com

LYRICAL PRESS BOOKS are published by

Kensington Publishing Corp.
119 West 40th Street
New York, NY 10018

All Kensington titles, imprints, and distributed lines are available at special quantity discounts for bulk purchases for sales promotion, premiums, fund-raising, educational, or institutional use.

Special book excerpts or customized printings can also be created to fit specific needs. For details, write or phone the office of the Kensington Sales Manager: Kensington Publishing Corp., 119 West 40th Street, New York, NY 10018. Attn. Sales Department. Phone: 1-800-221-2647.

Lyrical Press and Lyrical Press logo Reg. U.S. Pat. & TM Off.

First Electronic Edition: November 2018
eISBN-13: 978-1-5161-0139-9
eISBN-10: 1-5161-0139-1

First Print Edition: November 2018
ISBN-13: 978-1-5161-0140-5
ISBN-10: 1-5161-0140-5

Printed in the United States of America

Books by Judi Lynn

COOKING UP TROUBLE
OPPOSITES DISTRACT
LOVE ON TAP
SPICING THINGS UP
FIRST KISS, ON THE HOUSE
SPECIAL DELIVERY

Published by Kensington Publishing Corporation

Chapter 1

The house looked deserted, but Karli Redding knocked on her grandfather's door. Maybe the mean old coot had been carted off to a nursing home during the night and no one told them. He was lucky the house was still standing. It looked worse than the last time she was here. When was that? Ten, fifteen years ago? Its roof looked new, but paint peeled on the clapboards. The porch sagged where a column had rotted, and tall, dead weeds choked the yard.

She pulled her jacket closer. The air had a bite to it. When she exhaled, her breath misted, but it could be worse for the first of November. She knocked again, waited, and turned to leave, then decided she'd better call Mom first and check in. "I'm in Mill Pond. The place looks deserted. No one answered the door."

"Dad can't get around much anymore," her mother warned. "He's pretty much confined to his bed or wheelchair. Just knock and let yourself in. That's what everyone does, according to Keagan's phone call. Keagan was going to meet you there. Maybe he got hung up and is running a little late."

It was the first time Mom had given her a name. "Who's Keagan?"

"He lives on the farm next to Dad's. I'd have come to deal with this, but I'm in the middle of a project at work."

Yeah, right. That's what Mom kept saying. Not that Karli blamed her. Mom was a strong woman, and she'd overcome a lot, but memories of living with her dad still haunted her. No one wanted to be around him, and Mom couldn't make herself come back to face him again. Axel could make a saint want to strangle him. Thankfully, Karli had only seen him on rare visits when she was young. More than enough. Not so much that she couldn't do what needed to be done. It would be easier for her than

Mom and she was between traveling nurse jobs. Not that she'd meant to spend her time off dealing with a pain-in-the-ass geriatric.

Karli took a deep breath, bracing herself. What a depressing place! The farm fields spread as far as she could see, all of them neglected. The barn's roof needed to be repaired. It had taken all the determination she had to return to Mill Pond. No wonder her mom couldn't force herself to. Only bitter memories clung to this place. Mom had gotten out of town as soon as she finished high school and only drove back for visits until her youngest brother finally graduated and fled his parents, too. Axel Crupe was eighty-three years old now, and he hadn't improved with age. As far as anyone knew, he had no friends. His wife, Eloise, had given him twelve children, and Karli's mother could only remember her as pale and pregnant.

"She flinched a lot," Mom said, "because Dad liked to backhand her."

"Why did she stay with him?" Karli could hardly remember her grandmother. She'd died five years ago, but Karli had no clear memory of her. When the family visited Mill Pond, Eloise sank into the background, unremarkable and easily forgotten, never calling attention to herself. Maybe after having a dozen children, it took all of the oomph out of you. That, and living with Axel.

Her mother sighed. "I don't think Mom was too bright, and she was easily intimidated."

"A wimp."

"A sad shade of a woman," her mother corrected.

Understandable. Axel was a banty rooster with an attitude. Karli knocked on the door with more force, ready to push it open, when a tall, lean man cracked it wide for her. She stepped back and stared. Not hard on the eyes.

He nodded a welcome. "You must be Karli. Your mom said you'd come to help settle things with Axel. I couldn't come to the door earlier. I was helping him back in bed after changing his sheets." Karli raised her brows and he said, "They weren't wet, but he ate crackers and they were full of crumbs."

The house had that old-people smell. Keagan acted immune to it. He didn't look like someone who'd live in Mill Pond. He wore his golden-brown hair pulled back in a short ponytail. Looked artistic. Of course, plenty of artists owned shops in town. At least, that's what she'd heard. Her family never stopped by any of them, but that's why tourists came here. She stared, riveted by his cobalt-blue eyes and long lashes; hardly even noticed the puckered skin and scars on the left side of his face.

He shrugged. "When I was a kid, I pulled a pan of boiling water off the stove when my mom wasn't looking. It takes people a while to get used to how I look."

She blinked. "I was staring at your eyes. They're beautiful."

His lips curved in a smile. "Mom said your mother was short and plump with straight, blonde hair. Not a bit like you."

She raised an eyebrow. Was that an innocent comment? A compliment? Men noticed her coloring—thick, black masses of long, curly hair and brown eyes. She was a little overweight and didn't give a damn. If a man wanted a model, he was sniffing after the wrong girl. Most men didn't seem to mind.

She looked him up and down. Khakis instead of jeans. A thermal shirt that showed off his muscles. The man seemed awfully secure in his own skin. "Are you the Keagan my mom talked about?"

"Yup, that's me. Mill Pond's mailman. I know everyone in the area, and I notice changes when they happen. Axel hadn't emptied his mailbox for a few days, so I decided to check on him. Just down with the flu, thank God, but his stove was on. It's a good thing no pot was on the burner. I don't know the last time anyone's mowed the yard. He's reaching a point where he shouldn't be alone, so I called your mom."

A gravelly voice called from the back of the house. "Damn you, boy! Couldn't you just mind your own business? Leave me in peace?"

Keagan looked amused. "Sure, if I didn't bring you groceries once a week and watch your house fall down around your ears." He turned to Karli. "Don't let the old man fool you. He's like a kid. He has supersonic ears. I've found his stove on three times when I arrived, and the man doesn't even cook."

He was talking her language now. As a nurse, she liked assessments and specifics. "Hopefully, I can set up some kind of home care for him. If that's not enough, I'll help him choose a good nursing center."

Keagan raised an eyebrow, doubtful. "He's never made anything easy. You'll be lucky if he cooperates with you."

No matter. "If worse comes to worse, I'll have to call in health services, but thanks for alerting us to the problem."

He laughed. "I deliver mail. I'm Mill Pond's watchdog." He opened the door wider and stepped back. "Come on in."

She crossed the threshold and stopped. *Good grief.* The inside of the house was worse than the outside. The rooms she could see looked as though no one had set foot in them for years. No one had dusted in a decade and cobwebs hung from corners. It smelled musty, and a faint scent of urine drifted from a back room.

Keagan pressed his lips in a grimace. "It's not pretty. A woman comes in to clean his room every other week, but he won't let her touch anything else. I fetch groceries for him when he needs them, but I think he stopped cooking a while ago. The only empty containers I've seen in the trash lately held applesauce, cottage cheese, and Ensure."

Karli turned a serious gaze on him. "You're awfully nice to a mean old man."

The voice called again. "Mean, huh? Which one of Donna's miserable kids did she send? She was too much of a chicken shit to come herself."

Karli was glad she could spare her mom this. She could have dealt with it, but thankfully, Mom had put her growing up pains behind her. Why stir them up again?

"I don't see any other kids lining up to rescue you!" Karli followed the voice toward the back room—a depressing journey. The kitchen had worn linoleum flooring and a grease covered, four-burner stove. Flies buzzed around an open can of peaches. She shook her head. "Can he get around?"

Keagan nodded. "Everything's set up for his wheelchair, but he's moving less and less these days."

* * * *

Keagan kept walking until they stepped into a three-season room. Axel sat nearly upright in a hospital bed, cranked so that he could see out the windows. He had on stained pajamas, and his steel-gray hair hadn't been washed. A black garbage can sat close by, and the corner of an adult diaper drooped over its edge.

"For God's sake, shut the damn thing!" Keagan cracked the lid and let the diaper slide inside, then quickly shut it.

Axel looked a lot like she remembered him—average height, lots of long, messy, gray hair, and a stubbly chin. But his shoulders were stooped, his frame withered, and his legs thin and frail. Age was taking its toll.

He glared at her. "I don't need to be rescued!"

"The hell you don't. You need to be hosed down—and with lots of soap." She looked at Keagan. "Does he ever wash?"

"I help him in the shower every Sunday and lay out clean clothes for him."

"You go above and beyond duty. Why bother with him?"

The man shrugged. "We're neighbors. My folks live on the next farm, and I help out during the busy seasons. Besides, Mill Pond takes care of its own. Well, everyone but Axel. He never won any kindness awards."

Karli looked around. "Why is he back here? This is a three-season porch, isn't it?"

"He likes looking outside. It's glassed in and comfortable, at least, until winter. That way, he has a view, and he's close to a bathroom."

Not that he seemed to use it. "Does he change his own diapers?"

"Yup, and he makes it to the toilet for number twos." Keagan sounded so matter-of-fact, it surprised Karli.

"You've been through this before," she guessed.

"My grandmother lived with us for a few months before she passed."

That explained it. If Karli remembered correctly, there were five big bedrooms and a bathroom upstairs. When she stopped to think about that—a dozen kids and their parents in a two-bathroom house—she cringed.

Axel narrowed his eyes, studying her, and frowned. "Which kid are you?"

"Karli, Donna's older daughter."

He sniffed. "Your mom couldn't have a boy. Just two silly girls. Weak."

"Women are every bit as strong as men, so shut it."

Axel's lips turned down. "Are you sassing me, girl?"

"Maybe. I sure don't agree with you."

He moved slightly and winced, then rubbed his butt. "I think I'm gettin' another bedsore. It's starting to seep."

Every nurse's nightmare. She went to lift his light blanket to check on him, and he reached forward, grabbed her skin, and twisted it, hard. She remembered that from when she was little. He'd pinch her until she cried. Without thinking, she pinched him back, harder, and he yelped. Not a smart thing to do. She was a nurse. If he reported her, she'd be in trouble. But he didn't know that, and she'd be damned if he'd ever pinch her again. She held up a finger to get his attention. "Don't ever hurt me again. I don't like you, and I don't have to be here, but you're going to let me help you, whether you want it or not."

He looked stunned.

She put her hands on her hips. "Do you have a bedsore or not?"

He shook his head.

Keagan threw back his head and laughed. "You deserved that, old coot! You'd better be on your best manners. I don't think you're going to be able to bully your granddaughter."

Axel's shoulders stiffened and he turned away from them to look out the window.

Keagan shook his head. "What now? I doubt you want to stay in this place tonight. This is the only room that's tolerable—barely. What's your next move?"

"I saw a motel closer to town. I'll try to get a room there, then come here early tomorrow morning and clean some place to stay in. I brought an air mattress, in case. I'll set that up. There's no way I'm using one of the beds."

Keagan gave a small nod of approval. "My mom's going to send over a casserole tomorrow to get you started. I'll drop it off when I deliver the mail."

"Thank you."

He grinned. "You won't believe me, but Mill Pond's a pretty friendly place except for him. Here." He opened his cell phone and punched in the name of the local motel. "Nick and Meg own it. I hope they have an open room."

She was in luck. When she handed his phone back to him, she looked surprised. "They only had one vacancy tonight. They're full for the rest of the week."

"Tourists. Mill Pond is a happening place. You're lucky it's not leaf season. We're mobbed when people come to the National Forest to see the trees in their glory." Keagan grabbed an empty carton of microwaved mac 'n cheese off Axel's TV tray and carried it to the kitchen to throw away. "Good luck with everything. If you need something, holler." He gave her his cell phone number.

She watched him drive away, then went to make a slow inspection of the house. The refrigerator was clean inside, stocked with Axel's Ensure and cottage cheese. As for the rest of the house, she might as well have signed up to be a charwoman. She returned to the back room and noticed the TV remote on Axel's cluttered tray. The house might be ready to fall around his ears, but the flat screen mounted across from his bed took up most of the wall.

He glared at her. "The sooner you leave, the better."

"Then find a nice nursing home, and I'm out of here."

"Never gonna happen."

She smiled. "Then it sucks to be you. Until you show me that you can take care of yourself, I'm going to be in your business."

His hand shot out to pinch her again, and she raised an eyebrow. "Go ahead. Make my day." A Clint Eastwood quote, but appropriate. He folded his arms over his chest, and she said, "Let's get you cleaned up before I go to the motel."

"Keagan takes care of that."

"It looks like you need to be washed again."

"That's not gonna happen. No woman's touching nothing of mine."

"I'm a nurse."

"You're a girl."

She could argue, but he wouldn't change his mind. He'd been living alone and taking care of himself this long. Another day wouldn't matter. She started for the front door. "See you tomorrow."

"Not if a semi hits you first."

"You're not that lucky."

Chapter 2

At night, in her motel room, Karli called other motels around the area, hoping to find a place to stay, but Keagan was right. Mill Pond was a happening place. Every room was taken. Seems tourists came in November to buy handcrafted items for their Thanksgiving tables and to hike the trails in the National Forest before the snows fell.

She'd never been to the shops in Mill Pond. When her parents came to town, they drove straight to Axel's farm, stayed as short a time as possible, and then left. Even at its best, the farm had been nothing to brag about. Eloise kept the house clean, raised her children, and cooked food that filled bellies. End of story. Karli wondered if her grandmother had always been so dispassionate or if being married to Axel had drained her of all hope and stamina.

When hunger struck, Karli drove to a McDonald's. She usually avoided fast foods, but she didn't have the energy to engage with anyone at the local diner, and she had a feeling people around here were friendly. Probably far friendlier than she was.

Her room at Nick and Meg's Hotel had a pamphlet that listed local attractions, and she was amazed to read about the trendy resort on the lake, Harley's Winery, a microbrewery with specialty hot dogs, and the many shops on Main Street. Art's Grocery caught her eye with a long list of local offerings available in his Olde Time Store. The butcher's counter stocked ducks, Guinea hens, and fancy cuts of meats—all organic. She paused when she saw Handmade Dinnerware on display by Keagan Monroe. How many Keagans could there be in Mill Pond? Was it Grandpa's neighbor, the mailman? He did strike her as artistic.

She glanced at her watch and was surprised to see that it was already eight-thirty. It had been a long day. She called her mom on her cell. "Axel hasn't improved with age," she told her.

Her mom sighed. "I didn't expect him to."

"You never told me what a nice, little town this is."

"Mill Pond? We hardly ever interacted with anyone, except for school. Even there, we were sort of the odd kids out."

"I can see that. Is that why you always drove home to see your youngest brother?"

"I felt sorry for Charlie. Everyone left as fast as we could, and he was stuck there with Dad until he graduated. Then he left, too."

Karli wondered if Axel would be worse or better to the last kid in the family. She'd bet on worse, since Charlie wouldn't have anyone to defend him. "How did that go for him?"

"Charlie's a sweetheart. *Everyone* loves him. People had him spend the nights at their places most of the time. He wasn't home any more than he had to be."

The word "sweetheart" made her think of Keagan. "Your neighborly mailman's sure a decent guy. Do you remember him?"

"Never met him. I went to school with his mom, though, a wonderful woman. She'd smile at me whenever we passed in the halls."

Karli shook her head. "That's as good as it got for you?"

"We wore clothes about twenty years out of date, hardly ever left the farm, and everyone cringed when they saw our dad. My older brother, Kurt, and two of my sisters had Dad's temperament but worse. Kids avoided us."

Karli's heart hurt for her mom. "I'm sorry."

"Hey, it made me a stronger person, but don't let Dad bully you. He won't make anything easy about making arrangements for him."

"I'll manage. I don't have to take his crap, and he knows it."

There was another sigh on her mom's end of the phone. "Thanks for doing this, Karli. He won't appreciate it, but I do."

"I'm used to uncooperative patients." She didn't have to live with them, though. "Let me take care of this, and I'll see you before you expect it."

"If you need help, call me," her mom said. "I can drive to Mill Pond in half a day. We'll miss you in Indy."

"Miss you, too. 'Night, Mom."

With that, she turned off the bedside light and nuzzled into her pillow. She was tired. There was nothing to do but clean a room for herself at Grandpa's house tomorrow and get things settled as fast as she could. She'd wake up early and get a fast start. And since she was stuck here for a while, she might as well look around the town. It seemed as if Mill Pond had a lot to offer.

Chapter 3

Keagan drove to his parents' farm early in the morning. Heavy frost covered the fields, and fog swirled in the low spots on the way. It was only a twenty-minute drive from the two-story that he rented in town with his roommate, Brad, and he knew every inch of the way. He'd been looking for property to buy for a while now, but farms were too big and ranch houses in town with tiny yards were too small. He'd better find something soon, though, because his landlord was getting the itch to convert the rental into a bed-and-breakfast. He'd make more money, for sure.

No lights were on in either house—the old homestead or the ranch his sister and her husband lived in. The fields were all harvested. Hopefully, his dad and brother-in-law were sleeping in this morning. Keagan cut his headlights so they wouldn't shine in the windows and drove to the far shed where his studio was. He could only spend an hour here before he had to leave for work at the post office, but he'd hand-painted eight dinner plates last night. The paint would be dry by now, setting off the pattern he'd embossed in them, and he wanted to glaze them today. The woman who'd ordered them at Art's Grocery had chosen the fall leaf pattern with hues of rust, red, and gold, and she wanted to collect them this coming weekend when she made a return trip to Mill Pond.

When he walked into his studio, the smell of wet clay greeted him. The heavy blocks were sealed in thick bags, but somehow, the odor always permeated the room, and he loved it. He glanced at his pottery wheels and long, drying counters. The teapot in the shape of a cat sat ready to be painted in the corner. The customer wanted the teapot to look like a tuxedo cat—black with a white chin, nose, and paws—just like the picture she'd given him. He'd paint that after supper tonight.

He pulled on a work apron and got busy, finishing ten minutes before he had to leave for work. His cell phone rang and he glanced at his mom's number.

"Hey, K, when you stop to deliver mail for us today, come up to the house and I'll give you a casserole to drop off at Axel's place."

He grinned. This happened more often than he'd expected. People knew his route. If their houses came before a friend's, they'd often give him something to drop off on his route, besides their mail. Not technically allowed, but this was Mill Pond. Rules could bend here.

He closed up his workshop and started toward town, slowing by the house to give a quick honk, and his mom blinked the front porch light in a good morning signal. He could picture her, standing at the front window in her flowered terrycloth robe with the sash pulled tight around her slim waist and her chin-length hair slightly mussed—a smart, pretty woman. She worked as a paralegal for the town's main lawyer, but she must have taken today off.

When he got to the post office, Pete glanced up and grunted. "Heavy load today. More catalogues and ads than usual. That time of year, getting ready for the holidays."

If Keagan wanted to finish his route before supper, he'd better get a move on. It was after eleven when he pulled up to his parents' porch. He handed his mom their mail, and she handed him a cardboard box with a foil-covered, disposable pan inside it. He sniffed, and his mouth watered. "Tamale pie?"

She smiled and reached for a plastic container. "I made one for us, too, so you could have some."

"Thanks. You're the best." His mom was a wonderful cook. He knew his way around a kitchen, but cooking for one person wasn't that exciting, so he kept it simple. "Have a great day, Mom."

"You, too." She turned to go back inside and he heard his sister's voice, and then he remembered. Mom and Marcia were canning vegetable soup together today, using up the last of whatever vegetables they'd picked from their gardens. It was an annual event before they tidied up their gardens for next spring. This year, good weather had hung on longer than usual, so they were just getting around to it.

He followed his route up and down country roads until he came to Axel's house close to noon. Karli's Dodge Charger was pulled in the driveway, close to the front door. The car's trunk was open, and she was bending over to pull a box of cleaning supplies out of it.

Great ass. He shook his head, surprised at himself, but the woman was easy on the eyes. *Don't go there,* he warned himself. She was the type of woman who'd cause him grief. *Think with the right head this time.* Three more bags of groceries poked out of the trunk.

Keagan hopped out of his truck and went to help her carry things into the kitchen. If he kept her at a distance, they could be friends. Anything more, and he'd regret it.

"Thanks." She put the eggs and meat in the refrigerator, along with the milk. "I thought I'd stop in town and buy a few things before I came."

"Good idea, there's not much in the cupboards. My mom sent a casserole for you. I'll go get it."

She had most of the groceries put away when he came back—a bag of potatoes, a few cans of vegetables, and a can of coffee. She lifted the foil off the pan the minute he set it down. "This smells wonderful. What is it?"

"Tamale casserole. The bottom's a mix of ground chuck, onions, diced tomatoes, and black beans. The crust's a corn muffin mix."

"I want some. How about you?" She tore the plastic off a stack of paper plates she'd bought. "I don't trust any of the old man's dishes until I wash them."

He wouldn't either. "I can't stay, have to finish my route, but Mom said to tell you *hi.*"

Axel's voice interrupted them. "If you two ever stop yapping, I'm hungry out here."

"You haven't gotten out of bed yet?" Keagan called.

"Don't be daft. Had to use the bathroom, didn't I? Then I got a bottle of Ensure."

Karli rolled her eyes. "Tell your mom thanks. I appreciate the food."

With a nod, Keagan left and returned to his truck. For the rest of his route, though, he thought about the casserole. And Karli. She was one cute girl, and she didn't put up with any flack. A good thing, or Axel would run over her.

He thought of the house and felt sorry for her. She was one determined woman to stay in a place in shambles with an old man who was mean as spit. He didn't think she had a prayer of convincing Axel to go to a nursing center, but she might be able to come up with something else. He wished her luck.

Chapter 4

Karli took a plate out of the cupboard and washed it. Axel would need something sturdy to eat on. She searched the kitchen drawers for silverware and washed those, too. While she rinsed and dried them, her mind drifted to Keagan. He was plenty attractive, despite the scars on the left side of his face. There was something about him that intrigued her. He was quiet, secure in his own skin. She glanced at her reflection in the kitchen window. Guys always hit on her. Always. But he acted indifferent. It bugged her.

She dished the hot food onto Axel's plate. She'd see Keagan tomorrow when he delivered the mail. Maybe she'd wear a V-neck shirt, show a little cleavage. Maybe he was a boob guy and not into legs. When she started her new job in Indy, it would last three months. She could easily drive down here a few times a month if she and Keagan connected. She shook her head. What the hell was she thinking? She didn't have to chase guys. *They* chased her. She'd better get a grip.

"Hey, what the hell are you doing out there? Eating the casserole without me?" Axel shouted.

"There was steam coming off it. Too hot. It should be okay now." She carried the food into his room. An empty carton of cottage cheese sat on his TV tray. Good. He'd wheeled himself into the kitchen last night to get it and then wheeled for Ensure this morning.

"Did you clean a spot for your lunch?" She reached for the remote to turn down the volume on the TV, but he snatched it first.

"Leave my things be. I like it this loud."

"I'll turn it up later. I'd like to talk to you while you eat."

He got a mulish look on his face and pulled the remote closer to his chest.

She looked at the full plate of tamale pie she'd carried in and shrugged. "Fine." She turned to carry it back to the kitchen.

"Where are you going, girl? I said I'm hungry."

"Then turn down the TV."

He glared. "It don't matter what you say. I ain't gonna do anything you want."

"Then I'll bring you a carton of applesauce."

His gaze riveted on the hot food, and he tossed the remote on a nearby chair. "There. You happy now?"

He wouldn't hand it to her, but she didn't care. She'd dealt with worse. She'd had patients in hospitals that she'd had to restrain so they wouldn't yank all of their IV tubes out. She put the food on his TV tray and went to get the remote. After pushing the mute button, she sat across from him. She'd eat her food later, couldn't make herself eat with him. He was too disgusting with his stained shirt and leftover food stuck in his beard. "I know you don't want to leave your home, but you're reaching a point where you need to."

"Bullshit." He shoveled another forkful of food into his mouth.

She sighed. "Your house is in terrible shape. So are you. You can't get around very well. If a fire started, you wouldn't make it out of here. And you're not eating right."

"That's my business, not yours."

"What have you got against a nursing center? You'd get three squares a day and a shower once a week. They'd let you have your TV in your room and they have activities. You'd be moving up in the world."

"People would think they had the right to boss me around. No one tells me what to do."

"Even if it's for your own good?"

"I do what I want."

He did indeed. "Why not go now when you have a choice rather than waiting for poor health to make it for you?"

He stuck out his chin. "Let them try."

She shook her head and rose. "What if I try to arrange for you to get Meals on Wheels and some in-home nursing?"

"I don't want some strangers sticking their noses in my business."

She was losing patience. "Well, you'd better cozy up to the idea, because you're not safe on your own."

"I can make it outside if a fire starts. The door's right there and Keagan put a handle on the doorframe that I can use for support."

He'd finished his meal, gave her a look, and tossed his plate against the far wall. He'd eaten every bite, and the plate was plastic, so it didn't do any harm.

She laughed at him. "Are we two?"

"*We* aren't anything. Go home, girl. I don't want you here."

She bent and picked up the empty plate. Then she put his remote on the chair she vacated. "Learn some manners, old man."

"Hey, I can't reach the remote there."

"Use your wheelchair since you can do so much." She went in the kitchen and dished up a plate of food for herself. After eating it, she took out the stack of six more dishes and the rest of the silverware to put in the soapy water. No dishwasher. Why would Eloise need a modern convenience when she had twelve children to help her?

The TV blurted to life in the back room, so Axel had gotten his remote. Karli wondered how much he actually could do. When everything was in the drying rack, she wiped down the cupboards and counters. She groaned when she looked at the stove. Axel was lucky he'd never had a grease fire. She emptied the dirty water in the sink and refilled it. It took an hour and a half to get the stove clean enough to use.

When the kitchen was tolerable, she concentrated on the parlor. The room was a decent size with only a wooden rolltop desk in it. The desk was nice. There was plenty of room for her queen-sized air mattress to sleep on. She opened the window to let in fresh air, found a dust mop in a broom closet, and swiped down the walls and ceiling. Then she brought in a broom. A few hours later, the room was clean, but dingy.

Someone knocked at the front door. She glanced at her reflection in the glass doors that closed off the parlor from the living room. Her hair had gone a little wild, since it was damp with sweat. Her top clung to her. So did her jeans, but she was presentable.

A heating and air conditioning truck was parked in the driveway. Axel's furnace worked, so she wasn't sure why it was here. A stocky guy with a headful of blonde curls and sparkling green eyes stood at the door. His nose was a little big and his hands were huge. When she hurried to greet him, he grinned. "Hi, I'm Brad King, Keagan's roommate. He told me you'd come to town." His gaze raked her body, and his grin grew wider.

She got it. He'd come to check her out. Keagan must have told him that she was attractive. Wait a minute. Why did he send his roommate instead of hitting on her himself?

Brad held out a large pizza box, and the smell of pepperoni made her mouth water. "I thought I'd come bearing a gift to welcome you to Mill Pond."

Time had gotten away from her. It was later than she'd thought. Her stomach felt like an empty cavern. She opened the door and welcomed him inside.

Chapter 5

Keagan pulled his SUV behind Brad's truck in Karli's drive. His friend hadn't wasted any time, but then, Brad was partial to pretty, single girls. Keagan walked to Axel's sagging porch and gave a quick knock on the door.

Karli opened it and settled a frown on him. Had he upset her? How? She looked pretty damned appealing with her dark curls scraped back in a ponytail. She was a little thing, didn't quite make it to his shoulder, but her pissed-off energy still carried weight. He nodded to the big foil tray of fried chicken and another with fried potatoes that he carried. The aromas had to make her happy. "You're in luck, neighbor. Supper from Ralph at Ralph's Diner." He glanced inside at Brad with his pizza. "Oh, you already have supper. Maybe you can save the chicken for tomorrow."

She opened the door and motioned him into the dining room with Brad. He noticed she'd dusted the sturdy, cherry table that was long enough to seat twelve kids and their parents. Everyone in Mill Pond had heard she was here, and they all felt sorry for her. Soon, that table could be lined with all kinds of goodies.

She looked surprised. "I don't even know Ralph. Would you tell him thank you from us?"

"Sure will." He set the food down and nodded. "I'll be right back."

Her frown deepened as he ran back outside. This time, he carried in a set of four plates and coffee cups he'd designed. She lifted the lid on the box he'd packed them in and inhaled a soft breath. Her frown melted. "You made these? They're beautiful."

Nice. She liked them. "I had them on display at Ian's resort, but I just took him my winter design. These are for fall, so I thought I'd bring you these. I wasn't sure what Axel's dishes were like, if he still had any."

She rubbed a finger over embossed pumpkins, acorns, and leaves. "This was so nice of you. They're stunning."

"Thanks."

Her lips pinched together, and her brows narrowed into a scowl again. "Do you have any ego at all? You're giving these to Axel? They're art. He won't appreciate them."

Keagan glanced at Brad, confused. He was trying to be nice, but he'd irritated her again. "I came at a bad time. I interrupted you and Brad and your pizza. I'll let you get back to it before it gets cold." He turned toward the door. He'd ticked her off, and he wasn't sure why. And then he got it. Brad had dropped onto her doorstep with his golden curls and easy smile. He'd probably already turned on the charm, made her feel special, and then he'd swooped in with his chicken and interrupted. Keagan had learned from experience that when he was with Brad, he might as well be invisible. Some women even cozied up to him just to get close to Brad. He needed to get the hell out of here and let Brad do his thing.

She followed him out onto the porch. "I didn't thank you for the dishes. I love them and don't want them ruined. I'll only use them for special occasions."

Would there be special occasions with Axel? He didn't know what to say, so looked everywhere but at her and that made him *really* look at the porch. It was his turn to frown. "You know, this is downright sad. It wouldn't take much to fix it. All we'd have to do is jack up this corner and replace the column."

She looked surprised. "You can do that?"

He nodded. "People in town are pretty tired of how dismal this place looks. It's not a great selling point for Mill Pond. I can call some friends, and I'll probably get more help than I need."

She seemed genuinely confused. "Why would you do that?"

Brad cleared his throat behind them. "If you're serious, I'll sign up to help." Keagan had suspected he would.

She turned to him. "Really?"

Brad's smile returned. "For you? Anything."

Keagan rolled his eyes. He'd heard his friend's lines before, but this was a doozy. He gave Brad a look. "Saturday morning, it's on."

"I'll be here."

"Good enough." Keagan went to his truck and drove away.

Chapter 6

Karli took Axel a slice of pizza before she sat at the dining room table to eat with Brad. Keagan's roommate had perfected charming and funny, and she enjoyed his company, but after an hour, she was relieved to see him go. He was good at the boy-girl flirting ritual, she had to admit, but she'd met plenty of men like him.

When she went to check on Axel, the old man sniffed. "All that boy wants to do is get in your pants."

Karli raised an eyebrow. "Sounds better than spending time with you."

Axel threw back his head and laughed. "You aren't one bit like your mother, are you?"

"I was reared with love."

He gave her a sour look. "Babied."

"Yeah, and I liked it."

"Your little sister's probably even more pampered."

"Sure is. Her husband's crazy about her."

Axel looked surprised. "She's married?"

"Two years ago. They live in Florida now. Her husband got a job there."

He narrowed his eyes to study her. "How old are you? Why aren't you married?"

"I'm twenty-seven, and I don't want to be. I took the job as a traveling nurse to go anywhere I want, whenever I want. A husband would get in my way."

"Smart girl. A wife and kids are just a bother."

"Then why have twelve of them?" He'd messed up the blanket on his bed and she straightened it for him. Habit. Patients always needed something.

"Eloise didn't like condoms, and I wasn't good at pulling out."

She blinked. More candor than she'd expected.

Cheering came from the TV and his attention returned to the football game. "The other team made a touchdown."

Karli took that as her opportunity to leave. She grabbed his empty paper plate and went to straighten up the kitchen. Before she headed to the bathroom to wash up, she went to check on Axel. "What if I help you get in your wheelchair so you can freshen up for the night?"

"Freshen up?" He snorted. "I wouldn't mind brushing my teeth."

"Let's do it." She put a hand under his elbow and helped him to his feet, steadied him when he turned to lower himself into the chair. He could do it on his own if he had to, but she could tell it wore him out. The more he moved, the better off he'd be. She pushed him into the bathroom and handed him his toothbrush and toothpaste. She got a clean washcloth for him. When he'd finished, she wheeled him back to his room and helped him settle back in bed.

"You're not too bad at that," Axel said.

"I've had practice."

He grunted. "Wouldn't mind doing that most nights."

"No problem." She didn't make a big deal out of it, or he'd refuse. When she'd finished up, she turned out lights as she headed to her room. Once there, she changed into her pajamas, got comfortable on the air mattress, and called her mom.

"How's it going?" Mom asked.

"About what we expected. Axel doesn't like anything I suggest. I'm going to call different social services tomorrow to see what's available. Axel doesn't want to leave this place."

"It's in bad shape, though, isn't it?"

"It looks horrible, but the house itself is really solid. Once you get past how it looks, you realize that it could be a really nice house if someone did something with it."

There was silence on her mom's end for a minute, then Mom sighed. "Someone told me once that the house was beautiful when my grandma was alive. I can't picture it that way, too many bad memories growing up, but I suppose you're right."

"I can see it," Karli said. "It has simple, clean lines."

It was a large, two-story house with the open porch that ran across its entire front. Six, straight columns ran from the roof to its cement floor. A wide chimney was centered on the left exterior for the fireplace in the living room. An eyebrow arch let light in the attic.

"Keagan said he'd bring friends over on Saturday, and they'd fix the porch column. Can you believe that?"

"No." Her mom sounded surprised.

"People are really nice around here. Mill Pond isn't what I expected."

"I'm glad it's better for you than it was for me."

"I don't have Axel for a dad, or Eloise for a mother." She was beginning to think that Eloise was no prize, either. When they hung up, Karli thought about her family. All twelve of Axel's kids had run from him as soon as possible. Her sister, Nora, had sort of done the same thing. She'd wanted to leave Indianapolis for some place more glamorous for years. Karli loved Indiana, loved being close to her mom and dad. She was happy to travel, to stay in some new place for a few months, but Indiana always called her home.

She looked out the parlor's long, narrow window at the side yard. Dead weeds bent at odd angles in the beam of the security light near the mudroom's door. Frayed ropes hung from the branches of two trees. *What was left of a hammock?* It would be a perfect spot for one.

She pulled the drapes and reached for her book. She couldn't help but smile at Catherine Bybee's romance, *Not Quite Mine*. Would she ever find her happily ever after? Maybe. Maybe not. And it didn't matter. She didn't need a man to make her happy. But even as she told herself that, her thoughts drifted to Keagan.

Chapter 7

While coffee brewed the next morning, Karli made eggs and toast for herself and Axel. The old man was sitting up in bed, watching the History Channel, and he looked like he'd been awake for a while. "Couldn't sleep?" she asked.

"Nah, didn't finish the football game. Called it an early night, woke before the roosters crowed, and couldn't go back to sleep." He raised an eyebrow at her. "'Bout time you got up and moving."

She glanced out the window at the barn at the end of the driveway. "Do you have chickens?"

"Don't be daft, girl. Not anymore. Used to, though. They crowed at first light."

She was unimpressed. "You only got up half an hour ago then. First light doesn't happen until after eight this late in November."

He finished his eggs and swallowed his pills, then pushed his plate toward her. "Don't you have something to do?"

"Lots of things. I'm making calls to see what I can line up for you today."

"Knock yourself out."

She took a napkin and swiped at the toast crumbs in his beard. "Consider your options, old man, while you still have them. Want me to help you to the bathroom to clean up?"

"I did that last night, didn't I?"

She shrugged. "Suit yourself. I just thought it might feel good."

He waved her away, too caught up in his TV show. She'd let him pass this time, but she'd try again later. If he didn't use his legs, soon they wouldn't hold him.

After she tidied up their dishes, she took the industrial broom she'd found at the back of the closet and swept the dining room floor. It was probably meant for the front porch, but it would save her time now. It got the top layer of dust, so that she could use the kitchen broom to remove the finer layer. She finished with the dust mop, and the floor was passable. She settled at the long, cherry table with its sixteen chairs. Two corner cupboards, one on each side of the front window, held cut glass vases and pitchers, fancy pieces that hadn't been dusted since Axel's mom died, she'd guess. She spread all of her papers and notes over the table's surface. She could look into the living room across the hall. This house would be easy to entertain in. She wondered if Axel's mom invited people over a lot.

She liked the downstairs layout. Off the entryway to the left was the parlor, behind it, the living room with the fireplace, and then the bathroom. To the right was the monstrous dining room and behind that, the kitchen. Two rooms jutted out the back: a mudroom on the left and the three-season room on the right. There was a basement, but she had no desire to go down there. If the main floor was this bad, what would it be like? She pictured spiders and mice scampering across crumbling cement.

It had taken longer to clean than she expected, so she called: "Hey, Axel, I'll reheat some of the tamale casserole if you come out in the kitchen to eat with me."

"Save it. Just bring me a carton of cottage cheese and some applesauce."

"I know you can get those yourself."

"Never mind. I'll just eat some crackers."

She sighed. Baby steps, she told herself. She'd get Axel moving and motivated one step at a time. She carried his cottage cheese and applesauce to him, then made herself a peanut butter sandwich. Once she ate that, she shook her head. Enough stalling. Time to get to work.

Karli checked her list and began making calls. She learned that a home nurse would come and check on Axel once a month, so she made an appointment for her to come to make her first assessment. She learned that Axel was eligible for Meals on Wheels at a slight fee, and after several more calls, that he could hire a housecleaning company to come once a month. When she finished marking appointments on Axel's kitchen calendar, she went to tell him what she'd arranged.

The myriad of calls, trying to chase down the right people to talk to, had taken every bit as long as she'd dreaded, but at least, she'd accomplished something. She was happy with herself.

Axel shook his head. "I'm not doing it."

"You don't want meals delivered to your house?"

"I can live on cottage cheese, applesauce, and Ensure."

"Why would you want to?"

"I'm not paying for food that has no taste."

"Have you ever tried it?"

"No, but it's for old people, right? They always make our food taste like mush. Figure we can't chew and can't have salt. I'm not doing it."

She let out a frustrated sigh. "Okay, what if *I* pay for it for a week to see what they bring?"

"No skin off my back. It's your money, but I won't like it."

She gave a nod. "It won't start right away. They have to work you onto their delivery route."

"A lot of bother for nothing. I'd rather heat mac 'n cheese in the microwave."

"I don't see you doing much of that." He only used his wheelchair when he absolutely had to, but that was going to change.

He waved her comment away. "Keagan makes it when he delivers my groceries once a week."

She wasn't going to win this argument. Maybe when the meals came to his door, he'd change his mind. Maybe. "Okay, what about the housecleaners? They'd only come once a month. They'd keep your house in decent shape."

"I don't give a shit what the place looks like."

"You don't need flies and mice. You have to keep it a little clean."

He shook his head. "No mice have made a nest in my beard yet."

"I don't know why. It's a freaking mess. When are you going to let me clean you up?"

"Not gonna happen. Keagan takes good care of me."

"Do you ever wash your hair?"

"I wet it."

She sighed. Every time she'd tried to clean him, he'd had a fit. In most nursing centers, the patients only got showered once a week, so she was probably fighting a losing battle. She shuffled the papers in her hand, aggravated. "Are you worried about money? Are you living in poverty or something?"

He snickered at her. "I have plenty stashed away, girlie, but don't think you're getting any of it."

She gave him a level stare. "You can shove your money, as far as I'm concerned. I'm trying to help you. If you want to stay in this house, you need to get home care."

He leaned forward. "I don't *have* to do nothing. I was doing fine before you came, and I'll do better after you take your scrawny ass out of here."

She stood and stalked away. She wasn't getting anywhere. She needed to find something to do to distract herself, or she'd be tempted to beat the old man's head against the window. She glanced at the clock. Almost six. She went to the kitchen and reheated the chicken and fried potatoes that Ralph had sent. Maybe food would put Axel in a better mood. Hell, maybe it would make *her* feel better.

When she served it to Axel, he wolfed it down. She shook her head. "You love good food. If you really do have money, why not spend some to make your life nicer?"

His lips curled down in a sneer. "I'd rather leave everything in a mess and let all of you kids fight over it when I'm gone."

"Dream on. I don't need your money."

He got a sly look. "I have twelve kids. When there's money, there's squabbles."

"And you'll be dead. A little late to enjoy the action. You're an idiot. You go out of your way to drive people away, but you're only hurting yourself."

He chuckled. "You're preaching to the devil, girl. Save your breath. A man has to have his dreams."

She gathered his dirty plates. "Your dreams are too perverse to interest me."

She rinsed his dishes, then carried her food to the dining room. She opened her laptop and watched an earlier episode of *Dancing with the Stars* while she ate. It was too early to call it a night. She was too restless, so she found a bucket, filled it with hot soapy water, and mopped. By the time she finished, the parlor, dining room, and kitchen floors were clean, and she was dragging.

"My teeth aren't going to brush themselves!" Axel called.

She bit back the first thing that came to mind and went to help him into his wheelchair. He motioned for her to roll him into the kitchen, and he stared from it to the dining room.

"Mom always kept this place spotless. She made this house a home."

"She must have loved it then."

"She did." His voice turned brusque. "Enough of that. I'm an old man. I need my rest. Let me clean up and get back in bed."

She shook her head. His mellow mood had last more than a few seconds. She should celebrate.

After she got him settled, she went to the parlor, sagged onto her air mattress, and crashed hard.

Chapter 8

She wasn't quite sure what to do the next day and decided to clean the living room. She needed to keep busy or Axel would drive her nuts. He didn't want eggs for breakfast. He didn't want cottage cheese or Ensure.

"I could make you toast," Karli offered.

"I like French toast."

"If you come to the kitchen to eat, I'll make it for you."

"Never mind."

She was determined not to give in this time. If she caved and took him breakfast every time he refused to get up, he'd *never* get up. That irritated him, so he turned up the volume on his TV.

Fine. Let him. If she dusted and swept the living room, she'd have a room to relax in. There was so much dust she tied a handkerchief over her nose and mouth. She dug in the broom closet and found an old vacuum cleaner with attachments. She picked the closest corner and started sweeping. She got the cobwebs and walls first. Then she started on the sofa and overstuffed chairs. Two hours later, she still hadn't gotten to the wooden floors.

When she switched the vacuum off, Axel called, "There's no TV in there. If you want to watch something, you'll have to watch what I pick."

He really was a pain in the ass. She called back, "You're behind the times, old coot. I brought my laptop and I can watch TV on that. Movies, too. And I brought a stack of books to read. I have plenty to entertain myself."

She heard him grumble. "Enjoy it while you can. Just wait till the kids hear that you're snooping in my business. They'll roar in here, ready to line their pockets."

"You talk too much." She went to the refrigerator and grabbed one of the beers she'd bought. She carried it to the parlor and closed the door.

While she sipped, she wondered: *Would people come like Axel thought they would?* If they did, she could get out of this place. Someone else could take care of him, and Axel could stir the pot all he wanted.

Her thoughts settled, she went to finish cleaning the living room.

"Hey, girl! Was that a beer in your hand? A beer would sure taste good right now."

She started to say *Screw you*, but changed her mind. If a beer would make him happy, why not? She'd hated the old man for as long as she could remember, but he wasn't as bad as she'd remembered. Or else she was older and didn't have to put up with his crap anymore. She wasn't sure which.

She opened a bottle and took it to him. "Only one. You're on meds. You're rotten enough sober. I sure don't want to see you tipsy."

He grinned.

"I'm happy I can entertain you."

"Cool your jets. You're working yourself into a tizzy."

She plopped two pieces of cold fried chicken on a paper plate and took it to him. She grabbed two more for herself. She hated to admit it, but Ralph's chicken was even good cold. Her mom would turn green with envy. She went to the long, wooden worktable in the kitchen to eat it.

Ansel called: "Don't nurses care if someone eats healthy? I could use some applesauce."

She took it to him, rolled her eyes, and stomped away. Okay, first impressions weren't that off. The old man was a damn nuisance. After lunch, she started on the floors. She had to empty the sweeper bag twice before she could finish when it clogged with dirt. She swept the floor a second time, too, just in case, and then damp mopped it. The oak planks needed to be refinished, but they were in good shape. When she was done, the room was spotless, but it looked downright sad. The paint had faded to a colorless hue. The furniture's cushions were long dead. But there were two oak rocking chairs drawn by the fireplace with floor lamps next to them. She could sit there.

The sun dimmed outside, and she turned on lamps to brighten the room. Glancing at her watch, she saw that it was six.

"An old man could die of starvation with you as his nurse," Axel called.

"I should be so lucky!"

Axel had managed by himself before. He could now, if he had to. But Karli was starving after all the cleaning she'd done.

The kitchen was buried in shadows, so she flipped on the switch for the overhead light. She warmed up the tamale casserole that Keagan's mother had sent and carried a dish out to Axel. Supper tonight finished it off.

He sat in the dark, too. Maybe a good thing. Then she didn't have to look at him. He didn't care as long as his TV was on.

Karli turned on the lamp by his hospital bed and arranged his plate on the TV tray. "Eat up."

He frowned at her. "Why don't you ever eat out here with me?"

She handed him two napkins. "Gee, I don't know. Maybe it's the spills on your shirt or the yolk smear in your beard." She gave him a long look. "Or maybe it's your crappy disposition. Who wants to spend time with you?"

He squared his shoulders. "I told you I wasn't dirty. Keagan gets me in the shower every week."

"Whether you need it or not." She shook her head. "Lucky him. I won't fight him for the honor."

Axel's gray eyes sparkled. "You've got some mouth on you, girl."

"I've heard that before."

He laughed. "I bet you have. Well, shoo now. Let me eat in peace."

She turned and went to the dining room to eat her supper. They had plenty of leftovers, but she liked a little variety. She decided to run to the store tomorrow to buy a few things. Beef and vegetable soup sounded good.

After she cleaned up their supper dishes, she went to her room and called her mom. She wasn't doing this for Axel. She had nothing but bad memories of him. She was doing it for her mom, trying to spare her another unpleasant memory. She'd move heaven and earth for her parents. "No luck today," she told her. "Axel vetoed everything I thought of. I have a nurse coming to do an assessment in a few days, but he won't pay for Meals on Wheels or a cleaning service."

"There's only so much you can do. He won't trust anyone, even if you're trying to help him."

Karli paused before asking, "He says once your brothers and sisters hear that I've come to Mill Pond, they'll think I'm after their inheritance and come, too."

"Oh, God." Her mom groaned. "I sure as hell hope not."

Her mom hardly ever cussed. Unfortunately, Karli was known for having a potty mouth. "How bad are they?"

"Most of us turned out better than we deserved." She could almost hear her mom counting on her fingers. "Jackson tried his best to protect the rest of us. He's the oldest, sixty-three. He worked for the railroad and bought a small ranch in Oklahoma when he retired. He won't care about Dad's money."

"You don't either, but that leaves ten more." With that many kids, there had to be a few who were financially struggling.

Her mom said, "Ronnie's sixty. He works construction, walks on high, steel beams. He never married. I don't think he'll care either."

"Okay, that leaves nine."

Her mom took a deep breath. "Kurt's sixty-two and as mean as Dad. Always went from job to job, always broke. If he comes . . ."

"I might leave."

Her mom chuckled. "I wouldn't blame you. Sylvie's next, fifty-four. Meaner than Kurt. She's been married and divorced three times."

"No one can live with her." How did women like that keep attracting men?

"Maureen's next," her mom said. "I feel sorry for her. Sylvie bullied her so much, she turned out like Mom—scared of her own shadow. She married a controlling husband and jumps when he says jump."

Karli played with a strand of her hair, wrapping it around her finger. "I don't remember meeting her at your mom's funeral."

"She didn't come. She doesn't do anything without her husband's permission." Her mom paused. "I sort of lost track of my middle brothers and sisters. That's sad to say, isn't it? But I have no idea where they went and what they're doing."

"Where are you in the pecking order?"

"I'm kid number ten. Mom had a miscarriage after me, so Ida's five years behind me. She was a whiner, moody and bossy. She always thinks she's been wronged. We weren't close."

"And then there was Charlie?" Karli had fond memories of Mom's youngest brother. They drove down to Mill Pond every summer when school ended to pick him up and take him to their house for the summer. He was thirty-eight, only eleven years older than she was. He was sweet and funny, and Karli adored him. Eloise had miscarried three times between Ida and him. After Charlie, she went through her change, and her childbearing days were over. Karli was only seven when Charlie graduated from high school and moved away.

Mom's voice had a lilt in it. "He's still teaching in Oregon, married with three kids. I'm so happy for him."

Mom had paid his way through college at a regional campus in Indianapolis. She and Charlie were still close. They talked to each other once a week. "I told him about Dad. He won't come, doesn't want anything to do with him."

Karli thought through the list. "So, if someone comes, who do you think it will be?"

"The ones you don't want to meet: Kurt, Sylvie, or Ida."

Wasn't that the way it usually worked? "Oh, well, if it gets too messy around here, I'll pack my things and come home."

"Hey, you gave it your best. Dad has a choice. If he doesn't take it, that's not your fault."

That's the way Karli saw it. If he didn't want her help, that was his problem.

After their conversation, Karli grabbed her romance novel and headed to the living room. Axel's TV still flickered in the back room, but she could hardly hear it. He'd turned it down so that she wouldn't take his remote and punch mute. He was a fast learner. She yawned and opened her book to where she'd left off. It had been a long day, but she wouldn't be able to sleep if she didn't relax first. It was time for a little fantasy escape.

Chapter 9

When Keagan stopped at Axel's place on Friday, he delivered the mail and a ham loaf that Betty, who worked at Ian's inn, had made. Karli let him in and motioned him toward the kitchen. Her dark hair hung loose today, halfway down her back; she wore jeans and a thin, black sweater. As always, she looked good. Brown bags covered the worktable.

"Just got back from the grocery. I'm putting a few things away. Thought I'd fix you guys something to eat tomorrow since you're working here for free."

He glanced at a dozen cube steaks stacked to be put in the refrigerator. "Swiss steak?" he asked. Ralph made a mean version of that dish at his diner.

She shook her head. "Thought I'd go for chicken-fried steak with gravy."

"Now you're talking!" His mouth watered. When she opened the refrigerator, he saw stew beef and frozen vegetables on the top shelf. "Do you like to cook?"

She got the impression this was a serious question. Food must matter to him. "Once in a while. When I'm in the mood. Not every day. You?"

"I can manage the basics." He set the ham loaf on the stove. His mom loved gardening and cooking. Some of his favorite memories were spending time in the kitchen with her.

Karli stopped putting groceries away and turned to look at him. "I've never tasted ham loaf. Will you thank Betty for me? I have a thing for international food—Thai, Italian, and Mexican. Is there anywhere around here I can find those?"

He frowned. "Not in Mill Pond."

"I love food, but I'm just as happy if I don't have to cook it. Do small towns offer much variety? I've been spoiled in Indy. Ethnic restaurants are scattered everywhere."

"Tyne makes all kinds of international food, but only guests can eat at Ian's inn. I'm guessing you could find them in Bloomington, and I know you can in Indy." He thought a minute. "Tyne's coming tomorrow. I bet he'd give you some easy recipes."

She shook her head. "I don't want to cook the food. I want to pay for it."

When she looked disappointed, he said, "I'm not bad at Italian."

Her brown eyes glittered. "What's your specialty?"

"Chicken carbonara and spaghetti with meat sauce."

"You'll have to invite me for supper some time or stop by to cook for us." She said it casually, but he got the feeling she was going to hold him to that. Did he mind? Not really. It had to be more fun than cooking for Brad.

He glanced at the clock. "Well, I'd better get going. I have to finish my route."

She gave him a quick wave goodbye, and he'd started for the door when Axel yelled for him.

"Hey, boy, I need you. I could use a favor."

Keagan frowned. Did he still expect applesauce and cottage cheese when Karli was cooking for him?

"A favor?" Karli shook her head. "He never words anything like that for me."

"You're a blood relative. It's different." Keagan stalked toward the back room. "I'm only a neighbor. I can ignore him."

"So can I, when he gets too feisty."

Keagan went to see what Axel needed. He did a double take when he saw the old man. He'd actually tried to comb his hair. Not that it helped. It was too dirty with too many knots, but at least he'd made an effort. "How can I help you?" he asked.

"I'm getting a little ripe. I could use a shower," Axel told him.

Keagan expected the floor to open up and swallow him. He usually had to bully his neighbor into washing up. "When?"

"Tonight, if you have time."

Keagan narrowed his eyes, suspicious. "Is a social worker coming to the house and you want to trick her, pretend you keep clean and tidy?"

Axel's expression went sour. "Will you wash me or not?"

"I'll be here." If the old man would soap himself up, Keagan would get him under some hot water. "What if I come by when I get off work?"

"Fine." Axel flicked at his beard. "Why don't you find some scissors and trim this up, too?"

"Do you have a hot date? Is something going on that I don't know about?"

Axel sniffed. "Don't get too full of yourself, boy. I just need a little cleanup."

"No, you need a do-over, but I'll be here. I washed all of your sweat pants and T-shirts two weekends ago. We'll get you in some clean clothes, too."

"If you say so."

Keagan cocked an eyebrow. "You're feeling all right, aren't you?"

"Don't push it." Axel turned back to his TV show, and Keagan started for the front door.

Karli called, "Since you're coming, why don't you stay for supper? I'm making vegetable soup."

"With beef?"

"I'm putting it in the pressure cooker now."

That's what his mom did, too, to get it tender. "What if I buy a loaf of bread at Maxwell's? And I'll bring wine."

"Perfect." She looked smug, but immediately turned to grab onions, potatoes, and carrots out of the refrigerator drawer.

Once back in his truck, Keagan thought about the look she'd given him. He must have been mistaken. Why would she look smug? Maybe because he was going to scrub Axel, and she wouldn't have to smell him anymore. A bowl of soup would be worth that.

With a satisfied nod, he pulled away, reminding himself to stop at Maxwell's when he got to town.

The rest of the day went quickly, and he found himself driving back to Axel's by five-thirty. The rich aroma of beef stock and simmering soup wafted through the house when he knocked and Karli called for him to come in. He handed her the long loaf of French bread and a bottle of red wine when he found her in the kitchen. He sniffed and was sure he caught the scent of apples, too.

She smiled and said, "The apple dumplings will be finished soon. Why don't you clean Axel first, wash up, and then we'll have supper?"

That worked for him. He'd get the crappy job out of the way, and then he could enjoy the rest of the night. He helped Axel into his wheelchair and then pushed him into the bathroom. He rolled up his sleeves and supported him under his arms to scoot him from the wheelchair to the bath chair made for invalids. It sat in and out of the tub, so he helped Axel strip down, and then lifted his legs to scoot him across the seat to the side behind the shower curtain. He tinkered with the water until it was the right temperature, then hit the button for the shower and closed the curtain most of the way.

When Axel's hair was soaked, he squirted shampoo on it and scrubbed, then rinsed. Next, he soaped up the wash cloth and scrubbed Axel's back and bottom. He shook his head. Yup, he'd seen more of Axel than he ever wanted to see, but the old man couldn't reach behind himself. He soaped the cloth again and handed it to him. "Go to it. Don't miss any spots."

He waited until Axel gave him a call, then gave him a quick once-over, turned off the water, and dried him with a thick towel. He dried his hair, too, and ran a comb through it. "You're nothing to brag about, but you're clean."

The old man snorted. "Don't forget the beard."

Keagan draped the towel over him and trimmed the wiry whiskers as well as he could.

He grabbed a clean, disposable diaper and slid it on him, followed by the clean sweatpants and shirt. He pulled slippers on Axel's feet and started to roll him back to his room.

"I want to eat in the dining room."

Keagan stared.

"Karli said I could if I cleaned up."

Was that what this was all about? "We're eating out there," Keagan told him.

"I know."

Keagan scowled. "One nasty comment, and I . . ."

"I know. You'll hike me back to bed."

He would, too, damn it. He and the old man had an understanding.

Karli carried a giant tureen to the cherry table, along with a platter that held the sliced bread. She put a trivet on the table and carried out a nine-by-thirteen dish filled with apple dumplings.

Axel's jaw dropped. So did Keagan's. His mom made wonderful meals on Sundays, but he loved this combination. While she dished up food for Axel, Keagan opened the bottle of red wine he'd brought. When he paused over Axel's glass, the old man nodded.

"You sure?" He turned to Karli. "Do we have to worry about any of the medicine he takes?"

"Let him have a glass. Tonight's special," she told him.

Keagan didn't think it was possible, but Axel was on his best behavior while they ate. Well, he didn't say much, mostly shoveled food into his face, but he seemed to enjoy listening to their conversation. Karli asked about the different farms in the area, and Keagan happily told her about the families and the specialties they raised.

"Mill Pond's changed a lot in the last five to ten years," he said. "People got together and decided to up their game. We wanted to bring more tourists and money into town, and it's worked out better than we thought."

"Do you sell a lot of your dinnerware?" Karli asked.

"Almost more than I can keep up with. I've never wanted to own a shop of my own. I'm happy displaying my work at Ian's inn and in Art's grocery, but I'd like a bigger studio someday, so that I can make more inventory and products."

Axel paid attention to that and pointed a finger in his direction. "You've got to be close to having enough money by now."

Keagan nodded. "I live on my mailman wages, but I've socked every penny I make from the dinnerware in the bank."

"For how long?" Axel asked.

"Eight years now. It wasn't anything to brag about when I started out, but I could almost live off it now. If I find the right property, I can afford it."

"Good. You've earned it."

Karli glanced at Axel, surprised, but didn't comment. When they finished the soup, she went to the kitchen and brought back a gallon of vanilla ice cream. Keagan loved apple dumplings, especially a la mode, and had to stop himself from asking for seconds. By the time they ate the last bite, Axel sagged back in his chair, tired.

Keagan laid a hand on his shoulder. "The food and the wine's done you in. Ready for bed?"

"I changed your sheets while you were in the shower," Karli said. "You should sleep well tonight."

Axel grunted and Keagan rolled him to his room and got him into bed. A few minutes later, they heard the TV turn on. Keagan shook his head. "Always with the TV."

"He needs something to distract him," Karli said. "But he won't last long tonight."

"Neither will I. After we clean up, I'd better go home. We plan to be here early tomorrow to work on the porch."

When the last dish was dried, Karli yawned. "I'm going to call it an early night, too."

On his drive home, Keagan had to admit he'd enjoyed himself at Axel's. Karli was good company and one hell of a cook. Too bad she was only going to be here for a short time. He felt comfortable with her. He liked most people, but he wasn't very social. He spent most of his free time in his studio. His mom bugged him about being too private. Maybe he was, but the idea of growing old alone didn't bother him. Not after Cecily. He chuckled. Maybe he'd turn grumpy and stubborn like Axel in his old age.

Chapter 10

Karli set her alarm and got up early on Saturday morning. She pulled on an old pair of jeans and a lightweight sweater but took care with her hair and makeup. Keagan would be here, after all. In a hurry, she'd fixed overnight oatmeal for Axel and was surprised when he asked for seconds.

"That's what my mom made for us kids when I was little," he told her. For being such a curmudgeon, the old man sure put his mom on a pedestal. She liked that.

"Want me to help you clean up before everyone gets here?" She thought he'd turn her down, but he nodded. She supported him so that he could slide into his wheelchair and then he waved her away.

"I can do the rest."

"Okay, go for it." The more he did for himself, the better. After she cleaned up their breakfast things, she got out the ingredients for the chicken-fried steak and had to laugh at herself. Good God, she was turning into Suzie Homemaker! She rarely cooked three days in a row, but she wanted to impress Keagan and his friends. And if food really was a way to a man's heart, she'd cook up a storm.

The men pulled into the driveway as soon as there was sunlight. Keagan came with Brad and introduced her to Tyne and Harley when they arrived. *Be still her heart.* But they both wore wedding rings. Someone had already scooped them up.

What the hell was in the water in Mill Pond? Harley had a rocker look with his dark, shaggy hair and long, lean build. He made her think of an Italian on steroids. Yum! He also had a thick, gold band on his ring finger. Hands off! Brad dazzled with his golden curls, and Tyne . . . Tyne looked like a walking sex commercial with his dirty blonde hair, stubble, and awesome body. His ring was silver, but married was married. To her, not one of them was as appealing as Keagan.

She did her best smile-and-greet routine. Every man responded but Keagan. Go figure, but she was genuinely impressed with how nice each man was. Good looking *and* decent human beings. And faithful, if she read them right. She respected that. A triple whammy. Keagan was ready to plow right into work mode, though, so she retreated to the kitchen.

This was shaping up to be a great Saturday. Harley and Tyne were taken, but they were great eye candy. Might as well enjoy. Brad was easy on the eyes, too, but he was a player. She'd been there, done that. What she'd never done was get too serious, too attached to move on. She frowned. Did that make her a female player? She'd never worried about it before. If she plugged into Keagan, would she be able to walk away?

She wouldn't know until she tried, right? Not that she was making any headway. She was striking out with the man. Time to up her game. And if that meant appealing to what was important to him, like food, so be it. That's what seemed to make Axel happy, too.

She mixed flour, salt, pepper, garlic and onion powder, and a pinch of cayenne pepper for the dredge. She was going all out. She coated every cube steak, then pan-fried them. She put them in the slow cooker with a little beef broth and set it on low to keep them warm. Then she started on the gravy. There were more than enough pan drippings to give it flavor. When she dipped her finger in and liked the taste, she turned it off. She'd reheat it when the men were ready to eat. She wrapped potatoes in foil and tossed them in the oven, then opened three cans of green beans and added them to crumbled bacon and sautéed onions. Nothing too fancy. She didn't want Keagan to think she was trying too hard.

The men plunged right into work. They started by jacking up the front porch. There was no way for her to help them, so she concentrated on dusting and sweeping upstairs. She didn't plan on spending any time there, but it had to be healthier eliminating so much dust from the house. The second-floor bedrooms were all good-sized. She wondered when someone had walked up here the last time. Before Charlie moved out? Enough cobwebs hung in the corners that Mill Pond could have used Axel's house for their haunted castle. The bathroom had been updated at some point. Maybe a pipe had leaked, because Axel didn't do any more than he had to, by the looks of it. The tile and fixtures were dated, but there was a toilet, tub, sink, and shower.

She was sweeping the second bedroom when Brad touched her shoulder to get her attention. "Sorry! The vacuum's so loud, I didn't hear you come up the stairs."

He grinned. "You're a brave woman, trying to take on Axel's house."

"Not really. I'm not good at sitting around with nothing to do, and this definitely needs doing."

"You're using a vacuum on wooden floors?"

She gestured to the side of the room she hadn't gotten to yet. "Too much dust for a broom or dust mop."

"Are you going to move your mattress up here?"

"No, but since I'm here, I might as well get something accomplished."

His smile dazzled. "I could help you fill some of your spare time. What if I picked you up and we went to Chase's bar some night? I could introduce you around."

She loved bars. She'd love to meet more Mill Pond people, but she didn't want to encourage Brad. "That sounds like fun. You know I don't expect to be here much longer, though, right? Either Axel lets me help him, or he doesn't. Are you okay with just drinks and a kiss good night? Because that's as far I'll go."

His smile grew wider. "One night with you? Sign me up."

She pursed her lips. Maybe she'd worded that wrong, but it would be nice to get away from Axel for a while, to have fun and meet people. She nodded. "Next weekend?"

"Done. You're mine on Saturday night." He looked pretty happy with himself.

She glanced at her watch. "Boy, time's gone fast. Are you guys ready for drinks? I bought lots of beer and pop."

He wiggled his eyebrows. "It's not too early for me to down a beer."

She motioned toward the stairs. "Let's see if the others are ready for a break."

When she invited them in for something to drink, they all sniffed and glanced at the kitchen. "Are you hungry?"

Silly question. She nodded toward the kitchen. "Everything's ready. If you want to serve yourselves, I have plates and silverware on the counter top."

They stood as one. She frowned at the mismatch of plates she'd washed, but she was lucky she'd found six in the cupboard.

"Don't forget me!" Axel called from the sun-room.

"Want to come and join us?"

The men cringed, but luckily Axel turned her down.

She had his plate in hand. "You guys go ahead. I'll take this to Axel, then grab one for me and join you."

The men were chatting comfortably among themselves when she brought her food to the long, cherry dining table.

"Damn, I love chicken-fried steak," Harley said. "I'll have to mention how good it is to Kathy. She never makes it."

"She's probably afraid to make anything that isn't Italian," Tyne said, teasing him. "Your dad makes a point of letting everyone who visits the winery know about your Italian heritage."

Harley laughed. "Yeah, but I was born in Mill Pond. I'm a melting-pot kid. I loved chicken nuggets at school lunch. I like it all."

Keagan turned to Tyne. "Is there any food you don't like? You've traveled so much, you like it all, don't you?"

Tyne grimaced. "No bugs. I've been to places where they're considered tasty but not to me."

"Even if we doused them in coconut milk?" Keagan asked.

"Even then." Tyne's brown eyes twinkled. He turned to focus on her, and she felt a flush tinge her skin. Damn, he was hot. "How's it going with Mr. Meany? You okay?"

She shrugged. "We're getting along all right, but he won't sign up for any home care. I have a visiting nurse coming today to assess him, but he's pretty set in his ways. I don't know if I'm going to be able to help him or not."

"His choice." Tyne obviously didn't mince words. "If he wants to stay here and stink and let the house fall around his ears, it's his own fault."

"I heard that!" Axel called.

"Good, but I bet you don't waste time thinking about it." Tyne must know Axel better than Karli realized. "Keagan tried to get you help, too, but you're too damn stubborn."

"Hmmph!"

The TV volume got louder, and Tyne shook his head. "Stubborn, old man."

"There's more food in the kitchen," Karli said. "I made plenty if you want seconds."

That must have been the invitation they were waiting for. They all went to fill their plates again. Karli noticed that Keagan took seconds of everything. When he sat down, she saw that his golden-brown hair had sawdust in it. Her fingers itched to brush it out, to touch him. His worn jeans showed off his muscular thighs. She bet he'd be great in bed.

"Everything's delicious," Brad told her, capturing her attention.

"Thanks." Her gaze returned to Keagan. He was *so* not her type. She usually fell for guys like Brad. But there was something about her friendly mailman, something self-contained.

Tyne finished his food and pushed to his feet. "I'd better get started again. I can only stay till two. I work tonight."

She stared at him, surprised. "You work tonight and you're working here all day?"

"So does Harley, but we're so happy someone's making this old place look better, we were thinking of sneaking out here at night to fix it up in the dark."

She laughed. "That's pretty desperate."

Harley stood with Tyne. "Old Mill is trying to make itself into a tourist town. We're doing a good job, but this place is an eyesore. At least, it looks like it might not collapse now."

Tyne turned to Keagan. "I'd love to get rid of the peeling paint. Bare wood would look better than that."

Harley nodded. "Most of the paint's gone anyway. If we had a full crew, it wouldn't take long if we had two men per side. Would Axel let us scrape it?"

"Knock yourselves out!"

"How in the hell do you hear everything we say back there?" Keagan called.

Axel chuckled. "I know when to turn the TV down."

"I'm game," Keagan said. "Are you going to set this one up, Harley?"

"I'll put my old man on it. He'll offer everyone a free bottle of wine for a full day of work."

Karli blinked, surprised. "You guys are serious about this house."

"We have to strike while the old man's in a good mood." Tyne stood. "But right now, I have to get back to the porch, or I'll have to leave you guys to it without me."

Keagan finished the last bite on his plate, and he and Brad rose, too. "Let's do it," he said.

While the men went back to work, Karli cleaned up after their meal. Only two steaks remained, enough for a quick lunch someday, then she returned upstairs. She was finishing the fourth bedroom when the doorbell rang. She ran down to greet the visiting nurse. "Thanks so much for coming. Axel's in the three-season room at the back of the house. He doesn't want to see you, but he needs some kind of in-home care."

The woman, in her late fifties, smiled. "No one wants to admit they can't care for themselves, but once he hears the benefits we can offer, he'll change his mind."

Karli wasn't so sure but guided the woman back to him.

Axel's expression went sour. "Go away. I don't want another damn nurse bothering me."

The woman gave a pleasant smile. "I didn't come to bother you, Mr. Crupe. I'm an RN. If you need medicine or equipment, I can help you with that." She took out her stethoscope. "Let's listen to your heart for starters, okay?"

He pinched her. Hard.

She jerked back. "Now, now, we can't have that. I'm only here to help you."

He turned his back on her.

"There's no reason for that."

He turned to glare at her and raised his middle finger. "This is my house. I don't want you here. Go away."

Her expression hard, she gathered up her things and started to leave. "I can't help him."

"Wait!" Karli jumped up to follow her. "He needs in-home assistance."

"He needs to learn manners. I don't have to deal with him." The nurse stomped from the house.

Karli crossed her arms over her breasts and returned to Axel. "You think you're pretty damned clever, don't you? Well, you just blew that."

He crossed his arms, too. "You're bad enough, but I told you. No more people. I don't want any little Nurse Nancy traipsing in and out of my house."

"Fine! What are you going to do when I leave?"

"Throw myself a party."

She wanted to throttle him. That would look bad on her nursing record, though, so she stalked out of the room instead. She worked upstairs until she finished the last bedroom, then came down to start a batch of ham sandwiches, the kind her dad made for football Sundays, on Hawaiian buns with Swiss cheese, ham, and a seasoned butter coating.

She took two sandwiches in for Axel and plopped them on his TV tray. "Enjoy real food before you're scraping applesauce out of plastic containers again."

"Wait till my kids get here. They'll compete to make me happy, hoping I'll leave everything to them."

She snorted. "Good luck with that. When I talked to Mom, they didn't sound like the type."

She left him to carry the food out to the men on the almost-finished porch. Tyne and Harley had already left, but Keagan and Brad climbed down their ladders to join her.

"The porch is about done," Keagan said. "It should last another fifty years." He sounded awfully happy with himself.

Brad dipped right into the sandwiches. "Damn, these are good."

Keagan ate half of his in one bite and gave her a nod of approval.

She smiled. "My dad makes them for football Sundays when buddies drop in."

Brad gave her a look. "I bet I'd like your dad."

"I bet you would, too. He's pretty damned likeable." She tossed a glance at Keagan. "You'd like him, too."

Keagan blinked, surprised. The idea obviously hadn't crossed his mind. He frowned. "Is your family thinking of coming to Mill Pond to see Axel?"

"Hell, no." The words spilled out before she could edit them.

Keagan laughed. "I don't blame them. Axel's a pill."

"That's putting it nicely. How do you put up with him? He just chased the visiting nurse away."

"That's not good. Who does he think will take care of him when you leave?"

"His kids who come home to rescue him and inherit all of his money."

"Like that's going to happen. I guess I feel a little sorry for him. It sucks to get old and have to depend on people when you've never had to."

Brad shook his head, nodding toward Keagan. "This guy's too much of a softy. He can be had with a sad story."

"And that's a bad thing?" Karli had gotten the impression people could only push Keagan so far.

Brad thought about his answer. "Sometimes, he should put himself first. He's happy staying in the background."

Keagan chuckled. "I don't have a choice when I'm with you. When we're around women, I might as well be invisible."

Brad reached for another sandwich. "Well, I wasn't talking about the ladies, but really, you don't even try. They come to our table because I flirt with them. You don't make an effort."

Keagan shrugged, unconcerned. "I want to get my studio up and going first. I'm not ready for women."

Not what she wanted to hear. Karli raised an eyebrow. He'd better get ready, because she had him in her crosshairs, but it was going to take more work than she'd expected. She gathered their empty plates—his plates, the ones he'd made. She motioned to them. "I love these. I wanted to use them for lunch, but there are only four of them. How many patterns do you make?"

"I try to do something new for each season, painted any way the customer wants. You should come to the studio on my parents' farm. I can show you my lines."

Just herself and Keagan? "I'd love that."

Keagan finished his beer and wiped his mouth with the back of his hand. "We'd better finish up. We're almost done. Once the sun gets a little lower, it gets damn chilly. Thanks for the food."

They climbed back up their ladders and half an hour later came to say goodbye to her. She walked out to see the finished work and smiled. She'd expected bare wood, but the men had painted it and all of the other columns so they matched. "The house looks sturdy again—neglected but solid."

"It's a good house." Keagan's voice sounded wistful. "I always think it's sad to see a good house left to die."

"Die?" Brad laughed at him, but Karli nodded agreement.

"A house is more than wood and nails on a foundation. It shelters people, becomes a home."

Keagan locked gazes with her. "That's how I feel."

Brad laughed at both of them, then started to his pickup. "Gotta go. I'm meeting some people at Chase's tonight. Wanna come, K?"

Keagan gestured across Axel's dry, weedy field. "Mom invited me for supper tonight, since I'd be so close."

"You had a choice," Brad called. "You could hit Chase's with me."

"Maybe next week."

"Yeah, right, you'll probably hole up in your studio." Brad pulled away.

With a wave, Keagan climbed in his SUV and left, too.

Karli had enjoyed their company. She grimaced as she walked back into the house. She got to spend Saturday night with Axel. Woo-hoo! She took a deep breath. So far, she'd struck out on everything she'd tried with the old man. Maybe she was going about things wrong.

She went out to the sun porch to straighten his TV tray and asked, "Can you drive?" She'd seen an oversized gray pickup in his garage.

Axel gave her a look. "What do you think?"

"I'm not sure. But if you don't want people in your house, maybe you should go to them."

Axel turned back to his TV show. "Doesn't matter. Can't drive, and I'm not paying."

Back to square one. "Then we haven't made any progress."

"Speak for yourself. I've been eating high on the hog."

If looks could kill . . . She took a deep breath. How could she make him understand? "I didn't come here to pamper you. I'm a nurse, but I'm not *your* nurse. I came to help you find a nursing home or get you live-in care."

"No worries. You're doing that, missy. You just being here will bring some of the others, and then they can knock themselves out, trying to win my favor."

The old man just didn't get it. She put a hand on his forehead and shook her head. "Nope, no fever. You're not delirious, just deluded."

He sniffed and turned away. "Just you wait and see. They'll be here."

As she carried his things to the kitchen and began putting them away, she slammed doors a little harder than needed. But if any of his kids were like him, the old fool might be right.

Chapter 11

On Sundays, Keagan went to his parents' house for their big meal. Last night, his dad had tossed hamburgers on the grill, and it had been just him and his mom and dad. He'd been glad they kept it simple, because he'd eaten two helpings of chicken-fried steak and four of the small ham sandwiches Karli had made for them.

On Sunday, his sister and her family were there, too. He gave a quick knock before walking into the long living room. It was empty, but the TV blasted *Dora the Explorer*. Marcia's kids must have claimed it while the adults did their own thing. He heard voices in the kitchen, then decided to walk through the dining room to the kitchen at the back of the house. Sometimes, the two women went crazy and cooked enough food for an army. Today, thankfully, he saw a pot of soup on the stove and cornbread cooling on the counter. Marcia saw him and came to wrap him in a hug. "Hey, bro."

His mom turned from rinsing a pan. "Not sure why, but I get hungry for soups when the evenings get chilly."

"Where are the kids?" Keagan didn't see any sign of the two rowdies Marcia called hers, but the minute they heard his voice, they came roaring up from the basement. Jenna attached herself to his left leg, and Jack took the right. He walked back and forth with them, and they giggled when he pretended to try to shake them off.

Marcia rolled her eyes. "Stuart roughhoused with them before we came this morning, and they still haven't settled down. Then they went down in the family room to play foosball. They're all wound up."

Keagan smiled. He and Marcia had spent plenty of time in the family room in the basement when they were growing up. He grabbed each kid by the back of their sweatshirts and lifted them into the air, swinging them to and fro. Screams and laughter filled the kitchen, and his mom smiled at him. "It's time all of you headed to the dining room so we can eat."

Keagan let out a long sigh. "I probably don't have time to get anything out of my SUV then."

Marcia gave him a wary look. "It's nothing that makes noise like that awful Halloween telephone you bought them, is it? The howls and cackles about made me nuts."

He smiled. He'd done better than he'd thought if he could irritate his sister *and* entertain the kids with one present. "No noises come out of this one."

She narrowed her eyes. "That's a cagey answer."

"I know." He went to his vehicle and returned with a long box. While the women carried things to the table, the kids ripped it open, and he used his dad's air pump to blow up the giant turkey that served as a punching toy.

Marcia laughed. "Maybe they'll hit that instead of each other."

"Fat chance. They'll just learn to punch better." At four, Keagan thought they had pretty solid form.

His mom carried the big soup pot to the table. "It's time. Come and get it."

Stuart and his dad wandered in from wherever they'd disappeared to, and everyone took their seats at the table. His dad bowed his head and said a quick prayer before Mom started passing the food. Keagan snagged a big piece of cornbread, then handed his dad his soup bowl to fill. When the salad made it to him, he loaded his plate and drizzled it with honey mustard dressing.

Marcia fussed with the kids' plates before serving herself. She looked prettier than usual today in a pink sweater that showed off an interesting necklace. Keagan nodded toward it and said, "That's an eye-catching piece. I like it."

His sister broke into a huge smile. "I made it. Lefty Morgan asked me to sell some of my pieces on consignment in his jewelry shop."

Keagan nodded, impressed. Lefty used to strike him as a shifty name until his mom explained that he'd gotten it in school because he was left-handed. "Lefty mails a lot of jewelry to customers. I'm always picking up orders to deliver at his shop, a lot of them from out-of-state."

Stuart beamed at his wife. "Lefty wants to have more variety. He sells plenty of his silver and gold jewelry and class rings." He held up his right hand to display the ring he'd gotten when he became an Eagle Scout. "He'd like to have more fun pieces like Marcia's, made from polymer or polished stones."

Keagan was happy for her. She might not have made it to Chicago after art school to design jewelry, but now she could do it in Mill Pond. Before she met Stuart, who loved farming, she'd always talked about moving to a big city and hitting it big. After she married him, they'd built a house close to Mom and Dad's and helped them work the fields. Even then, Marcia still designed jewelry for local craft shows and sold a lot in Indy, but then she had the twins. No more jewelry. To Keagan, it looked like no more dreams.

Keagan swore that would never happen to him. Not a second time. When he'd been with Cecily, she'd demanded most of his time, craved attention. Pouted and fussed when he spent time in the studio. She constantly wanted to be doing something. It had been a struggle to get any pottery done. When she'd met Ryan, he was happy to work alongside her every day and then take her out every night. Keagan couldn't compete with that.

After she left and he got over her, he discovered he was happy delivering mail and selling his dinnerware. He never wanted to be joined at the hip with a woman ever again. He grinned at his sister. Her personal passion had been put on hold, but she was back at it again. "Way to go, sis."

He looked at his dad. "What have you been up to? Are you and Stuart done for the year?"

"If the weather holds, we're going to plow the back fields, get them ready for spring. We'll probably start on them tomorrow."

"A head start is always nice." He grinned at his mom. "Are you done canning and freezing for the year?" She was a paralegal and worked for a lawyer in town, but she always took off work to put up pint and quart jars for the year.

"I took off two days next week. I have more eggs than I'll ever use, so Marcia and I are making and freezing egg noodles."

His parents raised chickens, and even though they shared the eggs with Marcia and her family, his dad got tired of eggs for breakfast once in a while. Sometimes that meant a flurry of lemon meringue pies, pavlova, or custards. Noodles were always good. If Keagan got lucky and his mom decided to make chicken 'n noodles, she'd send him a quart to heat up for supper.

Adult conversation ended when they finished their meal and the kids were excused from the table. Squeals ensued while Jack chased Jenna around the table. Keagan pitched in with clean-up, and then he went to watch football with his dad and Stuart while his mom and sister came and went. The kids disappeared into the basement with their blow-up punching bag.

When it was time for him to leave, his mom handed him a bowl of leftovers to deliver to Karli and Axel. Keagan frowned. "I used to get the leftovers."

"Buck up, buttercup!" his sister teased. "This way, if Karli doesn't want to cook lunch for the curmudgeon, she doesn't have to."

He knew better than to complain. He took the leftovers and drove home to the house he and Brad rented. Soon, he thought, he'd have a place of his own. A studio of his own. He couldn't wait.

Chapter 12

Karli slept in on Sunday. When she finally got up, she pulled on her robe and wandered to the kitchen, flipping on lights as she went. It was a gray, dreary day.

"Do you know what my electric bill will be next month?" Axel called from the sun-room.

"Shut it! Do you know how much free food you've gotten? It balances out." She'd set the coffeepot last night, so poured herself a cup, took a long sip, then poured a cup to take to Axel.

"'Bout time you got your ass out of bed. I'm starving."

She shrugged. "There's still cottage cheese and Ensure in the refrigerator and plenty of leftovers. Roll yourself out there like you used to."

He pouted. "Aren't you gonna fix something for breakfast?"

"When I damn well feel like it."

He looked out the long bank of windows. "Crappy day today. Good thing it's football Sunday."

"If you were a smart man, you'd get up once a day and exercise a little. Muscles are for moving. If you don't use them, you lose them."

He gave her an odd look. "Doesn't really matter to me. What does it matter to you?"

She sighed. "Some people only think about quantity of life, but I'm a nurse. Quality matters, too. I'd like you to stay healthy enough to enjoy whatever days you have left."

"You don't want me to drop over and get the hell out of your hair?"

She grinned. "Where would the fun in that be?"

He laughed, caught off guard. "Good, then feed me."

"Nah, I believe in tough love. Get in your wheelchair and move a little."

He studied her. "You're not all that tough. I can wait till you're ready to cook."

He was in an odd mood this morning. She nodded and motioned to his coffee cup. "It's getting cold. Drink it while it's hot." She returned to the kitchen and stared out the window over the sink. Gloomy, gloomy day. Dead fields stretched far into the distance, and she could see a big, white house with a red barn and a few outbuildings as tiny dots before more fields stretched out of sight. Keagan's parents' house? He went there most Sundays, didn't he? She glanced at the clock. Too early for him yet. She wondered what he was like around his mom and dad, his family.

Family. She thought about her mom and dad in Indianapolis, and opened the cupboards to pull out the ingredients to make pancakes. Her mom made them every Sunday when she was growing up. When she carried a stack of them, drizzled with maple syrup, in for Axel, he actually licked his lips.

"My mom used to make these every Sunday."

"So did my mom." She frowned. "You always talk about your mom, never your wife. With twelve kids, didn't Eloise cook a lot?"

"She made toast every morning. That woman didn't cook any more than she had to. Didn't like it." He grimaced. "Not sure she liked anything. Mom loved cooking, loved working in her gardens and flower beds. Loved sewing." His eyes lit up when he talked about his mother. "She loved this house, and then she went and died way too early."

Karli could almost feel his pain. "Mom said your dad was a nice grandparent. He was loving, wasn't he?"

"He was okay. Weak. When Mom died, he did what needed done, like Eloise, and that was about it." He finished his pancakes and ran his finger over the empty plate to lick off more syrup. "Whoever said that people marry their parents knew what he was talking about. I ended up with a woman just like my dad."

Karli pursed her lips. Was Keagan like one of her parents? Was that why she was so attracted to him? Her mom was warm and lively, her dad easygoing and steady. Hmm, if Keagan had some of her dad's virtues, that wasn't a bad thing. She asked the first question that came to her mind. "If Eloise didn't make you happy, why have twelve kids with her?"

"The woman loved sex." When Karli almost choked with surprise, he shook his head. "Once I had four kids with her, it's not like I could kick her out. How the hell could I farm and care for them? I figured I was stuck and might as well make the best of it."

"But you knew she was lazy. Why not spend more time with the kids when you could?"

"I can't stand kids. They're whiny and always want something."

She put her hands on her hips. "Then you were as bad as Eloise."

"Never said I wasn't."

Damn, he was annoying! She took a deep breath, grabbed his plate, and started to the kitchen. She called over her shoulder, "I'm driving to Bloomington today. I want to do a little shopping, and everything closes in Mill Pond on Sundays."

"Good, you'll be out of my hair while the big football game's on this afternoon. Just leave me a bottle of Ensure."

He was a pain in the ass, so why did he get to her? On top of that, this house was just plain depressing. While she washed up, she decided to go to a home improvement store and buy paint for each room downstairs. If the townsmen were willing to fix the outside of the house, why couldn't she make the inside look a little better?

Okay, that wasn't her most brilliant thought. Paint wasn't cheap, and she didn't plan on staying here much longer, but she'd go crazy if she didn't have something to do. Why not paint? She'd give Axel an ultimatum and then call health care services, tell them what she'd done and why it hadn't worked, and then let them decide what to do, but she didn't want to be blamed for neglecting Axel.

Was that the only reason?

She thought back to Keagan saying that he hated to see a good house die. She *liked* this house. It was warm and inviting, even when Axel wasn't. It deserved better.

Lord, she was losing it! Since when did she care about cooking and cleaning? But the sad truth was that she *did* care. Was she just playing house? Playing make-believe? Not her style. For some reason, though, right now, it made her happy to be in this house, so she was going to go with it.

On the ride to Bloomington, the road curved and dipped, full of beautiful scenery. She found a complex on the outskirts of the city with a home improvement store and headed straight to its paint aisles. She chose a soft rose color for the parlor, a rich cream for the dining room and living room, and robin-egg blue for the kitchen. She bought a ladder, paint brushes, and rollers, and lots of edging tape. Then she found all kinds of safer grip handles that Axel could use.

On the drive back to Mill Pond, she stopped at Art's Grocery to buy a pork loin, a bag of mini-carrots, two onions, and fingerling potatoes. Once home, she tossed everything in a cast-iron Dutch oven, sprinkled them with a package of French onion soup mix, a little soy sauce, and some chicken broth, then threw them in a hot oven. She added a box of sliced mushrooms for good measure. Nothing fancy, but good.

Football blared from Axel's room. He didn't look at her when she carried in a cup of tomato soup for lunch, so she changed into old clothes, opened windows in the parlor, and started painting—the white ceiling first, then the rose-colored walls. Thankfully, it was a small room, and she'd bought expensive paint so she didn't have to prime, but she was still tired and covered with paint spatters by suppertime. The room looked beautiful. The paint set off the wood floors and wide trim. She took a quick shower before heading to the kitchen to dish up a late supper.

Axel frowned when she put his dish on the TV tray. "I don't like mushrooms."

"Then don't eat them. I'll get you a carton of applesauce."

She reached for his plate and he said, "You could heat up some of those leftovers people brought."

"So could you. Do you want this or not?"

His lips turned down, but he picked up his fork. "I'll eat around the mushrooms."

"Whatever." She carried her dish to the dining room table and flipped on her laptop to scroll through her e-mails while she ate.

By the time she'd finished cleaning paint brushes and supper items, it was a little after eight. She was too tired to read, so went to her room and sat on the air mattress to admire its fresh look. She was watching a DVD she'd brought when her mom called.

"Is Dad cooperating any more lately?" she asked.

Karli paused her show and settled against her pillows. "It's not going to happen. I'm giving him an ultimatum, then calling Home Services. They can deal with him."

"He probably wouldn't like live-in help, would he?"

Axel? "He'd probably pinch them."

"Well, you tried," Mom said. "Your sister called and she and Rob are thinking about flying home for Christmas."

"Really? That'll be fun. I'll try to get a couple of nights off work to see them." If she remembered right, she worked both Christmas Eve and Christmas night. She'd worked the night shift for so many years, it felt natural to her now.

"We can have our family dinner on whatever night works best for you," Mom told her.

Her parents were wonderful about that, always willing to be flexible to fit her schedule. They talked a few more minutes, then Karli finished watching her movie before curling on her mattress and pulling her blankets close.

"Hey, girl! I want to brush my teeth."

Karli shut her eyes and counted to ten. Helping her mom had seemed like a good idea at the time . . . before she met Axel. She laughed at herself. She could handle this a lot better than Mom could. That's why she'd come. She didn't want her mother to have to deal with crap like this. Pushing to her feet, she padded to the back of the house. Tomorrow, she was going to start painting the kitchen, and it was time to have a serious talk with the old man.

Chapter 13

On Monday afternoon, when Keagan stopped at Ian's inn to deliver his mail, Tyne ran out of the kitchen to hand him a big, plastic tub of chicken and dumplings. "For Karli and Axel."

Keagan raised his eyebrows in surprise. Tyne worked the morning shift on Sunday and Monday, and he rarely left his stainless-steel domain. "You've never sent food to Axel before."

"That's because I don't care if the old bastard starves or not." Tyne had a way of speaking his mind. Sometimes, it caught Keagan off guard. "I like Karli. Is she going to stay in Mill Pond a while?"

Keagan breathed in the aromas coming from the inn's kitchen. Onions and garlic mingled with what must be a tomato sauce. His mouth watered. He'd grabbed a bagel and cream cheese before he started his route, but by now, it was a distant memory. He hadn't stopped for lunch either, munching on cheese and crackers in his truck instead. He usually packed his mom's leftovers for lunch on Sunday, but she'd asked him to give those to Karli, damn it.

Tyne raised an eyebrow. What had he asked him? Oh, yeah, about Karli. "She only plans on spending a month here, trying to get health care set up for Axel. Small towns aren't her thing. She's a city girl."

"A close city." Tyne tilted his head, studying him. "Indy's only an hour and a half away."

Uh-oh. Keagan could feel a lecture coming on and thought he might be able to avoid it. He glanced down the inn's hallway to the kitchen. "Don't you have to cook or something? On Mondays, you do the breakfast and lunch crowd, right?"

Tyne's dimple showed. He was amused. "Both over. I'm fixing my dish for Paula to heat up for supper tonight. Lasagna."

"God, it smells good." His stomach rumbled. "Shouldn't you get back to that? Bet you want to finish up to get home to Daphne."

Tyne laughed. "I'm just saying when I came to Mill Pond, I didn't plan on staying either, thought I'd move on once I got some experience, but look what happened."

Keagan gave him a look. "I know what you're up to, but it won't work. I'm not Karli's type. Brad is."

"And you know that . . . how?"

"By the way she looks and talks to me. Not one bit interested."

"*I've* seen the way she looks at you, too. If she bent you over and kissed you senseless, you'd still think she'd rather have Brad. You're practicing avoidance, my friend."

Keagan glanced around the lobby, hoping for Ian to wander to the desk and save him, but no one was in sight. "Okay, let's be honest. She's too much woman for me." He'd gone that route before. It hadn't ended well.

Tyne's gaze turned serious. "Harley told me about Cecily. That was three years ago."

"Not long enough." He never talked about her. Didn't want to, but Tyne was persistent. He'd bring it up again if Keagan didn't satisfy him now. "After living together for two years, she ran off with a guy who worked on the line next to her at the factory. They both liked to party. That's what each of them did—worked and went out. We did that when we were dating. I thought she'd settle down once we moved in together, but I was wrong."

"Did you try to keep up with her?"

"She wore me out. I tried to put in time at my studio every morning before I delivered mail, then go out with her every night. And the sex—she wanted it all the time."

"Most men's fantasy."

"Until they get it. I couldn't keep it up." He realized what he'd said and grimaced. "The pace was too much for me. It felt exciting at first, but I got tired of it really fast. Ryan had no problem with it."

"He worked eight hours and did nothing else?"

"He worked, showered, changed clothes, then went out to eat and have fun."

"Sorry, man. That's why you're afraid of Karli?"

"Damn right. She'd use me up like Cecily did and then leave town."

"Why did Cecily leave?"

"The factory shut down. She and Ryan took that as a sign to find some place with more to offer—more bars, more fun."

Tyne let out a long breath. "Okay, this sounds sleazy, but why not enjoy Karli while she's here?"

Keagan scowled. "I'm not good at playing love 'em and leave 'em. I suck at casual affairs, get too attached. And it hurt too much when I found out Cecily was seeing Ryan on the sly. The next time around, I want someone for keeps, someone nice and quiet who'll want to stay."

Tyne narrowed his eyes. "Sweet, young things are around here. I've seen them. So why aren't you going after one of them?"

Keagan huffed out a sigh. "Don't judge me, but they don't interest me much."

"Yeah, not your type, you're just trying to play it safe. All I'm saying is that Karli's into you. I can tell. Give her a chance. You might click."

Keagan backed toward the door. "I appreciate the advice. I really do, but a woman would mess up my plans right now. If I find the right place, I can buy it."

Tyne added one last parting shot before letting him escape. "You act like you have to choose, but maybe you don't. Maybe you can have it all. Maybe Karli would move in with you."

"Maybe, but it would be like living through Cecily all over again." He turned and bolted for the door. Karli wasn't looking for a relationship. How could she do long term as a traveling nurse? Nope, she and Brad both liked short and fast, not Keagan's style.

When he reached Axel's place, he hopped out of the truck to take him his mail and to deliver Tyne's food. When he saw Karli, he'd be careful. But when she opened the door for him, he frowned. "I smell paint."

"Really?" She pulled out a strand of her dark, curly hair to show him the blue speckles on it. "I put a scarf over my head, but my hair keeps getting loose."

He loved her hair. She was one of the most attractive women he'd ever met. That only made her more dangerous.

She motioned him inside. "Come see what I've done." She showed him into the rose-painted parlor. He'd have never thought of that color for the room, but it was perfect. It fit the old-time elegance the house had once had. Then she led him to the kitchen with three of its walls painted blue. It was a good-sized room with a long, butcher-block table in its center. The fresh paint showed up how dated the blonde-wood cupboards were, but it was still an improvement.

He handed her the chicken and dumplings. "This was the perfect time for Tyne to send you these."

She looked relieved. "Good, this room is taking forever. I started early, and I'll be lucky if I get it done. Thank Tyne for me. I won't have to stop to make something for supper."

Keagan smiled, happy to see the improvements she'd made. "I've always liked this house. It has a natural charm about it. Axel's mother made sure it was pretty."

Karli looked surprised. "It always looked rundown when my family came for visits."

"That's because Axel didn't care about it, and neither did Eloise." He held up a finger. "Give me a minute. I have something to show you."

Karli watched him run up the stairs and looked surprised when he came back with a small stack of pictures to show her. They were black-and-whites of the house when the yard was landscaped and it was well taken care of. "Was this when it was first built?"

Keagan nodded. "Its bones are still good. It just needs some work."

She gazed at the pictures and then looked around at the dingy rooms. "It was a really pretty house." Its exterior was painted white with darker shutters.

"They were sage green," Keagan said. "They're faded now, out in the garage." Its landscaping hugged its foundation with flowering bushes and perennial flowers. Inside, the parlor had an upright piano on the long wall. The dining room had fancy dishes displayed on the plate rail.

Karli pointed to the dishes. "Your plates would look pretty displayed like that. They're art."

Her compliment pleased him, and before he could stop himself, he blurted, "If you'd like to see my studio, I could drive you there some night this week."

"I'd love that." Her answer was too quick.

Oh crap, what had he done? But he'd invited her, hadn't he? "Will Thursday work?"

She motioned to her surroundings. "It's not like I have big plans."

It must suck, staying here with Axel. "Maybe we could go out for supper, too. You could meet some of the people in Mill Pond."

"Perfect. Should I dress up?"

He laughed. "Not for Joel's microbrewery. I thought we'd keep it fun."

"I like fun."

He bet she did. Well, Mill Pond was a fun place to be. He'd show her a side of the town she'd never seen before. And then he'd stay the hell away from her.

Chapter 14

On Tuesday, Karli was finishing painting the kitchen when the Meals on Wheels truck pulled into Axel's driveway. Karli had paid for one week of food as a trial for him. If he tried it, he might like it. The man brought the packets of food to the door, and she paid him. It was close to suppertime, so she removed the lid and sampled a small piece of the meat. Not bad. She probably used more salt when she cooked, but the food tasted good. She took it out for Axel.

He stared at the disposable container. "What's this?"

"Boneless ribs, and mashed potatoes and gravy."

He took a bite and spit it out in his napkin. "Disgusting."

Karli fought down her temper. "I tasted it. There's nothing wrong with it. It might taste better when I'm not here and you're eating cottage cheese and applesauce again."

"At least I can recognize those." He pushed the tray away.

"Fine." The word was clipped. "What do you want now? Applesauce or Ensure?"

"Some of the leftovers folks sent."

"Those won't happen when I'm not here." She crossed her arms over her breasts, ready to argue. The front door opened and closed, and someone stomped toward them. Karli stopped bickering to glare at whoever had invited himself in.

A man with salt-and-pepper hair and a beard as messy as Axel's stood in the doorway to the sun porch. He pointed a finger at Karli. "I heard you were here. Donna's daughter, right? Don't think you can swoop in here and butter up Dad to get my inheritance."

She wasn't in the mood. "You must be Kurt."

"That's me, and I'm onto you, girlie. You're sniffing after the money, but it's mine. I'm staying here to protect my rights."

"Good, you can have him. Knock yourself out." She waved a hand toward Axel. "Whatever you come up with is between you two. I don't give a damn. Now you can take care of him."

"Hold on now. I never said anything about taking care of him. I don't owe this old guy anything. I survived him, and that's enough."

"Well, I'm tired of him. And I'm sure not going to wait on you."

Kurt studied her, caught off balance. "You're a feisty, little gal, aren't you? Right now, I'm temporarily out of work, so thought I'd stop to check on Dad a while. Don't want to get your dander up, as long as we understand each other. I'll take my things upstairs and stay out of your way. How's that?"

Temporarily out of work, her foot! He came for free room and board and a shot at his dad's money. What did she care? She put her hands on her hips. "Unless you're going to take care of the old coot, stay out of my way, or I'm gone, and he's yours."

Kurt looked at the food on Axel's tray. "Is someone going to eat that?"

"No!" Axel pushed it toward him.

Kurt picked it up and dug in.

Great. A freeloader. He and Axel deserved each other. But Karli was supposed to go out with Keagan on Thursday night. If she stormed out of here now, she'd miss that, so she nodded at Kurt. "We'll call a temporary truce."

Axel looked Kurt up and down. "Thought you were married."

"Was. Got a divorce."

"Kids?" Axel asked.

Kurt shook his head.

Karli pinched her lips together so that "lucky them" didn't escape.

"You still doing odd jobs?" Axel asked.

"Off and on."

Karli gestured to the rundown barn. "This place could use a little work. You'd be the person to do it."

"Not me. I don't give a shit about Axel or the farm. All I want is the money."

"What money?" Karli motioned outside at the miles of weeds. "This place is a wreck."

"Don't play dumb with me. A hundred acres can probably fetch six hundred thousand dollars."

"You're kidding."

"Don't think you're getting a share. Neither are my brothers and sisters."

The man sounded like a broken parrot. "And why is that? How many times did you come to visit Axel?"

"I'm here now. That's all that matters."

Axel laughed. "The fun's just starting. Your sister called yesterday. She's going to drop in soon, too."

Kurt's eyes darted to the driveway. He looked nervous. "Which one?"

"Sylvie."

"Christ almighty! Not her!"

Karli stared. "What's wrong with Sylvie?"

Kurt jammed his hands deep in his pants pockets. "She's a bitch on steroids; as hard as nails and greedy as sin."

It sounded as if Kurt and Sylvie were a perfect match. She turned to go to the kitchen. "What difference does it make? There are twelve kids. Twelve into six hundred thousand . . ."

Kurt cut her off. "You don't get it, kid. That money's mine."

"Yeah, right." She carried Kurt's empty container into the kitchen and dumped it in the trash, then she nuked the last of Ralph's fried chicken to take to Axel.

"What about me?" Kurt asked.

"The leftovers are in plastic containers with red lids, and there's a microwave. Don't touch the chicken and dumplings. That's for supper tomorrow."

"And if I eat them?"

"I'll throw every damn leftover away and you can buy your meals in town." She fixed herself a plate of the leftover pork roast and vegetables and headed to the dining room. Kurt heated up the rest of the roast and went to watch TV with Axel.

She grimaced to herself. How lucky could a girl get! She had Axel and his mirror-image son. They'd better not push her too far. After her night on the town with Keagan, she'd decide what to do, if she wanted to stick it out a little longer or throw in the towel and go home.

Chapter 15

Karli pulled her robe tight around her and slipped on warm footsies in the morning. The old house got cold during the night, so she padded to the kitchen to start the coffeepot. On her way, she glanced at the fireplace in the living room. Piles of wood sat in straight lines beside the driveway, but she had no idea how to start a real fire. Her apartment had a gas fireplace. All she did was switch a flip to light it.

She turned on overhead lights as she went. The rooms she'd painted made her so happy, the dingy rooms looked even sadder. She decided to paint the dining room. It was a beautiful room with lovely built-ins. She'd feel like she was doing something constructive. If nothing else, the fumes should keep Kurt away from her; that, and the fact that he seemed allergic to labor of any kind.

She sipped her coffee, then pulled on her paint clothes. Axel still wasn't stirring, and Kurt only roamed downstairs when he was hungry. The bread she'd left on the counter was gone, so she assumed he'd made himself a snack in the wee hours last night. He'd better enjoy it while he could. She didn't think Sylvie would be as generous with him.

She heard Axel stirring after nine, so stopped to take him a cup of coffee and some applesauce. He frowned at her. "Are you painting again?"

He had a valid question. Even she was beginning to wonder about herself. But it took so little effort to make the old house look good, why not do it? She could almost feel each room smile when she finished it.

"Might as well. The dining room's so pretty, it deserves a little attention. Besides, I like to spend time there. The living room's next."

He shrugged but looked pleased. "My mom made us eat every supper at the dining room table. Insisted on us sitting down as a family."

"That was my dad's rule, too." Karli pulled up his blinds and let sunshine spill into the room. "Are you warm enough?"

He reached for his wool robe. "I'm fine. Keagan's been making noises to move me inside the house to a warmer room, but I like it out here."

"It has to get really cold in January and February."

Axel snorted. "You'll be gone by then and I can have the parlor."

He looked too pleased with himself. "Probably sooner," she said, and he glowered. The old poop. He'd miss her when she was gone. "Hungry?"

"Not much. Toast and jam would be enough today."

After they ate, she helped him into the bathroom and back, then returned to her painting. She had the ceiling and one wall finished by eleven and Kurt still wasn't up. Must be nice to keep whatever hours you wanted. She looked in the refrigerator, and there weren't as many leftovers as she'd thought. The men would need those for supper Thursday night, so she stopped work to cook a huge pot of chili. Soon, she'd run out of ideas. She only knew how to cook a limited number of things. She kept the chili mild for Axel, and when she carried his bowl to the sun-room, Kurt was sitting in the spare chair, watching TV with him.

Axel took a quick bite of his lunch and nodded. "Can I get some crackers?"

Kurt followed her to the kitchen and dished himself up a bowl to carry to the porch. He balanced it on his lap, took a bite, and called, "Not spicy enough. I like jalapenos in mine."

Really? What is he—a food critic? "Ask me if I care."

The man wouldn't win any awards for brains or charm. She rummaged through the cupboards for a sleeve of crackers to take to Axel.

Kurt returned for seconds before she could dish up her own food. She decided to eat in the kitchen. She'd cracked the dining room windows to keep the paint smell from being too overwhelming, so it was chilly in the front of the house. She ate, standing at the window over the sink, looking out across dead fields. How long would it take to get used to seeing nothing but weeds and crop stubble for miles? In her apartment in Indy, she could hear neighbors tramp up and down the stairs, hear their cars start in the morning, and fuss when they played their music too loud. She felt isolated here.

By suppertime, every wall was painted, and she'd started the living room ceiling. She was tired. She heated up Tyne's chicken and dumplings. Both men loved it, but who didn't like anything Tyne cooked? He could make gruel delicious. After she tidied the house, she showered and changed into her pajamas and robe, then settled in her room for the night. Kurt wandered to the parlor to find her.

"My room smelled a little musty last night. It needs to be dusted and swept."

She stared at him. "You don't remember where the broom closet is?"

He tugged at his shaggy beard. "I thought you were taking care of the house."

"You thought wrong. I'm painting because I got tired of looking at these sorry walls, but I don't spend time upstairs. Have no desire to. It's as clean as I'm going to make it."

"But you're a woman."

"Yes, I noticed, and I still won't clean up after you."

He turned on his heels and walked away. A little later, she heard him rummaging through the refrigerator. He called, "Why don't you ever buy beer?"

"If I did, it would be *my* beer. Buy your own."

He returned to stand in front of her. "My car's not running so well right now."

"It got you here, didn't it? If it conks out, you can probably hoof it into town."

He glared and went back to sit with Axel. Finally, he returned and held out a ten-dollar bill for her. "When you go to town for groceries tomorrow, pick me up some Bud Light, will you?"

She glanced up from her laptop. "I'm not your delivery girl, and I'm not going to town. You two are on your own tomorrow night. Keagan's taking me out for supper."

Axel heard her. What was the deal? Did the man have radar ears? Most people his age were hard of hearing. He called, "What are we supposed to eat?"

"There's plenty of cottage cheese and applesauce."

Kurt pinched his lips in a tight line, but didn't argue. "We have lots of leftovers, don't we?"

"More than you deserve *if* you don't eat them all tonight." She went back to reading her e-mails, and Kurt took the hint and left.

The next morning, she pulled on her paint clothes with less enthusiasm. Her arms and back hurt. Her neck ached. What the hell had she been thinking? But she only had one more room to go and the downstairs would be finished. Not the bathroom. That was more work than she wanted to expend, so she painted the living room and thought she'd never get it done. There were too many windows and doors to tape around. She covered the front of the fireplace. When she finally finished, she swallowed two Advil. By four-thirty, the parlor, dining room, and living room looked as good as they were going to get, so she quit to get ready for when Keagan came.

"What about supper?" Axel called.

"Kurt's here. He can heat up leftovers."

"We had those for lunch."

"There are still some left. There are packets of Meals on Wheels in the refrigerator, too." She'd bought a week's worth, but Axel wouldn't touch them. "And we have . . ."

He finished for her. "Applesauce, cottage cheese, and Ensure."

"Bon appétit, boys!"

Once in her room, she grimaced at the clothes she'd packed for her stay. *What to wear?* Keagan seemed to favor the natural look, but she liked to make more of a splash. He was taking her to a microbrewery, so she didn't want to overdress. She decided on a pair of tight jeans and a V-necked, black shirt with a mustard-colored cardigan. The mustard yellow looked good with her dark coloring. She rimmed her eyes with brown liner and added peach lipstick, then studied herself in the mirror. She'd do.

His blue SUV pulled in the drive at five-thirty, and she ran out to meet him. He grinned. "Are you ready to get away from Axel for a while?"

Fastening her seat belt, she shrugged. "I can stomach Axel. It's Kurt who drives me nuts. Sylvie's supposed to be on her way, too. If they're willing to watch over the old fart, he won't need me. I can leave him to them." She waited for his reaction.

"When I told Mom that Kurt had shown up, she didn't have anything good to say about him. We all think you've done more than anyone expected to try to help Axel."

Not what she wanted to hear. She wanted Keagan to be sad she might leave soon. Instead, he gave her a running commentary of the shops they were passing on the way to the brewery. "This way is a little longer, so you can see some of the town. My sister just started selling her jewelry at Lefty's shop," he said, pointing. "She works with polymer, beads, and polished stones."

"I love jewelry. I'll have to check it out." Karli had a thing for necklaces. She hadn't packed any to come here. No need to doll up for Axel, but since she'd met Keagan, she wished she'd brought a couple.

He gestured up and down Main Street. "This is the main drag. Ralph's diner is down there."

They passed a florist shop that sold honey. Karli shook her head. "That's an odd combination."

"Not really. They grow a lot of their own flowers in the summer, so they keep bees."

Joel's microbrewery was close to the highway—a great location to attract tourists on their way to the national forest. The parking lot wasn't full, but there were a decent number of cars. The inside of the old building surprised her with its bright colors and warehouse feel. Keagan led her to the bar side, and people waved as they chose a table.

"We go up to the counter to place our orders," he told her. "I'm getting the sausage sandwich. Joel gets the sausage special made from Carl Gruber. You'll never taste sausage this good anywhere else."

They went to the counter, and she ordered a sausage sandwich, fries, and beer, too. Back at the table, she bit into the sandwich and almost moaned. She loved sausage, anyway, and Keagan was right. This was better than anything she'd ever tasted.

He gave a satisfied smile. "Well?"

"I'm eating two of these."

He laughed. They were halfway through their meal when people started dropping by to say *hi*. Two women came first.

"Hi, I'm Daphne. You've met my husband Tyne. I own the stained-glass shop in town."

"And I'm Miriam," the tall woman said. "My husband owns the brewery, so you'd think I'd be sick of eating here, but Daphne and I aren't the best cooks."

More people followed, every one of them friendly, welcoming her to town. By the time she and Keagan were on their own again, Karli had finished her meal.

"Ready for another sandwich?" Keagan asked. "I am."

When he went to the counter to order, she went to help carry their beers. An older man turned to introduce himself to her. "Hi, I'm Buck Krieger. I own the landscape nursery a little outside of town." Before they got back to their seats, a half dozen other people greeted her.

"Is everyone always this nice?" Karli asked when they sat down.

"Mostly." He squirted mustard on his sausage. "Every town has a few clunkers, but we like to watch out for our own."

"But I'm not your own. I'm only here for a little while."

He shook his head. "Your mom grew up here. We have partial claim on you. It made my mom happy to know *your* mom turned out happy, so people are glad to see you."

That made sense. Karli sipped her beer and studied Keagan over the rim of her glass. "Since you didn't want to farm, did you ever want to leave Mill Pond?"

"Nope, never." His brows dipped in a frown. She'd obviously brought up something unpleasant.

She fidgeted, uncomfortable. "Did I say something that annoyed you?"

He scratched his head. "Not your fault. I sometimes wonder if I'd have left Mill Pond with Cecily if she'd have stayed with me, that's all."

Uh-oh, did he still have a thing for an ex-girlfriend? "How long has it been since you broke up?"

"Three years. We lived together for two years, but she left town with a coworker from the factory. Well, after the factory closed down, that is."

Three years was a long time. He should be ready to move on by now. Karli reached out to touch his hand. "I'm sorry. It must have hurt."

"I could never make her happy." He took a deep draught of his beer. "Anyway, it was for the best. I need to get my business secure before I settle down with someone else."

Settle down? That was the last thing she wanted. She'd become a traveling nurse for a reason. She wanted to be able to pick up and move whenever the mood hit her. "You're pretty close to getting your own place, aren't you?" She'd gotten the impression he was ready to buy a house and set up a studio.

He nodded. "I've been saving. I'll have low monthly payments, so I don't have to worry about debt. Now, I just need to find the right property."

Karli decided to let the conversation rest a minute. They'd gotten on some dicey subjects and she wanted to shift back to a cheerful mood. They finished their meals in comfortable silence.

He had beautiful eyes and eyelashes. She could stare at him for hours and hardly notice the scars on the side of his face. Odd, how they faded away when she started talking with him.

When they finished eating, he left a tip and led her to his SUV. "Ready to see my studio?"

"I sure am." Damn, how she wished the invitation was a come-on, but she was pretty sure it wasn't. He really did want to show her his work. Too bad. She could think of lots of creative ways he could use his hands besides molding clay.

Chapter 16

By the time they drove back past Axel's farm, darkness blanketed every field and country road. Keagan turned into the long drive that led to his parents' house—a big, white four square with a porch swing hanging on the narrow front porch. Karli couldn't help comparing it to Axel's. His porch was long and wide with columns that marched across its front and turned a corner to meet the side of the house. She loved it.

Lights spilled from his parents' living room windows. More lights beamed from a back room.

"Mom's in the kitchen," he said. "Mom and Dad must be eating a late supper tonight. Dad probably worked outside until it got dark."

Karli thought of her parents. They ate supper at six-thirty. When she was growing up, she was expected to be home every night unless she got special permission to skip or be late. "That's when families catch up with each other," Dad always told them. "Supper is sacred."

Karli had fussed and fumed about that rule when she was younger. Now, she cherished it. Dad's rule *had* made their family bond.

A little farther down the drive, a ranch house sat back on a deep, front lawn. "My sister and her husband's house," Keagan said.

Keagan drove past a freshly painted, red barn to a long, narrow shed that must have held yard equipment at one time. He parked and led her to the door. He unlocked it, flipped on the bright overhead lights, and led her inside. It felt good to get out of the chilly night air. In November, when the sun dipped, so did the temperatures.

The studio's walls and ceiling were painted white. The wooden floor was painted green. Long, butcher-block counters lined all three walls with pine shelves mounted to the walls above them. A sturdy oak table occupied the center of the room with a pottery wheel at each end. A kiln took up one corner of the room. But what caught her attention was the beautiful products drying on every available surface.

She couldn't help it. She walked to the shelves holding the displays to study them, drawn by Keagan's beautiful work. In a large cupboard that held one dish of each design he'd ever made, she studied the new lines for every season. He had six plates on the bottom shelf for spring. For the first, hyacinths, daffodils, and tulips were hand painted on a white plate. On the next, the entire surface was embossed with different spring flowers and then glazed with a butter yellow. She loved each year's pattern, then looked at the plates he'd made for six summers. One featured daisies and lilacs, another violets and green leaves, another roses, and one featured an embossed sun design that covered an entire dish. Fall had colored leaves on a white background, another plate was embossed with pumpkins, gourds, and acorns, another featured mums and sedum. Each was so special, she didn't know which she'd choose if she was going to order a set. Winter took her breath away.

"They're all gorgeous," she told Keagan.

He came to stand next to her. "You must love snow."

"I love the seasons, but these just make me happy." One entire plate was embossed with snowmen, sleds, and mittens, then glazed a glossy red. Another had a white center and was surrounded by vivid red poinsettias. A third was rimmed with pine trees with cardinals perched on their branches. Her favorite might have been the plate rimmed with fruit pies and steaming mugs of coffee to warm the cold winter days.

He nodded toward the shelves with specialty items. "I paint cookie jars and teapots to order."

There was a wide of variety of those, too. Some were shaped like cats with the tail curved to be a handle. One teapot was a fat Carolina wren with its beak open to form a spout. She shook her head in wonder. "I love them all."

The rest of the shelves and counters were filled with work to fill orders. He sighed. "I really could use more space someday, but this works for now."

She noticed plates and bowls drying on drop cloths in the back corner. She gave a seductive smile and bent over, pretending to study those. Her neckline plunged. Her jeans were tight. His expression said that he'd noticed. And then there was a quick knock on the door, and Brad strode inside.

He smiled at her. "Keagan said you were coming to see his work tonight. Thought I'd stop in, too."

Were the heavens mocking her? Why did he show up when Keagan had actually noticed her?

Karli pointed to a squat, fat, embossed tureen with a matching platter. "I want a set of those. I love to cook soups and stews."

Keagan looked surprised. "You travel a lot. I didn't think you'd want a lot of baggage to drag with you."

"Those are worth the bother."

Brad grinned. "Do you cook at home?"

Why don't you go away? She couldn't say it. Brad was Keagan's friend, his roommate. She had to be nice to him. She forced a smile. "Sometimes, when the mood strikes. One-dish meals are my favorites."

"I love beef stew." Brad looked at her, hoping for her to follow through.

She didn't. She looked at Keagan. "Beef's heavy. I like chicken stew. Have you had it?"

He blinked, caught off guard. He obviously thought he could melt into the background since Brad arrived. "I don't think so."

"Do you like chicken wings?" Brad asked. Karli had to give him credit. He didn't discourage easily. "Our pizza place makes really good ones."

"I'm a little picky about wings. My favorites are grilled citrus-chipotle. I get them at The Tower Bar at home."

Brad glanced at Keagan, still undeterred. "My buddy says you've been doing a lot of painting lately."

She nodded. "Axel's house is starting to look better."

"Maybe I can take you out after a long day of painting. You wouldn't have to worry about cooking supper that way."

He really was a nice guy, but he was only looking for a good time. Usually, that's all she wanted, too. And maybe that's all she'd get in Mill Pond. She smiled. "That would be nice. Kurt goes through more food than Axel ever did. And Sylvie's coming soon."

Keagan shook his head. "Mom talked to me about Axel's kids. Sylvie's name came up. Nothing good."

Karli sighed. "Yeah, that's the impression I got. Two of the worst are coming to duke it out over Axel's money."

"Some families are like that." Keagan shrugged. "Not mine. We all try to help each other." He looked at Brad.

"Beats me," Brad said. "My family's kind of live and let live. None of us have enough to fight over."

What Brad didn't know was a lot. Karli had lost a patient whose two daughters squabbled over who got which knickknack.

Keagan looked at his watch. "Hate to say it, but I'm on the clock early tomorrow. Are you ready to call it a night, Karli?"

She faked a yawn. If they left now, she'd have a little more time alone with Keagan. "Works for me. It's been a nice night."

"I'm driving right by your place," Brad said. "What if I give you a ride home?"

"Thanks." Keagan glanced out the window at the lights shining in his parents' windows. "That way, I can stop to say a quick hi to Mom and Dad."

Damn, she'd been shanghaied, but she had to put a good face on it. "Thanks for the tour of your studio," she told Keagan. "And I really do want your tureen and platter with the coffee mugs and pies on them."

He nodded. "I'll make them for you."

Brad turned up the wattage on his smile. "It's you and me, pretty lady. Let's go." He led her to his truck and held the door for her. "No need for a seat belt. You can sit close to me."

Oh, brother. This was so *not* how she wanted to end the night. And she had no intentions of getting cuddly with Brad.

"How many more days will you be in Mill Pond?" he asked.

She shook her head. "Not sure, it's according to how miserable Sylvie is to live with."

He lost a little bit of his flow, but recovered quickly. "Indy isn't that far from Mill Pond. If we click, I'd still like to see you."

She wasn't going to make it that easy for him. "I don't know where my next job will be. I've been thinking about the East Coast."

That caught him off guard. "Where on the coast?"

"Maybe somewhere in New England in the summer and someplace warm in the winter, like Florida."

"It would be nice to be able travel like you do."

She raised her eyebrows. "Would you really leave here?"

He laughed. "Probably not. I'm happy in Mill Pond."

Just as she'd thought. When he pulled into the drive, she leaned closer and gave him a quick kiss on the cheek, then slid out the truck's door. "Thanks for the ride."

"Any time. Someday, I'm taking you out on the town, and we'll get to know each other better."

Like hell they would. She smiled and made a dash for the house. If she showed any interest in Brad, Keagan would wipe his hands of her. And Keagan was going to start taking her seriously, whether he knew it or not.

Chapter 17

The next day, when Keagan drove down his parents' long, gravel drive to deliver mail, he glanced at the far fields, looking for the dust cloud that followed his dad's tractor. Nothing. What was Dad waiting on? The weather was good, but there were no guarantees how long it would last this time of year.

When he pulled up to the house, his sister hurried out onto the porch to hand him an open cardboard box with a covered, aluminum foil pan inside it. "Thanks for stopping for this. Mom took it out of the freezer and thawed it last night, then baked it this morning."

Keagan inhaled the aroma. "Really? Mom made one for Karli and not for me? She knows I love sausage and spinach pie."

Marcia pulled her jacket closer and grinned at him. "Sorry, bro. There was only one and Karli beat you out."

"I'm protesting." He put the box on the floor on the passenger's side of the mail truck. Then he gestured toward the dry fields. "I thought Dad would be turning over the sod by now. Did he change his mind?"

Marcia's gaze darted away from his. "Dad decided to go into town with Mom today. They thought they might grab lunch there."

"I smell a rat." Dad never went into town to lunch with Mom. "Is there anything wrong I should know about?"

"Like what?"

She still didn't make eye contact. Was she trying to keep a secret? A good one or a bad one? "You tell me."

"Nothing to tell."

He hesitated but had lots of deliveries to make so didn't argue. When he pulled away, though, he felt uneasy. His sister was a terrible liar, and he knew her telltale signs. Her eyes always slid away from his, but Marcia hadn't out-and-out lied to him today or she'd have rubbed her nose—her sure giveaway. She hadn't told him the whole truth either.

On the way to the road, he glanced at the far fields again. Something wasn't kosher, but he'd wait. Were Mom and Dad planning something special for the holidays this year? Was one of them sick with something that needed treatment? If it was something serious, they'd have told him. So why the cloak and dagger this morning? But secrets didn't last long in Mill Pond. Eventually, he'd find out what was going on.

He changed his route a little bit so that Karli would be his last delivery for the day. He told himself it was because it would be more convenient, but he knew that was stretching it. If he were like Marcia, he'd be rubbing the bridge of his nose. Before he pulled into Axel's drive, he told himself that he'd better be careful around Karli. She was way too attractive, and he was a little bit too attracted to her. She acted like she might return the interest, but she'd be leaving Mill Pond soon. And that might be a good thing for him. All he had to do was wait it out.

When he knocked on her door, it took her longer than usual to answer it. When she did, she looked frazzled. She was makeup-free with her hair pulled up in a messy ponytail, and she looked like she could spit nails. He stared. "Looks like I came at a bad time."

She glanced at the foil pan he carried and motioned him inside. "I want to wash my hands again before I touch food."

Uh-oh. That didn't sound good. He went to the kitchen and put the casserole on the long, wooden worktable. He laid the mail beside it. She went to the bathroom and came to join him a few minutes later.

"Do I want to know?" He wrinkled his nose. A rank smell drifted from the three-season room.

She glowered. "Idiot Kurt drove to town to buy beer and brought back tons of chocolate candy bars. He and Axel ate them all at one sitting."

"Chocolate gives Axel diarrhea. I never give him straight chocolate."

"That's because you have a brain." She turned to glare at the back room. "And the dumb ass who provided the chocolate can't stomach anything unpleasant, so while I was changing Axel's diapers, because he couldn't make it to the bathroom in time, Kurt was throwing up in the trash can."

Keagan felt sorry for her. "You're made of stern stuff. Most people would turn and run."

"I'm a damn nurse. I've seen lots worse, but I'd like to strangle Kurt right now."

Keagan didn't blame her. "My mom sent supper if you're not in the mood to cook."

"Those two get broth and crackers. And if there's one more accident, they won't see good food for another week."

He nodded. "What about you? How are you doing?"

"They ruined my appetite. It's tea and crackers for me."

He tried to think of a different subject, something pleasant. "Are you looking forward to Thanksgiving? It's not that far away. Bet you'll be ready to head back to Indy to celebrate with your parents."

She grimaced. "Mom and Dad are flying to Dad's parents' house in Milwaukee. I usually go with them, but it felt like too much this year. If I'm still in Mill Pond, I'll just stay here."

He was appalled. "With Axel?"

"And the moocher moron." Her voice dripped with sarcasm. "If I'm really lucky, Sylvie will get here in time, too. This Thanksgiving's going to be fun."

The words sprang out before he could stop them. "Come with me to my parents' house. We always have enough food."

Her brown eyes sparkled. "Really? You don't know how nice that would be. Thank you."

What had he done? Damn it! Didn't he just tell himself to stay far away from this woman? But no one should have to eat frozen turkey dinners with Axel and Kurt.

She smiled, and he was happy to notice she seemed to be getting in a better mood. "Is your parents' farm as big as Axel's? It probably keeps them busy, doesn't it?"

"Farms are a lot of work. Things are slowing down now, but their farm's bigger than this one. Seven hundred acres." They'd had a family summit in the spring when the Bransons' fields, across the road from Mom and Dad's, went up for sale. They were prime acres and wouldn't be available long. If his parents bought them, they'd be overextended, but if they didn't make an offer, someone else would. Each family member got a vote, and Keagan voted to buy. Everyone did but Dad.

Karli looked surprised. "Axel owns a hundred acres, right? Kurt thinks it's worth $600,000. He expects to be rich soon."

"A little high, but close. It's not going to be that easy, though. Axel's kids were always like a dog with a bone. They'll fight over it."

She started toward the dining room. "I need to get away from the smell."

A good idea. "I bet you're going to be happy to leave here. Where have you been as a traveling nurse?"

She perched on a wooden chair and stretched her legs. She had damn nice legs. "I spent some time in Florida. My sister lives there, and I got a job close to Tampa. Then I went to California for a while, but the cost of living is too expensive, so I went to New Orleans. I love the food, but missed my mom and dad, so came back here for a while."

"You have a great lifestyle."

She gave him a thoughtful look. "Would you travel?"

"Travel, yes. Move, no. I'd love to go someplace special for a couple weeks once a year, see the country, more of the world. All I've been doing lately, though, is saving money."

He'd love to hear about the places she'd been, but he was pretty sure the more time he spent with Karli, the more time he'd want to spend with her.

She locked gazes with him. "I like to travel, but I always miss my family. I like seeing new places, then I always come home."

"And I always stay home, but I'd like to see new places. If you'd put us in a blender, we'd be perfect." He wondered how well they'd fit together, but even her stay in Indy was temporary. Everything about her was short-term. He had to remember that.

She raised a dark eyebrow, studying him. "We might be perfect, as is."

He was getting in over his head. Time to run. He gave a breezy smile. "I doubt it. You're more adventurous than I am. I hope your day gets better, though. And I'd ban chocolate from the house." He started for the door.

She called after him, "Thanks for inviting me for Thanksgiving!"

Thanksgiving. She probably wouldn't be here by then, and if she was, he'd have his family there to serve as a buffer. He'd be fine. He could do this.

Chapter 18

Early Thursday morning, Brad called to invite Karli to go to Chase's bar with him for supper. She couldn't think of one reason not to go. She was going to Art's Grocery before lunch to stock up on groceries for the rest of the week, and she'd agreed to pick up a case of beer for Kurt just to shut him up. She could reheat Keagan's mom's casserole for supper, so Axel wouldn't starve, and she could hardly wait to get away from both men and the house.

"I have to be back early," she told Brad. "Axel's been having some problems lately."

"Fine with me," Brad said. "I have an early appointment on Friday, need to install a new furnace. This way, we'll get to know each other a little better, and I'll have great company while I eat."

The man had an answer for everything. She was impressed. At the store, she bought deli meat to make sandwiches for lunch. Just to annoy Axel, she stocked up on applesauce, cottage cheese, and Ensure, but then she ruined it by buying a ham hock to make him bean soup. He'd told her how much he loved it when his mother made it. She bought some of his other favorites, too—pork chops, everything to make macaroni and cheese, and a whole chicken.

When she got home and threw sandwiches together, the old coot went on and on about how much he loved deli ham. He thought he was being sly, "buttering her up" as he called it, but flattery would get him nowhere.

"Enjoy it while you can," she said.

Axel looked smug. "Sylvie's been married three times. She probably cooked for her husbands."

Kurt snorted. "Either that or she cooks like shit and that's why they left her."

When Axel frowned, Karli shook her head. "There's always Meals on Wheels if you get desperate."

Kurt licked his lips. "Those were pretty good."

"Then you buy them." Axel finished his sandwich and turned back to his TV, flipping to his favorite station.

"Hey, I was watching Judge Judy," Kurt complained.

Axel shrugged. "You have a room. Buy a TV for up there and leave me alone."

Karli had noticed the two men were getting tired of one another's company. Maybe a nursing home would start looking better. She finished putting groceries away and turned her attention to the wooden floors. They were in remarkably good shape, so she spent the day polishing them. By six, though, she was showered and dressed, ready for Brad. She hadn't gone to a lot of bother, just mascara and lipstick, but he still looked happy to see her.

"You look great! Everyone at the bar's going to be jealous."

She'd pulled a jacket over her long-sleeved tee. Her sweater hadn't been warm enough last night. She wondered if Keagan stopped at Chase's to eat. Even if he did, he wouldn't come tonight, she was sure. He'd do his best to avoid her and let Brad work his magic. It wouldn't matter. Keagan couldn't get rid of her that easily.

When they walked in the bar, people looked up and waved. It was just like going to Joel's microbrewery. The town greeted her. Most tables and booths were full, and Buck Kreiger—Brad said he ran a landscape nursery—motioned them to his table.

"Is the place always this busy?" Karli asked.

Brad nodded. "This time of year. After New Year's, everything will slow down. Tourists stop coming and people hibernate. The shopkeepers count on it to build up new inventory and have some time off."

Chase himself came to wait on them. He frowned at Brad. "Where's Keagan?"

"He had an order he had to finish tonight." Another ready answer. Brad was full of them, but it was just as Karli suspected. Keagan was offering Brad a clear playing field, damn him.

Chase raised an eyebrow. He wasn't buying it either, but gave Karli a dazzling grin—the man knew how to dazzle. "What can I get you?"

They all went for burgers, but after Chase left, Brad laughed. "It's a good thing Chase is wearing that big, gold ring. Before Paula, when he asked, *What can I get you,* he never knew what to expect."

Karli could understand that. This town had its share of hot men and Chase was near the top of the list. "I've heard he makes great barbecue."

"True, that," Buck said. "His sauce is a guarded secret."

"He hasn't even told Paula?" Brad sounded surprised.

"He's told her, but she's not allowed to use it. As a chef, she gets that." Karli shook her head. "Does everyone in Mill Pond take food so seriously?"

Both men stared at her. Brad answered. "We're a foodie town. That's how we put ourselves on the map. Tourists used to stop here, look through a few shops, and then take off for the national forest. Now, they stop and stay for a meal or two, linger to go from shop to shop and spend some money. More people try to stay in town for the night. The farmers have all upped their game here."

Karli snorted. "Come on. Chase's bar, the microbrewery, and Ralph's diner are the biggest eateries in town. Ian's resort does gourmet, and it's always full."

Buck squared his shoulders, offended. "Have you tasted one of Chase's burgers? The beef comes from Carl Gruber. Carl supplies Ralph, too. And Cutter Rethlake farms the hogs for the specialty pork around here."

Karli pinched her lips together. "Should I call truce? I can tell you take farming seriously."

"Everyone should." Even Brad looked fired-up. "It's the difference between quality and quantity."

She put up her hands in defeat. "I get it. Even Art's Grocery has its local meat counter."

"People bring coolers to shop there." Buck sat back in his chair and chuckled. "But we'll quit giving you grief. You probably have plenty of fancy restaurants in Indy."

"We do, but I don't go to them very often. Too expensive."

Chase saved her by carrying their burgers to the table. "Here you go, guys. Enjoy."

An understatement. Boy, were they good! If burgers could be gourmet, these would qualify. Karli thought of all the food she'd eaten in Mill Pond and all of it had been delicious. When they finished their burgers and fries, Buck ordered dessert.

Chase grinned at Karli. "Buck never leaves here without a slice of pie. Ian's wife Tessa makes them. They're the best."

And that wasn't bragging. He was right. Mill Pond might not be fancy, but when it did something, it did it well.

When Buck finished his pie, he paid his bill and headed to the door. "I'll be here again next Thursday if you need a table to sit at."

Karli watched him leave, then turned to Brad. "He's a nice man."

"One of the best. Mill Pond's full of good people."

It was. No wonder Keagan didn't want to leave here.

Brad paid their bill, she left a tip, then they headed to his truck. On the drive home, he said, "Indy's not that far away. I could come up to visit you on weekends."

She laughed. Was that a definition of booty calls or not? "My schedule's not that convenient. Some weekends I work, some I don't. No set hours."

"No problem. We'll just have to keep in touch."

She didn't plan to, but she wasn't going to argue about it. "Why do I get the idea that you're already a busy man?"

He grinned. "I do get lonely, you know, and need company."

As in women. Exactly what she expected. "I wouldn't want you to wither away from lack of attention. Don't change any plans for me."

"Wouldn't think of it, but I can always find time for friends."

Oh, goodie, he could work her in between Girl A and Girl B. No thank you. When he dropped her off, he called, "This was fun. We'll have to do it again."

"I'd like that." She'd had a nice night, but that's all it was. He was never getting into her panties. He just didn't realize that yet.

Chapter 19

Karli scowled as she watched Keagan's mail truck slow at the end of the drive. He delivered a fistful of envelopes, then drove away. The damn scaredy-cat. To hell with him!

She scraped the leftovers of the spinach casserole into a bowl to nuke. No cooking lunch today! Then she glanced at her reflection in the window over the sink. Lord have mercy, it was a good thing Keagan ran for his life. She looked like she'd stuck her finger in an electric socket. Her hair could make Medusa run. But damn, she was practically throwing herself at the man and he pretended not to notice. Worse, he threw Brad in her path to distract her.

There had to be *some* way to get closer to him. Then inspiration struck. He'd known exactly where to find pictures of this house in its glory days. He hated to see it in disrepair. Every time she painted a new room, he loved it, loved seeing the old place look good again. But what if she went all out? The weather was still decent. What if she decided to scrape the whole damn exterior like his friends had mentioned?

Something had to impress the man!

She grinned at her reflection. If she played her cards right, he wouldn't want her taking on such a big project by herself. Second, it would knock his socks off that she wanted to try. And third, he'd probably volunteer to help her.

She glanced out the window at the poor barn. It looked worse than the house, and she realized how much it bothered her to see this place in such sad shape. She could almost feel how much Axel's mom had loved the house when it was built. It deserved to be treated better.

She'd only lived in apartments since she took her boards, and she'd never stayed in one place for more than six months. It surprised her how much she enjoyed restoring this house to a little of its former glory. Had all of her nesting hormones come unhinged when she came to Mill Pond? Or was she just having fun playing house?

The timer dinged on the microwave, chasing away her fanciful thoughts. She dished up their lunch. Axel didn't look as happy as she thought he would when he saw his plate.

"Not a fan of spinach," he told her.

"It's healthy, full of calcium and vitamins." She kept trying to sneak fruits and vegetables into his diet.

"I get those when I drink an Ensure."

She rolled her eyes. "It's not the same."

Kurt shrugged. "Spinach is okay."

Okay? If they had really liked it, the whole thing would be gone, so she'd better count her blessings. She was eating at the wooden table in the kitchen with the oven on, soaking in the heat, when a mouse ran over her foot.

"Holy shit!" She wouldn't let herself jump on a chair. She was a grown woman, and she wouldn't scream over a mouse. But she wanted to.

"You okay?" Words she never thought she'd hear Axel utter.

"A mouse just ran over my foot."

He grunted. "Yeah, they come in about this time of year when it gets cold outside."

She walked to the door to talk to him. "How do you catch them?"

"There are some traps in the broom closet."

She wrinkled her nose. "I'm not going around the house to collect little dead bodies."

"Suit yourself."

She frowned at him. "There must be something else."

"Mice leave when there's a cat in a house, but when you leave, you take the damned thing with you."

"I don't want a cat."

"Then kill the mice or start naming them."

She glowered toward Kurt. "Mice are a man's job. He should deal with them."

Kurt finished a beer and swiped at his mouth with the back of his hand. "They don't bother me."

"They're disgusting. They spread disease and multiply faster than rabbits."

He shrugged. "They don't eat that much. Put some cheese out for them."

She turned and stalked back to the kitchen. The idiots! She wasn't about to start every day by sweeping away mouse turds. She went to her room and called her mom. "Axel has mice. I heard about a gadget you plug into the wall that has a high-pitched sound that drives them away."

"You have to buy one for each floor," Mom told her. "I don't think there are any outlets in the attic."

Karli could picture every mouse running to the third floor of the house and partying there. "So what do I do?"

"We always had barn cats when I was growing up."

Karli sighed. "Axel says if I get a cat, it's mine. I take it with me."

"Cats are portable," her mom said. "Most apartments are okay with them."

Not what she wanted to hear. She'd have to buy a litter box and train the cat to stay indoors. And travel with it. Then she thought of Keagan. His parents had a huge farm with massive fields. They had a red barn and must battle lots of mice. Would they take another cat when she left here if she paid to have it spayed and get it all its shots?

"I'll ask Keagan if his parents will take it when I leave."

She could almost hear her mom's smile. "It's easy to get attached to cats."

"We never had one. You always had some kind of dog."

"That was your dad's fault. He doesn't like cats. I grew up with them. They're my favorites."

Karli had never known that. "I don't want a pet. Too much work."

"Okay." Mom had that *mother* tone in her voice. She didn't believe her. But she was wrong. Karli didn't want anything that was extra work in her life. "Good luck, hon."

"Thanks. If I don't see you before then, have fun in Milwaukee."

Mom laughed. "Has Sylvie come yet?"

"No."

"Then I hope she stays away until after Thanksgiving. If you get sick of it all, let my dad deal with Kurt and come home."

"Will do. Love ya." When Karli hung up, her thoughts turned to Keagan. She had another reason to talk to him. Any reason at all worked for her.

Chapter 20

The next day, Keagan saw the red flag standing at attention on Axel's mailbox, but there was nothing inside it. Still, Axel must need something, so he drove to his front porch and knocked on the door.

Karli opened it and motioned him inside. She looked cuter than usual today in tight jeans and a flannel shirt that wasn't tucked in. Her dark hair was pulled back in a hairband with a few bangs that had escaped curling on her forehead.

The old nursery rhyme popped into his head. *There was a little girl Who had a little curl Right in the middle of her forehead* . . . He smiled. He'd bet Karli could be really good when she wanted to be . . . and very, very naughty when she chose to.

He breathed in the aroma of bacon, sautéed garlic and onions. "*Mmm,* smells good in here. Are you making lunch?"

"Tomato soup and grilled cheese sandwiches, but I started the meatloaf for supper, wrapped it in bacon. Thought I'd fix mashed potatoes, too. Want to stop by?"

He glanced toward the kitchen, tempted, but shook his head. "I'm meeting Brad at Chase's for burgers tonight."

"Those are good, too." She shrugged, then frowned, turning serious. "I'm sorry I put up the flag to bother you, but I saw a mouse in the kitchen yesterday. Everyone I talked to said I should get a cat, but I'm not staying here much longer. I don't want to take in a pet, then leave it. I was wondering if I adopted a cat and paid for its shots and everything if your parents would take it when I had to leave."

He blinked. One more cat would hardly be noticed in the barn. "I'd guess so, but it wouldn't be a pet. It would have to stay outdoors. They like getting new barn cats every once in a while so their cats aren't so inbred. They'd prefer a male, though."

She frowned. "I was going to get it spayed."

"Then no problem. They just don't need a zillion kittens."

She nodded and he turned to leave. "Wait. I wanted to ask you about ladders, too. I thought I'd start scraping the house, get rid of some of the peeling paint."

He stared. "Axel will let you do that?"

"He'd better."

Keagan grinned. "Some of us have been talking about spending a Saturday scraping, but we're having such a warm November, we thought we might even be able to paint. Chase and Harley are on the town council, and they got a vote through to buy paint for this place. We thought we'd buy good quality products. Most of us already own spray guns. We'd like to finish as much of the exterior of the house as we can before it gets too cold."

"How in the world will you talk Axel into that?" Would the old man allow it?

"I think he'll go for it, since he's not paying for it." Keagan nodded toward the back room. "You know he's listening. The old bastard turned down his TV so he could hear us." He raised his voice. "What do you say, Axel?"

"Go ahead and waste the town's money! What do I care? The kids'll inherit more when I die."

Karli grimaced. "You're too mean to die any time soon, old coot!"

Keagan heard his laugh. Axel enjoyed heckling Karli. People had asked him about painting his house before and he'd sent them away. Karli could bully him into things he normally wouldn't do. Hell, he brushed his teeth twice a day now. "I'll call Chase and whoever can make it will show up on Saturday. No making food for us either. We'll cover that. There'll be too many of us."

"Will you be here?"

"Yup, so I don't want to see you climbing some high ladder. We'll put you in charge of the shutters."

"What shutters? There aren't any."

"They were falling off, so I put them in the barn. They're really nice, handmade."

She shook her head. "How long have you been taking care of Axel?"

"I don't. I just check on him once a week and bring him a few groceries. He's lost ground the last couple of months, though. That's why I called your mom."

"And now I have this damn girl living with me!" Axel yelled out at him.

Keagan chuckled, but his good mood vanished when he heard footsteps coming down the stairs. Kurt hadn't even changed out of his pajamas. His gray beard was scragglier than Axel's, and his long, unkempt hair grazed his shoulders. What a lazy-ass bum! Keagan glanced at the clock and said, "Good morning—what's left of it. Did you come down for lunch?"

"I smelled meatloaf."

"That's for supper. Don't touch it," Karli told him. "I made it early so I could drive into town today and buy a ladder."

Keagan turned to Kurt. "A few of us are coming on Saturday to scrape the house. We could use an extra hand. You worked odd jobs, didn't you?"

Kurt ran a hand through his hair, making it more mussed. He rolled his shoulders and winced. "I'd pitch in, but I lost my last job because my back's been bothering me. It's still not right. I have to take it easy."

"Yeah, I thought so." Keagan shook his head. He didn't know how Karli put up with him, but then, it wasn't her call, was it? Axel was enjoying himself too much. He started for the door again. "My dad and Stuart, my brother-in-law, both have spray guns. When we paint, I'll bring those, too. If we have enough people, we should be able to get the house done pretty fast."

She looked happy. "When I leave, I hope the house looks more like that picture you showed me. I think it will make my mom happy to know it's pretty again."

That was nice of her to think of her mom, to care about the house. There were so many things he liked about her. If only . . . He gave his head another shake. She'd be gone soon and then he could concentrate on his job, his neighbors, and his dinnerware.

Chapter 21

For a mid-November day, the weather was mild. Karli enjoyed the drive into Mill Pond and enjoyed talking to Meg at the hardware store even more. She'd decided to wait on getting a cat until after the house was painted. Having so many people coming in and out of the house might terrorize it, or it might slip out and disappear when the door opened and closed.

She bought an extension ladder, but hoped she'd never have to climb very far up it. Keagan meant to paint the house the colors of paint he imagined in the picture—gleaming white for the clapboards and sage green for the shutters. Mom often talked about the old place, how pretty it could have been if Axel had done much of anything to it. Karli hoped she'd still be here when they finished it.

She stopped at Art's Grocery since she was in town and visited with a few people she didn't know but who were friendly while she grabbed three rotisserie chickens, some deli meat, and a few loaves of deli breads. She'd freeze whatever she didn't use today.

When she got back to the house and dragged everything inside, she went to check on Axel. He was sitting up in bed with his arms crossed over his chest, his lips turned down, his eyes narrowed. The TV was tilted so that Kurt could see it better, and Kurt was leaning back in his easy chair, watching some judge who wasn't Judge Judy.

Her good mood vanished. Karli could feel the anger roil off of Axel. "Is everything okay?"

He nudged his chin toward Kurt. "He took the remote and won't let me watch my favorite shows."

It served Axel right. What did he expect? She should let him stew in his own poisons, but she could hardly tolerate Kurt, and this felt like the last straw. Her fists went to her hips. "Give him back the remote."

Kurt sent her a cursory glance, unconcerned. "Why should he get to hog the TV all day? Why can't I watch some of the shows I like?"

"Because this isn't your house yet. You don't pay for anything. If you don't like it here, leave."

Kurt crossed his arms, as stubborn as Axel. "I have every bit as much right here as you do, and you seem to do pretty much whatever you please."

She pulled her cell phone out of her pocket. Kurt sat up straight in his chair. When he reached to grab it from her, she raised an eyebrow. "Go ahead. Try to bully me."

He pulled his hand back. "Who are you calling?"

"Keagan."

"Hey, there's no need for that. If Axel wants his damn remote, he can have it." He tossed it to him.

Karli took a step closer to him, and Kurt shrank back from her. She pointed a finger at him. "You're not a guest here, and you're not a caregiver. You're a freeloader. If you don't annoy me, it's up to Axel if you stay or go, but don't push me. I'm not in the mood." She whirled on Axel, and the old man's eyes opened wide. "You think you're so clever, playing people against each other, but when Sylvie comes and I go home, this is the way you're going to be treated. Get used to it."

Axel relaxed. He looked cocky again. "Nah, I can have the likes of him evicted."

There was something about the way he said it that made her suspicious. "What do you mean *the likes of him*? Did you try to get *me* evicted?"

He pulled at his blankets, not meeting her eyes.

"You did, didn't you?" She wanted to smack him, surprised by how angry she felt.

"Sheriff Brickle wouldn't boot you off my place, said he'd talked to your mom and you'd only come to help and I should listen to you."

Her hands balled into fists again. "You old bastard, that does it!"

"I told you when you came I didn't want you."

"And I should have listened." She turned on her heel to stomp away. She was done talking to him, done with him period! He could sit and rot in this house for all she cared!

"Hey, where you goin', girl?"

"Home! I'm not getting anywhere with you."

He actually sounded upset. "Don't be like that. You just said it. When Sylvie gets here, I might rather be in a home than be stuck here with her and Kurt."

"Then call Sheriff Brickle and see if he can help you."

"Girl! Come on back here. You're the one who knows all that stuff. You're the one who'd make sure I like where I end up."

She was throwing two of the rotisserie chickens in the freezer, along with most of the fancy bread loaves. She hesitated. That's why she'd stuck around—to see how things went when Sylvie showed up. Okay, not the whole truth. To see Keagan, too. She pressed her lips together. She wasn't sure any of it was worth it.

Axel said, "Come on. You want to see them paint the house, don't you?"

"I *had* wanted to." She slammed the refrigerator door and walked to the sun porch to glare at him. She hugged herself, trying to squeeze away the anger. Damn, Axel could irritate her. She took a deep breath. "I'll stay until Sylvie comes. Then you have to decide—stay with her or get help."

He didn't argue. He gave a quick nod, then looked at the clock. "You made some meatloaf, didn't you?"

She glanced at the clock, too. After five. "Give me a minute. I like mashed potatoes with meatloaf. They'll take about half an hour." She needed to do something to work away her negative energy.

He nodded again. Kurt squirmed. No, he wouldn't. He would, she just knew it. Karli pressed her lips together and stalked to the refrigerator. Yup, just as she suspected. The foil had been messed with and a slice was missing. She came back to the sun-room and stabbed her finger at Kurt a second time.

He threw up his hands. "I'll never get into your suppers again! It's just that I love the damned stuff. Yours was perfect with the ketchup glaze."

She snorted and flounced back to the kitchen to start the potatoes. If she got started with Kurt, it would get ugly. Better to leave it alone. Her mom made the same exact combination every time she made meatloaf, always serving it with mashed potatoes, green beans, and an apple pie. Why she'd gone to the bother, she didn't know. She went to the dining room table where she'd left more shopping bags. She pulled out the pie she'd bought in town and slid it into the oven to warm with the meatloaf.

Half an hour later, she put the food on the dining room table and called, "If you want to eat, you have to come out here."

She almost regretted not letting them eat in the sun-room. The laptop was better company, but the more Axel moved, the stronger he'd stay. Supper was almost done when Brad knocked at the front door and delivered a loaf of pumpkin bread and a loaf of zucchini bread from Maxwell's bread shop.

"Maxwell and Steph—they work together—thought these would make an easy breakfast for you."

"They will. Tell them thank you, and thanks for delivering them."

Brad took a deep breath, inhaling the aromas of the food. "If I weren't meeting Keagan at Chase's tonight, I'd try to wheedle an invitation for supper with you. I'm going to Chase's tomorrow night, too. Want to come?"

She shook her head. She'd use the house as an excuse. "Everyone's coming to scrape on Saturday. I'm going to call it an early night on Friday."

"Gotcha. I'll try you again some other time."

He didn't sound too let down. His curly blonde hair was still a little damp, as if he'd showered after work, and a woodsy cologne drifted to her. He looked like he was ready for a little fun. She watched him hurry to his truck. Since he hadn't scored with her, he'd move to the next girl, and he'd probably get lucky.

Chapter 22

On Saturday, a small army of townspeople showed up to work: Tyne and Daphne came in his Jeep, Joel and Miriam brought a small keg of beer; Harley, Chase, Keagan, and Brad lugged hammers and nails. Keagan opened the door of his SUV and pointed to the back seat. "Ian and Tessa supplied the food—chicken enchiladas with shredded lettuce on the side." Hands reached in to help him carry the foil pans to the kitchen. Then everyone got to work.

So many people here offered so much kindness, Karli felt overwhelmed. When she started to tear up, Keagan reached to comfort her, but Brad hugged her first. He squashed her to him, a little too close for comfort.

"It's all right, hon. Mill Pond helps each other out."

Hon? Where the hell did that come from? She sputtered, irritated, but swallowed her protests. Keagan had taken a step back and gave her a look. He clearly thought she'd succumbed to Brad's charm. Damn the man! Damn both of them!

Keagan started to his SUV, his expression closed. "Let's get to it!" He'd brought a stretch ladder and Brad had another one. Joel and Harley had two regular ladders, so they decided that Keagan and Brad would scrape the highest clapboards. Tyne, Harley, and Chase would work from the bottom of the clapboards up, and the women were in charge of the shutters and trim.

When Karli dragged the paint cans Keagan bought to the barn to work with Daphne and Miriam, Miriam snickered. "Brad grabbed his chance to feel you up. Pun intended. That man's hands can do a full body search in less than two minutes."

Daphne lightly sanded a shutter and passed it to Miriam. "Let's hope he's not that fast at everything."

Karli grunted, still annoyed, but the women were funny. She pried the lid off a paint can. "Now Keagan thinks I've slept with his roommate."

Miriam finished dusting another shutter. "Does it matter?"

"A little, I don't like it when guys get notches on their bedposts they didn't earn."

Miriam blew out a breath and dipped her brush in the sage green paint. "I teach English. I see that all the time with high school boys." She chuckled. "Guess that says something about Brad."

"He lost points with me today." Karli opened another can while Miriam and Daphne slathered generous strokes of paint across the dry boards.

It was almost forty degrees outdoors, and even inside the barn, it was still plenty chilly. When they finished a shutter, they took it outside and leaned it against the barn to dry. By noon, Karli was starting to feel the chill down to her toes. "I'm freezing."

"So am I." Daphne rubbed her hands up and down her arms.

Miriam cleaned her brush and said, "Let's break for lunch before I get frostbite."

They only had two sets of shutters to go, so Karli nodded. When they stepped outside, the men were coming down from their ladders, and Karli was surprised by how much they'd already gotten done. The front and both sides of the house were scraped. They only had the back of the house to go.

She walked down the drive a little to look at their progress, and Keagan came to look, too. She sighed. "When I first saw this place, I thought a strong kick could knock it over."

"It could make someone a good home."

They walked toward the front porch together and she wanted to tell him that she wasn't interested in Brad, but that would sound dorky. He'd give her a look as if he didn't care one way or another, and she'd feel awkward.

When they got to the kitchen, people were already dishing up. She made a plate for Axel before she got one for herself, and when people went to the dining room to eat, Kurt came and dished up two enchiladas for himself, then joined Axel in the sun-room.

Tyne saw him and shook his head. "Does that guy help out with anything?"

"He didn't come here to work," Karli said. "He came to inherit."

Keagan sniffed. "He'll be lucky if Axel didn't leave everything to the wrestling federation for all the hours of entertainment they've provided him."

Karli tried not to laugh. "I could see Axel doing that just to annoy everyone."

Chase looked at Karli. "You've sure been nicer to him than he deserves. How long are going to stay here? Don't get me wrong. We're glad you came." He looked at the freshly painted rooms. "This old place looks a thousand times better."

She shrugged. "I told Axel I'd see how things go when Sylvie comes. Then he'll have to decide if he wants to risk having her and Kurt take care of him or if he wants some other help."

"Fair enough," Miriam said.

Brad looked sad. "Then you probably won't be here much longer."

"I might stay for Thanksgiving." She motioned toward Keagan. "He was nice enough to invite me to his family's get-together. Since my parents won't be home, I'd have someone to celebrate with if I stick around."

"That's still some little ways away." Chase nodded. "Until then, I'll send you some barbecue this Wednesday. Then you won't have to cook that day."

"Do you work on Thanksgiving?" she asked.

He shook his head. "The bar's closed."

"So is the microbrewery. Joel and I are going to my parents' place." Miriam looked at Tyne. "You'll probably be cooking your ass off for one of Ian's special resort packages, won't you?"

Tyne shrugged. "It's part of being a chef. Daphne's going to her mom and dad's, then we're celebrating as a couple on Sunday night after all the guests check out. We're ordering in pizza. The inn's pretty dead the next week. People stay home and eat light to recover."

They sat around the table and caught up with each other a little longer, then people threw away their paper plates and headed outside. Axel called out, "Boy! Keagan! I need you."

Keagan frowned and went to the back room. "What's up?"

"My remote won't work."

Karli had hovered close by in case something was wrong, but Keagan took the remote and punched a few buttons. "Your batteries are dead." He looked at Kurt. "Why didn't you help him?"

"I'm not his maid. Besides, I don't know where to find batteries."

Keagan went to a kitchen drawer and came back with new ones.

Kurt frowned. "You sure know your way around here."

"He should," Axel said. "He's been stopping in to help me the last few years."

Kurt's brows rose. "Might as well put on an apron and nurse hat."

Keagan picked up both men's plates to toss in the kitchen. "I'd rather help out than sit on my ass and do nothing."

"I'm tired of you taking potshots at me!" Kurt lunged to his feet, hands balled into fists, and Keagan spun to face him. Six-one, with lean whipcord muscles, Keagan looked intimidating. Kurt sat back down.

Karli blinked. Keagan was as nice as he could be, but no one had better push him too far. She liked him even more.

He turned and saw her behind him. "Is there anything else we need to do?"

Hmm, she heard a bit of a temper. She decided to sidestep his foul mood. "No, I was just going to get the picture you showed me. I thought the others might like to see it. It's in a drawer upstairs, isn't it?"

He nodded and started back outside. She got the picture and joined him.

After Karli, Daphne, and Miriam finished the shutters, they went to help with the house. Tyne had to leave at one thirty to cook at the inn, so they took his place. Two hours later, the scraping was done. Keagan moved his high ladder to the back of the house and looked at her. "The paint's dry on the shutters. You women did a good job on those."

Her heart did a silly thump at his compliment.

"Most of us are going to skip church tomorrow morning and show up here to paint. Can you stand us first thing in the day?"

Could she? She'd fix breakfast for him every morning if she could get him into her bed. "I'll fix stacks of sandwiches for lunch, nothing fancy."

The "nothing fancy" assuaged him and he nodded. "See you tomorrow then."

The men packed up and left. She hugged her arms around herself. Yes, she was chilly, but she was also happy. Keagan would be back in the morning.

Chapter 23

Early Sunday morning, truckloads of men showed up again. Ladders rimmed the old house, and the crew armed themselves with spray guns and got straight to work. There wasn't anything Karli could do to help them, so she busied herself dusting and straightening the house. Axel actually got himself into his wheelchair and rolled out in the kitchen to see what she was doing.

"There must not be anything good on TV on Sunday mornings," she said, teasing him.

"I heard you opening and closing doors, thought you were baking."

"Baking? I was wiping down the cupboards."

He let out a long breath. "I can't remember the last time I had a cookie."

She raised an eyebrow. "There's not much in this house to bake cookies with."

He gave a grim smile. "I don't need chocolate chips. They don't agree with me. But you always have peanut butter around, don't you?"

She'd just bought some, but she didn't have her favorite recipe with her. She reached for her phone, looked one up, and pretty soon, Axel was stirring. He licked spoons and licked the empty bowl. Soon, she and Axel were dropping dough onto baking sheets. He even talked her into oatmeal and raisins.

When the men came in for sandwiches, they grabbed warm cookies, too. After they ate and went outside, Axel tugged at his messy hair. "Don't suppose you know how to cut hair."

Karli snorted. "They didn't teach us any barber skills in nursing school."

"Do you think you could trim it up a little?"

She bit her bottom lip. "I could try."

When she finished, it wasn't the best, but she had to admit, Axel looked better. When she dusted off his shoulders, he yawned. "Might be time for me to watch some football."

She wheeled into his room and helped him into bed. The TV came on, and she went to the kitchen to clean up. When she looked out the window an hour later, it looked like the men were finishing up. She pulled on a hoodie and went to see.

Keagan's ladder leaned against the roof of the front porch. When he saw her, he called, "The paint's already dry up here. If you bring me the shutters you painted, I'll put them up at the two windows."

She gave him a thumbs-up and almost ran to the barn. He'd asked her, not one of the others, to help him. She hurried to grab a pair of shutters. When she got back, he'd come down for them and jammed a screwdriver and screws in his jeans pocket. Then he scurried up to the porch roof and stood on that to work. Karli squirmed. The porch roof slanted downward and didn't look safe to her.

"Be careful," she said.

He gave her a look. "I've been balancing on a ladder to paint the peaks all day. I think I'll survive this."

She went to get the shutters for the second window and climbed a few rungs to hand them to him. Once he'd finished installing them, he started down. He'd reached the ground when Karli noticed someone's paint brush lying on the roof. She scrambled up the ladder to reach it and then carefully retraced her steps. Before she reached the bottom, though, two strong hands lifted her and set her on the ground. Keagan's touch sent heat through her fleece hoodie.

She turned and found herself toe to toe with him. His solid chest was eye level. She looked up at his strong jawline, his lips. She sucked in her breath and tilted her head, staring up into his cobalt-blue eyes. She could smell his scent—clean and manly. His gaze burned with intensity. Her lips parted. One more inch and she'd be pressing against him.

"Good, that's where I left it." Brad reached for the paint brush.

Keagan gave his head a slight shake and stepped away.

Karli pushed back a scream. Damn it! Was Keagan's friend always going to ruin any special moment she had with him?

People began putting tools and equipment away. Keagan stuck his head in the house and yelled, "Axel! Want to see how it turned out?" He went inside to wrap the old man in a blanket, put him in his wheelchair, and roll him out to get a full view.

Axel's expression softened. "Just like when Mom was alive."

When people started to their vehicles, Karli tried to think of a way to keep Keagan with her a little longer. "I didn't get a chance to ask you, but could I come to your studio again? I'd like to order some plates to take home with me and another set as a present for my mom." She really did want the plates, but more than anything, she'd like some time alone with Keagan.

"Sure, any time." He gripped the wheelchair handles to push Axel back into the house.

She'd overheard Brad tell Tyne that he had to work Tuesday night. She looked at Keagan. "What about Tuesday?"

Brad looked disappointed, but Keagan nodded.

Chase turned to say his goodbyes and winked at Keagan. "Have you looked at the Yeagers' place east of town? It's about the right sized property for a house and studio, isn't it?"

"Is it for sale?"

Chase smiled. "Went up yesterday. It'll go fast. It's in good shape."

Harley winced and pressed his lips together.

Chase noticed and frowned. "What was that look for?"

"You haven't heard the news, have you? Beatrice Watson was in the bank when K's mom and dad applied for a loan. The office door was closed, but I swear that woman can hear through anything."

Keagan turned to Chase. Gossip whizzed through his bar, but he rarely shared it. "A loan for what?"

"I can't help you, haven't heard about it."

Harley didn't look happy to share the news. "Beatrice is going from place to place telling everyone. Their tractor's down. They wanted to buy a new one."

Chase looked relieved. "The harvest's done. They can wait till next spring."

They all looked at Keagan. "They won't have any more money in the spring. I'll go talk to them when I leave here."

Axel gripped the arms of the wheelchair. "Don't you bail them out, boy. You hear me? You've saved for years to buy your own place. Don't throw it away."

Keagan frowned, irritated. "When the Bransons' acres went up for sale, Dad didn't want to buy them, didn't want to overextend. He called a family summit. We all thought the tractor would last a few more years. I cast the deciding vote. We all knew it was a risk."

"Doesn't mean you have to give them your money."

Keagan shook his head at him. "You wouldn't understand."

"Damn right I do. You're being a damn fool."

"That's my choice." Axel's blanket had fallen off his shoulders. Keagan tucked it around him again. "Time to get you inside the house before you catch a cold. I'll get you back in bed."

Karli stayed outside to wave everyone off, then went in to check on Axel. Keagan lifted him into his bed and got him settled. Then he started for the door.

She trailed after him. Mixed emotions washed over her. Would he really draw out all of his savings to help his family? Would she do that for hers? "You've worked hard today, and you just got bad news. Want to stay for a beer?"

He took a quick step back from her. "No, I'd better get going. I want to get to my folks' place. I'd like to get this settled tonight."

He was pushing her away again. She'd seen the desire in his eyes when they were inches away from each other, but he was retreating to a safe distance. He was back to serious mode, worried about money and saving again. That would take years. She wasn't ready to wait that long. She wanted him now.

Chapter 24

On the short drive to his parents' place, Keagan's mind felt muddled. He'd wanted to kiss Karli so much today, he would have done it if Brad hadn't accidentally saved him. What had he been thinking? Duh! He obviously *wasn't* thinking. Chase and Harley would never let him hear the end of it. Gossip would have spread through Mill Pond faster than a tsunami.

She'd wanted it, too. She'd parted her lips, and he could feel her desire. But if he gave in to that urge, he'd be playing with fire. He already liked her more than he wanted to. If they got closer, intimate, he'd fall hard. And she wouldn't. That was the hell of it. She'd drive back to Indy and stop in for booty calls until she met the next guy who interested her. Not what he needed.

And then Harley had told him about his parents, and reality had smacked him in the face. If he'd played with the idea of being footloose and fancy free, he'd been mistaken. He'd voted for his parents to buy more property. He was partially responsible for their money problems. And once he helped them, what would he have to offer a woman? His charming personality? Like he had one! Karli could do better than that.

He pulled into the drive and took a minute to steel himself. Offering to help them was going to be a hard sell. He could show no signs of weakness.

When Keagan knocked on his parents' door, his dad only opened it a crack. He studied Keagan's face and shook his head. "No."

"You have to let me in, Dad."

"You heard, didn't you?"

Keagan nodded.

"Damn that big-mouth Beatrice! I don't want to talk about it."

Keagan took a deep breath. "Do I have to go around the house and knock on windows until someone lets me in?" It was dusk. Lights blazed in Marcia's house, a little farther down the drive. "I can go to Marcia's and talk to her."

His dad sighed. "Your sister and Stuart are here with the kids. They stayed later this Sunday than usual." He opened the door wide.

Warmth surrounded him when he entered the living room with logs burning in the fireplace. The evening newspaper sprawled across Dad's well-used leather recliner. Stuart sat in the big easy chair across from the recliner. Kids' voices squealed in the finished basement, and he heard Mom and Marcia in the kitchen.

"It's close to suppertime. Why don't we set another place at the table?" Dad asked. "We'll eat first, and then we can talk."

Keagan nodded. He was starving. Besides, he didn't want to ruin everyone's appetites. He went into the kitchen to see if he could help his mom.

She raised an eyebrow when she saw him. "I hope those are old jeans because you'll never get the paint off them."

He motioned to the frayed hems at his ankles. "My work pants. They come in handy."

Marcia looked wary. "You're not mad at me, are you? Mom and Dad didn't want you to know."

"I thought we didn't keep secrets. If I was invited to break the tie vote, I should have been let in on this news."

Mom waved that argument away. "We wanted to wait until we knew if we could get a loan or not."

"You've known for a while and Beatrice is spreading it all over town."

Marcia pulled breadsticks from the oven. "That woman's a hazard. Someone should staple her tongue to the top of her mouth."

Mom drained the spaghetti in the sink. "Now, Marcia."

It was all Keagan could do not to lick the sauce off Mom's wooden spoon. He loved her tomato gravy. Not that she was Italian, but her next door neighbor was when she was growing up. She'd learned to cook from her.

Marcia asked again, "Are you mad at me?"

"It wasn't her fault," Mom said. "We made her promise."

Keagan shook his head. "Who can rat out Mom?"

Marcia looked relieved. She opened the cupboard and handed him a plate. "You're staying for supper, right?"

"Of course he is!" Mom handed him silverware. Then she stirred the pasta into the sauce and said, "Let's eat!"

There was already a tossed salad on the table. Mom carried in the huge bowl of spaghetti, and Jenna and Jack hurried up from the basement. When the twins saw him, they came to hang on him.

"You can pester your uncle later," Marcia told them. "For now, find your seats."

Stuart helped settle them, and they began to pass food.

No one brought up the tractor during supper. After the meal, they all helped with clean-up, then the twins clamored for Keagan's attention. At four, they still thought he was special. He'd been warned to enjoy that while he could.

He got down on all fours and let them plow into him, trying to knock him over. Then they climbed all over him until Marcia said, "Quiet time. Put in a movie and settle down. I don't want you wound up for bedtime."

While they sprawled on the floor to watch TV, the adults gathered around the dining room table again. Dad said, "There are other places to get loans. We're looking into that now."

"They charge horrible interest fees." Keagan leaned forward on his elbows. "Dad, I voted for you to buy the Bransons' property. If you hadn't, someone else would have snatched it up, and we knew we were gambling that everything would go smooth for a couple years." His dad had argued that they'd made a good living off the farm all this time. There was no reason to expand, but Marcia said that farming was getting more and more competitive, that small farms had a harder time surviving than they used to. That's the way business seemed to be going. Bigger was better.

"We'll figure something out, K." His parents had called him *K* for as long as he could remember, their nickname for him, and a lot of his friends had picked up on it. He couldn't think of a time his dad ever used his full name, and Mom only did when he was in trouble.

Keagan looked at his mom. "Can you afford a high-interest loan?"

Mom wiped a hand across her face. "We'll cut back on a few things."

Keagan shook his head. "You guys make frugal look like a religion now. I have fifty thousand dollars saved. Is that enough for a tractor?"

"We're not taking your money." Dad's shoulders went rigid.

"If I rent for two more years, your money will be in good shape, and you can help me make monthly payments on my own place. It's only two years, Dad."

"It's not happening." His dad crossed his arms over his chest.

Keagan was every bit as stubborn. "Either take my money and buy a tractor, or I'll buy one for you."

Stuart looked alarmed. "You don't know anything about them."

"That's why it would be smarter if you picked your own."

Dad said, "We won't take it."

"Fine." Keagan laced his fingers together. "I'll park it in the front yard of our rented house."

He'd do it, too. They knew it. Once he made up his mind, there was little chance of changing it. That's how it had been when he left the farm to take a job as a mailman and when he started his own dinnerware business.

Mom tried again. "We'd rather you bought your own place."

"I know, and I appreciate that, but a farmer can't turn over his fields without a tractor."

"I said *no*." Dad was just as bullheaded as he was, probably who he got it from.

"Okay then, I'll quit my job as a mailman and drive the tractor to the farm every day to work your fields."

His dad stared. "You're not a farmer."

"I know how to plow."

"You love delivering mail."

"I know, and you love farming."

His dad pushed to his feet. "All right. You win. We'll look for a used tractor, save harder, and you'll look for a place in *one* year."

"Deal."

Marcia sighed. "In the meantime, what if Dad and Stuart add on to your studio, make it twice as big? Can they do that?"

He grinned. Marcia was offering a compromise. "I'd like that."

Dad and Stuart looked at each other. They knew they'd lost and might as well make the best of it. Dad nodded. "One year," he said, "and then we find you a house and some property."

"Fair enough."

Chapter 25

Karli took a shower to wash paint out of her hair and changed into sweats before she made sandwiches for supper. Axel was fine with the same thing for lunch and supper. Kurt took whatever he could get. She was cleaning the kitchen when the phone rang and Keagan's mom introduced herself and invited her to supper on Monday night. "Keagan will be here, too."

Had Keagan suggested that? Did he want to see more of her? Introduce her to his family? Excitement fluttered in her stomach. "I'd love to come. Can I bring something?"

His mom had a pleasant voice. "Just yourself. I didn't give you much notice."

"What time?"

"Five-thirty."

"I'll be there." Hope zinged through her veins. Maybe Keagan wasn't retreating. Maybe he'd just been thrown off stride when he'd heard about his parents' loan. She went straight to the refrigerator and took out a chuck roast to thaw. She'd throw it in the slow cooker for the men tomorrow.

Everything ready, she went to her room to call her mom. It was too soon to talk about Keagan, but she wanted to. Instead, she said, "I e-mailed you a picture of the house now that it's painted. Did you get it?"

There were some clicking noises, then her mom gave a small gasp. "It's beautiful."

"It looks like an old picture of the place Keagan found." She told her mom about all of the people who'd come to help with the work.

Mom sounded surprised. "I wish I'd have met more people when I lived there."

"They're really nice. Keagan's mom invited me for supper tomorrow. What have you and Dad been up to?"

Talk turned to her parents' upcoming trip to Milwaukee over Thanksgiving. By the time they hung up, Karli was in an especially good mood. The house was beautiful, her parents were happy, and she was eating with Keagan and his family tomorrow. She slept well that night and didn't have as many aching muscles as she expected in the morning.

She took her time getting ready to meet Keagan's family. Would his sister be as attractive as he was? He wasn't handsome or gorgeous, but she liked everything about him. Would they look at her and think he could do better? She was a little overweight. She decided to dress a little conservatively—a pair of black Dockers and a loose, burnt-orange sweater. She carefully applied her makeup. She wanted to look natural but to show off her features. She got the feeling Keagan didn't like black eyeliner and lots of blush.

The chuck roast was done at five o'clock, so she dished up Axel's food before she left. She got to Keagan's parents' farm about five minutes early. Keagan's SUV wasn't there yet. When she knocked, his mother pulled her inside to introduce her to everyone.

"You're Donna's daughter. We're so glad you came. Donna was such a sweet person. How is she?"

"Very happy. She has a great career, and my dad's a keeper."

"That's wonderful!" His mother motioned around the room. It screamed comfort with its worn, leather sofa and chairs, heavy wooden side tables, and fringed lamps. "I'm Joyce, and this is my husband, Abe. Our daughter, Marcia, and her husband, Stuart, help us farm and live close by with their four-year old twins, Jenna and Jack." Screams came from the basement and Joyce smiled. "They're playing downstairs right now."

Marcia stood and came to greet her. "I hope you're hungry, because Mom went all out. She made her pork goulash with buttered noodles and roasted vegetables."

"Pork goulash?" Karli could smell the rich sauce, heavy with paprika.

Joyce shrugged. "I wanted to play with the recipe a little, and we like it better with cubes of pork."

"Sounds wonderful to me. Can I help with anything?"

Joyce looked at the clock. "We can dress the salad. Keagan should be here soon."

At that moment, there was a quick knock on the door and Keagan stepped into the house. He looked surprised when he saw Karli. There went that fantasy. This clearly wasn't Keagan's idea, but attraction flamed in his eyes. He quickly hid it, but Karli had seen it. Hope tingled through her again. Keagan smiled and looked at his mom.

"I should have dressed up a little. I didn't know we were having company." He glanced down at his old jeans and loose, black sweater.

The man looked good to her. Edible. "No need to get fancy. You look great in anything."

He blushed under his tan, and his mom smiled at him.

"We're ready to eat," she said. "Come help us set the table."

The twins came up from the basement and took their seats. Jenna stared at her. Finally, she blurted, "Is your hair real?"

Karli laughed. She wasn't sure what she'd expected, but it wasn't that. "Why? Does it look fake?"

"You have a lot of it, and it's curly on the ends."

"My dad's part Italian, part Romanian," she said. "I get my coloring from him. He's tall, though. I didn't inherit that."

"Does he like kids?" Jack asked.

"Loves them. He loves most people, a friendly guy."

"What does he do?" Jenna asked.

"Owns a pizza parlor. I'd be thinner if he worked at a gym."

Jenna's eyes went round. "We like pizza."

"Then you'd probably like my dad, but you have to be careful. He's always trying out new recipes and testing them on me."

"You're so lucky!" Jack licked his lips.

"Quit grilling her," Keagan's sister said. "The food's on the table. Let the poor woman eat."

Karli spooned the pork goulash over the noodles and took a bite. The pork was tender. The onion and garlic mingled with the ketchup and Worcestershire sauce. "I've never had goulash like this."

Marcia smiled. "It's not family style. It's Hungarian goulash. There's a difference."

"It's wonderful." Karli noticed that Keagan had piled his plate high. It must be one of his favorites. For being lean, the man could eat. Maybe he burned a lot of calories jumping in and out of his mail truck all day.

His mom arched a brow at Keagan. "We thought Karli should see more of Mill Pond than Axel's farm, so we invited her over. You should take her to Ralph's some night for supper. And she should see Harley's winery, too."

"I took her to Joel's brewery."

His mom put another helping of roasted vegetables on Jack's plate. "A girl needs to get out more than that. You should give her a grand tour of the whole area."

Keagan leveled a look at his mom, but she put on an innocent face. Karli decided she liked this woman. He studied his mother a second, then smiled. "I'd better get to it then because she'll only be here another couple of weeks."

His mom's smug look faded. "Is that all?"

Karli nodded.

His mom perked up again. "We're not that far from Indy. She can always drive back to visit us."

"To see Axel?" Keagan's blue eyes sparkled. He was enjoying himself. "I bet she can't wait."

His mom's eyes sparkled, too. She looked irritated. Glancing around the table, she stood to gather dirty plates. "I made a New York cheesecake for dessert. Ready?" Keagan started to get up to help her, but she gave a quick shake of her head. "You've helped enough."

He heard the reprimand in her voice. They all did, so Karli hurried to take his place. So did Marcia. Once in the kitchen, the women quickly rinsed the plates and put them in the dishwasher. His mom looked at Karli and Marcia and shook her head. "There's no maneuvering that boy into anything. He's purposely giving me a hard time."

Karli smiled. "He goes out of his way to keep me at a safe distance. I've noticed that."

His mom cocked her head, curious. "Does he now? Interesting, isn't it?"

That's not the word she'd use to describe it. Frustrating, maybe. Challenging. "I'd say he's warning me off."

"But why?"

Was that a trick question? "There's no point in starting something when I'm only here a short while."

His mom shrugged. "It's not like he's found anyone in Mill Pond. Maybe he should expand his horizons."

He hadn't found anyone, huh? How long ago had Cecily left? Three years? Any man's hormones should be feeling deprived after that long.

Marcia huffed. "Quit it, Mom. You don't even know if Karli wants to spend time with Keagan, and you're stirring the pot."

His mom turned to her. "Are you interested in my son?"

Why play games? "I sure am."

"Serious or not?"

Karli blinked. "I don't do serious. I like to travel too much."

His mom's shoulders sagged. "Oh, well, that's the end of that then. Keagan's ready to settle down." She grabbed the cheesecake and Marcia carried the dessert plates. They returned to the dining room.

Keagan turned a thoughtful stare on his mother. "Satisfied now?"

She sighed. "Eat your cake, then you should still give Karli a tour of the area. She's earned that. We'll finish cleaning up."

Jenna pouted. "Are they going to leave already?"

"Afraid so, kid." His mom let them each sip a cup of coffee while they ate, and then she shooed them away. "Go! Have fun! Show Karli the sights."

Keagan fussed on his way to his SUV. "I'm twenty-eight and my mom still tries to fiddle in my life."

Karli strapped herself in and shook her head. "Give her a break. You can't turn off being a parent. That's what my mom tells me all the time."

He looked at her, surprised. "Your mom messes in your life, too?"

Karli snickered. "That's what moms do. It's in their DNA. Look at this way. What if your mom didn't give a damn? What if she said: *You're over twenty-one. Grow up. Do whatever?*"

He raised his eyebrows. "I guess I like it that she still cares."

Karli laughed. "So do I. You can't have it both ways."

"I never thought of it like that." He started his SUV and turned right on County Road. "We'll circle the lake and drive around town before we head to the national park."

She'd never seen the far side of the lake and the houses that circled it. The lake was larger than she'd thought. Then Keagan drove her up and down streets in town, explaining the many and different shops before he headed south to the national forest. There was so much on offer that it boggled her mind. Why hadn't Mom ever told her how wonderful Mill Pond was? But she already knew the answer to that question. Her mother had no idea.

When they passed a log cabin, Keagan said, "That's where Tyne and Daphne live. They both love nature."

Karli tried to pinpoint people she knew and where they lived. Chase and Paula lived above his bar near the lake. Miriam and Joel lived in a cottage on the west side of the lake; not that far from Axel's farm. Tyne and Daphne lived by the national forest. All good locations. She sighed. "Mill Pond has a lot to offer, doesn't it?"

Keagan smiled. "It's the best."

He was totally into playing tour guide, and she appreciated that, but the man was sitting within touching distance and they were alone. When he drove into the national forest, she reached across the seat to put her hand on his thigh. A bold move. But why not give it a try?

"You might want to be careful." He didn't turn his head, didn't look at her. "It's been a long time since I've been with a woman."

She moved her hand higher, and he pushed it away. "Stop it. I don't keep a condom in my wallet these days."

"I'm on birth control pills, no problem."

He turned onto a side road that led to an overlook of a small lake, parked, and turned off the SUV's engine. The lake's water was deep blue, like his eyes. The trees surrounding it were free of leaves. No one else was in sight. He locked gazes with her. "If you're trying to turn me on, you'd better mean it. Once I start, I won't be able to stop."

She blinked in surprise. Exactly what she wanted to hear. "Do you want me?"

"Blood still pumps through my veins and you're damn attractive. But do you really want to have sex, then leave, and that's it? Because that's all that's going to happen here."

Was this a test? If she said the wrong thing, would he start the engine and show her more trees? She shook her head. "If we're only a one-shot deal, it will be one hell of a memory. If we can have more, even better."

"But you're all right with whatever you get?"

It didn't sound very flattering when he put it like that. "I travel a lot. I don't expect forever."

"Right." His brows lowered. "I have a theory that the harder you have to work to seduce somebody, the more you want them."

"I'm not a player."

"Really? You could have Brad, but you want me because I'm not easy, don't you?"

Did he have to put it like that? Like he was a notch on her bedpost? He made her sound horrible. "I don't have a score sheet," she said. "I just like you, and if you like me, too, the sex would make me happy."

He was silent a moment, then shrugged. "Okay, from now on, that's how I'll think of you. Let's do this. Let's get it out of your system, and then you can move on." He started undressing. She stared.

"It's not like that." His sweater came off and he unbuttoned the shirt beneath it, letting it fall open. His torso was lean with corded muscle. "Wait! What are you doing? We can't go back to Axel's. He'll turn off the TV and listen to everything. Brad's at your place. Your studio?"

He chuckled. "Haven't you ever made out in a back seat before?"

"Here? Now?"

"You can't get more temporary than that." He stripped off his pants and his underwear. Jackpot! He raised a brow at her. "I've never made love to a fully dressed woman before."

She was panting. How pathetic. She pulled her sweater over her head, then fumbled with her slacks. Her hands were shaking.

"Too slow," he told her and motioned her to the back seat. He flipped a switch, and the seats flattened. She'd never made love in a vehicle before, but the minute she lowered herself onto the coarse fabric, he scrambled on top of her.

Bliss. She'd often imagined how beautiful a naked Keagan would be, and he surpassed her expectations. He lowered his face and gently touched his lips to hers. The kiss started soft and sweet and built in intensity. She was moaning, her body on fire, when he moved to her neck. She thought she might die of lust when he reached the base of her throat—that treacherous area that made her insides quiver. Then his lips moved to her breasts, nipping her through her bra. Inner spasms rocked her. His tongue grazed the top of her lacy bra. More. She wanted more! He reached behind her and unclasped it. He tugged until her breasts fell free.

"You're beautiful." His fingers found one nipple, his lips the other. He pinched and fondled. Passion exploded inside her, volts flying everywhere. It coiled in her stomach, building.

He unzipped her Dockers and slid them down. Her panties followed, and his lips trailed down to her belly button, then lower. His fingers still played with her nipple, and she took deep breaths. Her body tensed, needy. Everything he did felt wonderful, right. He kissed the top of her inner thighs, and her breath caught. Then his fingers slid into her folds, massaging her pleasure spot. Oh, god! She might climax before he entered her.

He kissed and licked and she thought she'd burst on the spot. Then his lips moved to her right breast and his fingers slid inside her. Nirvana! Could a woman die of too much pleasure? When he nipped a nipple at the same time his thumb caressed her sweet spot, passion flooded her. And the next thing she knew, he was inside her, pumping with a steady rhythm, building and building, until they both exploded at the same time.

"Oh, God!" She went limp beneath him.

He kissed her forehead, her temples. He nuzzled his face against hers, and then he withdrew. No, no, no. She wanted him inside her. Forever. No, longer. Then he turned to spoon against her.

His strong arms cradled her. She was safe in a cocoon of him. "You're wonderful."

He chuckled, a reassuring rumble in her ear. "Thanks! You're pretty good yourself."

She turned to stare at him. She always loved sex and was no innocent. She was twenty-seven, for heaven's sake. She wasn't promiscuous, but she'd never made a vow of chastity either. Still, she'd never felt like this. They cradled against each other until their pulses settled. Finally, he gently kissed her cheek, sat up, and started dressing.

"There. You've had me," he said. "Now you'll always remember Mill Pond warmly."

Remember? She didn't want it to end. She wanted Keagan three times a day. Maybe more. For a long time. Years and years. Oh God, what was wrong with her? Keagan had decided temporary was fine, and *she* was the one who wanted more.

Jeans on, he tugged his sweater over his head. "Believe me when I tell you, I'll remember you, too. I usually don't do one-night stands, but you were worth it."

No, no, no! She didn't want this to be a one-shot deal. But he went on.

"Now we can be friends. I'm a great friend." He waited for her to dress and climb into the passenger seat. Before he started the SUV's engine, he reached over to squeeze her hand. "Thanks, Karli!"

Thanks? Really? Slam, bam, thank you, ma'am? He had to be kidding! Screw friendship. She wanted more. She wanted Keagan. As hers. Always. What the hell had Mill Pond done to her?

Chapter 26

On the drive to town, after he dropped Karli at her car, Keagan had to chuckle to himself. Karli had looked so smug when she laid her hand on his thigh, he'd known he didn't have enough self-discipline to stand a chance against her. If he was going to cave, he might as well do it his way.

She'd been as surprised as he was. He'd decided he was going to enjoy himself and do it thoroughly. If he had to surrender, why not make the best of it? And damn, was it good!

When he parked at the two-story house he shared with Brad, some of his elation deflated. Since she'd had him today, would Brad be next? She made no bones about the fact that she wasn't a one-man woman, at least, not for long. He took a deep breath. He'd known that going into things. At least he'd finally moved past Cecily. That was a blessing in itself.

When Tyne had asked him why he hadn't found some sweet, young thing, he'd realized he was only passing time, deluding himself. Cecily had craved attention and excitement. Back then, all he wanted to do was keep her happy. It took constant effort. But he'd been there, done that. Never again. This time around, he wanted a partner, someone who cared about his needs as much as he cared about hers.

Karli could be that person, but she wasn't interested. And if he'd learned anything at all, it was that you couldn't change another human being. But Karli had been good for him. She'd jostled him out of his dismals. She'd pulled him back into the man/woman intrigue. And she was the best sex he'd ever had. Kudos for that.

Not this minute, not even this week or month, but it was time to start looking again. So what if he could only rent a house? Lots of people started out that way. Maybe he wanted too much, too many guarantees. Maybe it was time to take the plunge again and see where that led him.

When he walked into the living room, Brad was balancing a paper plate heaped with nachos on his lap, watching TV. Brad glanced up to say hi, then stopped and studied him. "Is everything okay?"

"For your ears only. Swear." Brad would be happy for him, and he knew how to keep a secret.

Brad crossed his heart and zipped his lips.

"Karli and I just made love in the back of my SUV."

"Finally! It's about time."

Keagan grinned. "It's nothing serious. She doesn't want that, but I didn't mind being used. It didn't break my heart."

Brad laughed. "I'll quit flirting with her. You can have an open playing field."

Keagan went to the kitchen and got a beer. "It's not like that. She might already be tired of me. It's strictly no strings."

Brad put his plate on the coffee table. "So you really wouldn't mind if I asked her out?"

"Karli will do whatever she wants. She made that pretty clear."

Brad raised his beer bottle in a toast. "Glad you're back in the game, bro!"

"Thanks." They clinked bottles and Keagan took a long swig from his. He'd never be like Brad, bedding a different girl every other month, but he'd put dating and romance on hold for too long. He was ready to find somebody.

Chapter 27

It was late when Karli got back home. She couldn't stop thinking about Keagan. She loved his hands. The fingers that molded clay were strong and creative. She'd never met a man she wanted so much. When she left Mill Pond, and he didn't see her a few times a week, he'd forget about her. She was more into him than he was into her. She had a nagging feeling that if she lost him, she'd regret it, but she had no idea what she could do to hang onto him. Even if she drove back here a couple times a month, he could make excuses to avoid her.

Axel interrupted her musings. He called from the back room. "Girl, where are you? Are you going to starve an old man to death?"

"Don't tempt me." She'd come home to an empty slow cooker, every shred of chuck roast gone. Kurt was nowhere in sight, so she assumed he'd finished off all the leftovers and left Axel to his own devices. How could the old man be hungry?

"Are there any of those cookies left?" he yelled.

So that was it. He wanted a bedtime snack. Well, why not? She'd put a dozen of them in a Ziploc and hidden them in her room so that Kurt didn't eat them all. "Want some milk?"

"It's good for old folks, isn't it?"

He was pushing it. When she took him his food, he studied her face and smirked. "Looks like things didn't go that well for you."

"Don't be so sure. I had a great day."

"Then what's eating at you?"

"Nothing's going like I planned."

He raised an eyebrow, curious. "Who else is giving you trouble besides me?"

"You're enough." She motioned to his cookies. "Eat up. I'm tired."

When he was finished, she cleaned the kitchen for the night and turned off the lights. Then she went to her bedroom and tried to distract herself on her laptop, but her mind kept returning to Keagan. She was going to his studio tomorrow night. If she plastered herself against him, would he throw her on the floor and have his way with her? Lord, she hoped so! But she got the idea he'd made love to her, and that was that.

She glared at her computer screen. Finally, she stomped to the kitchen and poured herself a glass of wine. She thought about calling her mom, but her parents would be watching their favorite PBS programs on a Monday night. Sighing, she typed *kitchen remodels* into her laptop's search engine. She was shocked how many sites came up, and she began to scroll through them. She found kitchens that were complete gut jobs, transforming cheap, horrid rooms into gourmet, open concepts. She saw modern kitchens, teak kitchens, and country kitchens until she finally landed on a renovation where the owners painted all of the existing cupboards and installed butcher block counter tops and stainless steel appliances. She fell in love with it.

She drained her wine glass. She could do that. Okay, she wouldn't pay for new counter tops and appliances—even though the old place needed it—but she could paint the cupboards. They were well-built, but she hated the blonde wood. She read the DIY directions. More work than she'd expected, but it's not like she had a life at the moment. Axel's cupboards reached all the way to the ceiling. She'd painted that the same cream shade she'd used in the dining room when she redid the kitchen walls to robin-egg blue. She frowned. The homeowners on the Internet project had painted their top cupboards light blue and the bottoms a darker shade. She liked the two tones, but she had no desire to repaint the walls. She decided to paint the cupboards a glossy white.

She was surprised to see that she'd spent two hours bopping from one site to another, so she turned off her laptop, changed into her pajamas, and switched off her bedside light. She'd drive into town in the morning and visit the hardware store again.

As she drifted to sleep, she worried that she was channeling all of her repressed sexual energy into painting to survive Mill Pond.

Chapter 28

She woke up, motivated. The TV was already on in Axel's room and when Karli glanced in to check on him, Kurt was there, too, slumped in his easy chair. Kurt noticed her and asked, "What's for breakfast this morning?"

"Oatmeal. I'm going to town after we eat."

Axel pushed the button on his hospital bed to sit up higher. "What are you up to this time, girlie?"

"I want to refinish the kitchen cupboards, paint them white."

Axel frowned and for a minute, she thought he was going to tell her *no*. "Like on *Fixer Upper*? That gal almost always puts in white cupboards."

Karli stared at him, surprised. "I didn't know you watched HGTV."

"What would you know about what I watch? You never sit out here with me." He shrugged. "There's not that much football on Tuesday nights."

She stared at him. Did Axel want her to sit with him once in a while? He could surprise her now and then. "Do you watch *Property Brothers*, too?"

"Yup, and they've got no use for blonde-wood cupboards. They'd rip them out."

"That's expensive," Karli said. "But your cupboards are solid. I think a fresh coat of paint will make them look good."

"No skin off my nose." He pulled his blanket a little higher. The three-season room was chilly in the mornings. "If it makes you happy enough to stay until Sylvie shows up, do whatever you want as long as it doesn't cost me any money."

She scowled. He'd ruined a nice moment. She turned on her heel and left him. If he choked on his breakfast, he deserved it. When she reached for the box of oatmeal in the cupboard, though, she stopped and grimaced. The box of Saltines next to it had been chewed through and she saw mouse turds on the shelf. *Ich!* She tore off paper towels to clean them up and threw away the box of crackers. It was time to look for a cat!

Axel didn't care if his home was overrun with mice. Stupid man! But what did she expect? As she stirred the oatmeal, she realized he'd never shown any interest in this house. Why should he start now? She added toast and orange slices to his food tray and carried it into him. She even brought a second tray for Kurt. It was easier than having him underfoot.

Karli ate looking out the kitchen window. A steel-gray sky brooded above the fields. Wisps of snow flew past the glass. When Karli went to collect the men's dirty dishes, Axel asked, "You're going to use glossy paint, aren't you? Make the cupboards look good?"

He cared more than he let on. "I was thinking about semi-gloss, something a little subtler."

"Why would you want to do that? It's a kitchen. It should look shiny." She hid a smile. "Okay, if you say so."

He narrowed his eyes. "You were going to do that anyway, weren't you?"

"Maybe."

He glowered. "You're an evil girl!" Then his lips curled into a reluctant smile. "I like that."

"Takes one to know one."

He laughed as she walked away. He liked it when she harassed him. He'd miss her when Sylvie took her place. For now, though, she hustled so that she could get to town and back before lunch. It took her a while to get ready and then she made the twenty-minute drive to town.

The weather might be brisk, but the sidewalks still held plenty of tourists. According to Chase, people came to shop for specialty holiday items and one-of-a-kind Christmas gifts. Daphne's quilts and wall hangings, displayed in Art's grocery store and Ian's inn, went quickly. So did stained-glass winter designs in her shop. Ester Thornton's weavings made from handwoven and dyed alpaca fleece—displayed in Art's grocery, too—usually sold out by the end of November. Keagan told her that he shipped more dinnerware in October and November than any other time of year. He made his Christmas and winter items ahead, hoping not to sell out.

She glanced at Lefty's jewelry shop as she passed it and was happy to see that it was doing a brisk business. Keagan's sister had locked herself in her workroom every chance she got to crank out earrings and necklaces in winter colors. Karli hoped her pieces were flying out of the store.

Soon, Karli parked in front of Meg's hardware. Karli had huge respect for Meg. Keagan had told her that the girl took over the store's reins when her dad had a serious stroke. He guaranteed her that Meg knew her stuff.

When Meg married Nick Hillegard and they teamed up to flip houses together, she'd expanded her knowledge base even more. Karli was sure she'd have plenty of advice for her project.

Meg gave her more than advice. When Karli explained about refinishing the kitchen cupboards, Meg wrote out a step-by-step list for what to do and recommended the right paint to buy. That, and a spray gun.

"It's the best way to get the finish you want," Meg explained.

While they assembled all of the products Karli needed, they gossiped. At first, it had appalled Karli how everyone in Mill Pond knew everyone else's business, but now she liked it. Everyone kept an eye on each other. Meg told Karli about how Grams had broken a toe playing kickball with Drew—Ian and Tessa's little boy—her great-grandson. "It's not slowing Grams down, though. That woman's unstoppable."

Karli had gotten that impression. She'd heard plenty of stories about Grams.

Meg rattled on. "Chantelle had her baby. Rumor is she's finally settling down. She and Eddie are nuts about their little girl, want to have more. I bet that's a relief for Keagan. Chantelle tried for Tyne before he met Daphne, then Joel, and then she settled on Keagan. Kept ordering things so that he'd have to deliver them to her house."

"Does that happen often to Keagan?"

Meg smiled. "More than you'd think."

"So women throw themselves at him a lot?"

"He's used to it, takes it in his stride. Truth is, I'm not sure he even notices."

Was that why he ignored her when she'd thrown herself at him? It happened to him all the time? Maybe she'd taken the wrong approach. Maybe she should have played hard to get, but she didn't have time.

She told Meg about the mouse problem at Axel's. "Do you sell anything that would get rid of them?"

Meg motioned to a shelf that held mouse traps, sticky paper, and poisons. "Your best bet, though, is to get a cat."

That's what everyone told her. "Is there a humane shelter around here? A pet store?"

"You can probably find a cat at the farm store on County Road. You can buy bulk animal supplies there for farm animals and pets." Meg gave her directions.

Karli drove toward the west side of the lake. The fields that had looked rich and vibrant bathed in sunlight looked bleak and empty with the gunmetal sky hovering over them. When she saw three silos clustered together, she turned toward them. A small, cement block building hunched at their base.

Karli frowned at her surroundings. Could she really buy a cat here? Only one way to find out. She got out of her car and went in search of a clerk.

A woman wearing a flannel shirt and overalls, her face weathered and creased, came out from behind a desk when she entered the building. "Can I help you?"

"I was told to come here for a cat. Do you sell them?"

The woman laughed. "Lord, no, but we've got plenty of them. I'll help you pick out one."

"How much will it cost?"

"The cat? It's free, but by the time you buy supplies for it, we'll make a profit."

Karli started to relax. Whatever cat she found here would be used to being outdoors, would be happy to live in a barn. "Mice are coming into Axel's house, and I need a cat to get rid of them."

The woman's eyes sparkled with interest. "You must be the girl who came to take care of him? That man's too cheap to feed a cat, but there are probably enough mice around his place that it won't matter."

Karli shook her head. "When I leave here, I'm taking the cat to Keagan's parents. He said they put out dry food for their farm cats. I'd worry if it didn't have someplace good when I'm gone."

"Good, then I like you even more. You've got to be a nice girl if you came to help an old goat like Axel."

Karli laughed. "I'm not making any headway with him, but at least I tried."

The woman shook her head. "The old fool never took care of anyone, not even himself." She motioned for Karli to follow her. "Come on. We'll find a few cats roaming around the pet food aisles. If you see one you like, you can have it."

They found an old, orange tabby first. It had a ragged ear. "Too many fights," the woman said. "Marmalade's been around here a long time."

"He looks happy. I'll leave him alone." The next cat Karli saw arched its back and hissed at her, then took off. She kept walking. In the fifth aisle, she saw a thin, young cat that was gray with a white chin and white toes on its back paws. She bent down, and he came to her.

"Dusty loves being petted. I think he was an indoor cat that someone dropped off, but he's a great mouser."

"Can I have him?"

The woman scooped him up and started to the counter. She dropped him in a heavy, cardboard box and closed it. "He's yours."

"What do I need for him?"

Karli ended up with a huge bag of dry food, a litter box, litter, and a cat bed. She added cat toys to the essentials and cans of wet food. "Just in case he can't find enough mice."

The woman helped Karli load everything into the back of her Dodge. "Don't get Dusty too spoiled, or Keagan's parents will have to deal with a prima donna."

But the damn cat was so cute, Karli couldn't help herself. Keagan's mail truck was pulling away from Axel's place by the time she got home. *Home.* She shook her head. When had she started calling it that? She carried the cardboard box in the house and released the cat. Dusty jumped out, then ran to hide under the couch in the living room. That room was in the back of the house, too close to Axel. Karli never went there. No one did. She left the cat to carry in the rest of the supplies. Sandpaper, paint cans, and a sprayer cluttered the foyer, along with the cat's things.

"You're late!" Axel called from the back room. "I had to wheel myself to get cottage cheese."

"Good, then you shouldn't be hungry." She listened for his grumbling, and he didn't disappoint. She carried two take-out bags into his room, one for Axel, one for Kurt. "I brought back Big Macs and fries for you. Better eat up now. I'm going out with Keagan tonight, so I'll heat up some soup for you for supper."

A streak of gray flew by the door.

"What the hell was that?" Axel stared. "How big are the mice these days?"

Karli laughed. "I got a gray cat—Dusty. It'll take him a while to get used to us."

The cat was under the table in the kitchen when she started to unload all of his stuff. He crouched and stared at her, but didn't leave. She put his bowls on the floor at the end of the counter and filled each of them—dry food, water, and a can of chicken and tuna, then put the cans of cat food in the cupboard and his dry food in the broom closet. The men were happy for a minute, so she went to the refrigerator to grab bread and peanut butter to make herself a sandwich. When she turned around, the cat was eating his chicken and tuna.

"You were hungry, weren't you?" She ate her sandwich, then carried his cat bed into a corner of the parlor, her room. She tossed his toys randomly. He'd find them if he wanted them. What to do with his litter box?

She pursed her lips, thinking. She didn't want it in the kitchen. Not in the dining room or her room either. The bathroom? She wasn't thrilled. The living room was actually attractive, since she'd painted it, so she didn't want to ruin it with a litter box. She took a deep breath and walked to the basement door.

Her thoughts turned to damp, moldy walls and crumbling cement floors as she pulled the door open. She flipped a switch on her right and five naked light bulbs illuminated the entire downstairs. Solid wooden steps with sturdy railings on both sides led to a large, open space. She grabbed the litter box and litter and descended to a room with high ceilings and a corner filled with wooden shelves. Mason jars and a pressure canner sat under them.

Karli was surprised by how neat and dry the basement was. She went to a spot behind the steps to put the litter box. Dusty followed a few steps behind to watch. She was filling it when something scurried in the shadows on the far wall. Dusty raced down the remaining steps after it. She heard a high squeak and then silence. One mouse down.

Ugh. She put the bag of litter on one of the shelves and started back up the steps, leaving the basement door open a crack.

She glanced at the clock and was surprised that Keagan would be here in half an hour. No time for a shower. She changed into a nicer top, slapped on a little makeup, and set two cans of soup near the stove. Then she met Keagan at the door.

The cat flew up the steps with the limp mouse in its mouth, saw Keagan, and then disappeared back into the living room. Keagan caught a glimpse of it and frowned. "Hate to say it, but your cat looks too sleek to be much of a mouser."

"Did you see the dead body in his mouth? He's a pro."

"Is that so?" Keagan frowned at the metal bowls on the floor in the kitchen and shook his head. "Three of them?"

"I want him to be happy."

"You have a lot to learn about farm cats." Keagan held her coat for her. The temperatures had plummeted during the day. "You hungry?"

"Starving."

He drove her to Ralph's, and they both ordered the Salisbury steak special. Meg and Nick walked in behind them and came to share their table.

"Meg tells me you're going to redo Axel's kitchen cupboards," Nick said.

Keagan looked at her, surprised. "Are you getting new ones?"

"No, just refinishing the old ones. I like them, but I'm not a fan of blonde wood."

"No one is anymore." Nick reached for his cup of steaming coffee. "Boy, it was cold working on Dad's new project. There's no heat in the building yet."

Keagan nodded. "I had to keep hopping in and out of the truck today, lots of special deliveries."

They made small talk while they ate and then went their separate ways. Keagan drove her to his studio to look at plates. She reached across the middle console to rest her hand on his thigh and felt him tense.

"Am I being too pushy?" she asked.

"Hell, no, I wish you could sit next to me like girls did in old-model cars." She moved her hand higher, and his voice turned hoarse. "Careful now. I'm driving. You're enough of a distraction, as is."

Her hand returned to his thigh, but her insides turned somersaults. Keagan considered her a turn-on. Finally! When he parked at his studio, she leaned across the seat to kiss him. He didn't pull away but opened his lips slightly, his tongue skimming her lips and teeth. *Then* he pulled away and circled the front of the SUV to open her door. "Work first, then play."

A promised reward! Now, she was motivated.

Heat welcomed them when they entered the shop. Good. It was warm enough for them to get naked.

"First things first," he said and motioned toward the shelves.

She chose a cream-colored set of four plates and salad bowls, embedded with a snowflake pattern, for her mom. Mom could use it all during the winter season. For herself, she bought a set of everyday plates with a different pattern and a different color on each one. The mustard-yellow set was embedded with a head of garlic in its center. Another was bright red with a tomato motif. Forest green glazed the broccoli pattern. There were eight in all.

Keagan went into a closet and returned with a slatted, wooden box, then began packing each plate and shallow bowl. "This is going to be heavy. I'll need the dolly to lift it." He pointed to a heavy, industrial one. "I'll put them in the trunk of your car."

To help, she wrapped a plate to hand him. The sooner they settled this, the sooner they could move to better things. When he reached for it, their fingers touched. Electricity bolted through her body. Keagan's gaze locked with hers, his eyes blazing. He laid the plate down and yanked her to him. His lips crushed hers, then his kiss deepened, hot and demanding. She slid her hands under his shirt. *Damn, the man felt good!* Keagan lifted her onto his wooden worktable and stepped between her legs. *Bring it on!* Then tires crunched on the gravel outside the door and an engine turned off.

Why? Why now?

Keagan groaned. He took a deep breath, fighting for control. His lips pressed into a tight line, he lowered Karli back onto the floor and stepped behind the table to hide his erection. The door flew open, and Stuart rushed into the shop. He stopped and blinked at Karli.

"Oh. Sorry. I saw Keagan's SUV and didn't know anyone else was here."

Keagan tried to grin. "You look like Santa came early. What's up?"

"We found a tractor today, got a great deal. I was coming home from the grocery store, saw your SUV, and wanted to let you know."

"I'm happy for you." So was Karli. Stuart might have interrupted a perfect moment, but he had great news.

Stuart clapped Keagan on the back. "Thanks so much. You saved our fannies. I'd better get home, though. Marcia's waiting on the milk to finish cooking supper. It's already late."

"Congratulations!" Keagan called after him as he left. Then he looked at the clock and sighed. "It *is* late. We've lost more time than I thought. It'll take a while to load these and get you home."

Double phooey and damn! But Keagan had to start his job early each morning, so she put on her good sport face and wrapped plates while he packed them. She waited in the SUV while he loaded them with the dolly, then when they got to Axel's, she watched him use the dolly to transfer them from his SUV to the trunk of her Dodge. The man was strong! When he finished, he came to bend low and give her a quick kiss.

"I had a great night."

"So did I." She started to the house—disappointed, but hopeful. They were making progress. He was more relaxed around her, more affectionate. She knew better than to push him. Instead, she stood at the door and waved him away.

It was so easy spending time with him. She could talk to him about anything. Would she ever get bored of looking across a table and seeing Keagan? She didn't think so.

Chapter 29

The TV was on when she walked in the house. Axel and Kurt must be watching something. She hung her coat on a hook in the foyer and Dusty streaked toward her. He wound around her ankles, then started toward the kitchen.

"Oh, I get it. You're hungry." She followed him and filled his cat food bowl. The cat crouched and ate greedily. Karli decided the woman at the grain store was right. Dusty had been an indoor cat until he grew past the kitten stage, then the person who was supposed to love him had loaded him in a car and booted him out on the side of the road. How could people do that?

She bent to pet him, and his purrs filled the kitchen. It was a good thing she'd never know who owned him before, or she'd be tempted to whack the bastard over the head and dump him in the middle of nowhere to see how he liked it.

She glanced at the clock while she yawned. It had been a long day—a nice one, but long. She took a roll of sausage out of the freezer to thaw and headed to the bathroom. She washed her face and brushed her teeth, then turned off lights as she went to her room to change into her pajamas. She had a new Julia Donner Regency on her Kindle that she couldn't wait to read. She'd settled in and tugged her blankets around her when Dusty jumped on the air mattress and curled next to her. How cute was this cat?

She wasn't sure when she fell asleep. She only knew it was almost nine when she woke, and Dusty was pressed against her chest. The parlor was chilly, so she pulled on her robe to go to the kitchen. Dusty hurried to sit at his food bowl.

She sighed. "I feel like all I do is feed people."

"Good, you're awake, because I'm hungry. Soup makes a lousy supper," Axel called.

"Give me a minute." She fed the cat first, then made a pan of scrambled eggs to split between herself and Axel.

"Will you sit out here and eat with me?"

She'd have to sit in Kurt's chair. It wasn't contaminated, and Axel would like some company. She shrugged. "Why not?"

"Keagan used to sit out here with me once in a while, but he doesn't like Kurt, so he doesn't stop in as much."

Karli grunted. "No one likes Kurt. It's your own fault he's here."

Axel grew serious. "When Sylvie comes, I'll know what I need to do. If she's as awful as Kurt, a nursing home will look good."

Karli smiled. Music to her ears. "I'll get my plate." While they ate, she asked, "Do you remember who put linoleum floors in the kitchen? Are they original?"

Axel shook his head. "Nah, my mom would only have wood floors. Eloise is the one who wanted linoleum. She said it was too hard keeping the wood clean, told me I could refinish the kitchen floors or install something she could mop."

"And you got the linoleum for her?"

"That woman could be damn stubborn when she dug in. It was easier to give her what she wanted."

Karli was silent a moment. "You two weren't right for each other, were you?"

"She wanted to be married, but it wasn't because she liked me. She wanted someone to keep a roof over her head. I was too stupid to know that." He finished his food and pushed his plate toward her. "She liked being pregnant and having babies, too, but she didn't much care about them once they could walk and talk."

"They'd only be one or two then."

He glanced at Dusty, sitting at the door watching them. "Sort of like whoever had that cat. Only liked it when it was little. Once Eloise couldn't hold them and coo over them, she lost interest."

Karli had trouble picturing a mother who got bored with her own kids. The moms she knew had signed up for life.

Axel looked out the windows at a tire that had fallen from a frayed rope tossed over a tree limb. "I put up that swing for the kids. Should have done more, but every time I walked inside this damn house and Eloise opened her mouth, I just about choked on my bile. Still, it wasn't the kids' fault. I should have done more."

She didn't know what to say. Axel's version of his life was so different from everything her mom had told her.

He didn't seem to expect an answer. He went on. "I worked morning to night to just keep food on the table, but it wasn't enough." He looked at her. "What about you? Do you ever want to tie the knot? Have kids?"

He sure didn't make it sound appealing. "Nope, I don't want to be tied down. I like moving from place to place."

"Seems like it would get old to me."

She put his empty plate on top of hers. "Really? Marriage and kids didn't make you happy."

"I chose wrong. You wouldn't."

She snorted. "I'm not choosing."

"Even if the right one was right in front of you?"

She gave him a hard look. "And who would that be?"

Kurt walked into the room and slumped in his chair. "Did I miss breakfast?"

Axel growled. "Do you see our dirty plates? You should have gotten up earlier."

"I'm all right with coffee for now." Kurt started to the kitchen.

When he was out of earshot, Axel pointed at her. "Girlie, there are all kinds of mistakes people can make. Being alone gets old, too. Remember that."

Kurt returned and Karli pushed to her feet. "I'd better get started on the kitchen. If I pull up that linoleum, will I find wood under it?"

Axel gave a long sigh. "You just keep busy, girl. That's what I did, too, but it didn't make things any better."

His problems were bigger than hers. All she wanted was to sleep with Keagan a few more times before she left. But as she rinsed the plates to put in soapy water, she knew that wasn't true. She wanted to keep Keagan in her life, but how would she do that? He wasn't the type to wait for her each time she came to town. She glowered at the floor. This was the perfect day to take out her frustrations on the sad, sorry linoleum.

She decided to cook supper first, though. The floor was going to be a big project, and she might not want to stop to cook before she finished it. She found a large, deep skillet and put the bulk sausage in it to brown. She added a chopped onion to the cooked meat, then cannellini beans and diced tomatoes to start building her ragout. When it was finished, she put a lid on it and set it on a back burner. Then she changed into worn work clothes.

She was on her knees, ripping up old linoleum that stuck to the floor boards when someone knocked at the front door. "It's open!"

Keagan came to see what she was doing. He carried a bakery box and put it on the dining room table. "An apple cake from Grams," he told her.

It's a good thing she loved apples. But it was November. It's not like there was lots of fresh fruit to choose from. She stopped working and sat up, balancing on her knees. "That's perfect. It'll go great with our supper."

Keagan sniffed. "Something smells good."

"A ragout. Want a bite?"

"Just a taste. I have lots more mail to deliver."

She handed him a big spoon and he took a scoop. He moaned when he ate it. "That's delicious."

"If I'd have made more, I'd send you home with some."

He looked regretful. "That's okay. Brad's cooking tonight."

"Is he a good cook?"

"Hell, no, but don't tell him that."

Karli laughed. "You're still alive. I guess that's a good thing."

He came closer to look at the wooden floor she'd exposed. "You've bitten off a big project. Do you have a sander?"

"I don't think so."

"You can rent one for floors in town. It'll save you a lot of time."

She showed him her plans for the kitchen cupboards. He glanced at the sandpaper in the foyer. "It'll take you forever with that. I have an electric sander. I'll bring it to you tomorrow." He frowned. "You'll have a mess, though. You'd be better off if you let me take the cupboard doors down so you can sand them in the barn, or else you'll have dust everywhere."

The man was a blessing. She grinned at him. "If you lend me your sander, I'll make you a big pot of something."

His eyes lit up. "Stew?"

She laughed. "It's one of your favorites, isn't it? Sounds like a fair trade to me."

Keagan might be tall and lean, but he loved to eat. She could use that. She decided she'd make a little extra when she cooked from now on and put some in a plastic container to send home with him. She caught him looking at her and glanced down at her ratty jeans and holey T-shirt. "Sorry I'm such a mess. These are my work clothes." She touched her hair. She'd pulled it up in a ponytail, but strands had escaped and curled everywhere.

"You look wonderful."

She did? He was the type of guy who loved girls with no makeup, who didn't dress up. She could use that, too.

By the time Keagan walked out the door, Karli had a game plan to win him. Then she laughed at herself. What did she intend to do with him? But she already knew. She wanted him for keeps. She just didn't know how she was going to make that work. If he fell for her enough, would he travel with her?

Chapter 30

When Karli walked into the kitchen the next morning, she glared at the patches of linoleum that had stuck to the wood floor and didn't want to leave. She'd tried sliding a butcher knife under them, a flat bladed shovel, and screwdrivers. No luck. She'd gone to bed last night irritated and frustrated. She turned her face, didn't even want to look at them, and got busy in the kitchen.

The floor felt bumpy underfoot. She fussed while she cooked.

"Settle down, girl," Axel called. "Ask Keagan for some advice. The boy's handy."

He sure was, but she'd wanted the floor finished by now, even though she knew she'd gotten lucky on her projects so far. She hadn't hit any major snags, and one was bound to happen.

Just as promised, when Keagan brought the mail, he brought an electric sander, too. Karli was still struggling with the kitchen floor, but she was ready for their trade. She'd already made two pots of stew—one for him and one for them. Dusty loved it when she cooked, waiting for her to throw him small morsels. Axel had asked for a second helping, and Kurt kept dipping into the kitchen for more, so she knew they both liked it. Hopefully, Keagan would, too.

Keagan frowned at the floor. "Giving you troubles, huh?"

"Pulling up Formica isn't as easy as they made it look on TV."

"Have you tried a crowbar? The tip's narrow enough, it's easier to pry with."

Now he told her. But she wasn't being fair. She hadn't asked his advice, had she?

He studied it closer. "I sure don't miss the swirl pattern in the linoleum. The wood's in great shape. It just needs sanding and refinishing. Be sure to tape plastic over all the doors before you start. Seal this room tight, or you'll have dust everywhere, but you've done a great job."

His praise went straight to her head. She felt like she could float around the house for the rest of the day. He went to their pot of stew on the stove and asked, "Mind if I take a taste; see what you're sending me for supper?" When she handed him a spoon, he took a bite and closed his eyes with a smile. "This is damn good."

She might have to pinch herself. It sure made her happy to make Keagan happy. They spent another few minutes talking about the kitchen project, and Keagan told her that she'd be better off finishing the floor before she tackled the cupboards. "You have a hell of a lot of cupboards in here. I'll come to help you when you take off the doors, or you'll be at it all day."

"That's awfully nice of you."

He shrugged. "I have an electric screwdriver. The right tools make everything go faster. I've worked on lots of projects with my dad on the farm. I like tinkering around the house."

And she liked having him underfoot. She'd have to finish the wooden floor as fast as possible. The crowbar worked, and soon all of the linoleum was pulled up. She hummed as she drove into town to rent a sander that looked a little like an upright vacuum. She hummed while she sanded the floor and returned the machine to town. She bought a maple stain at Meg's, then beat it for home. She'd stain the wood before she shut out the lights for the night, so that the floor would have plenty of time to dry.

Her good mood vanished when a woman knocked on the door. Karli opened it and saw someone with Axel's steel-gray eyes and wide nose. It had to be Sylvie, and by her downturned lips and glacial expression, Karli knew she hadn't come to spread joy.

The woman was taller than she was and looked her slowly up and down. "You must be Donna's kid."

Karli wouldn't let her know how intimidating she looked. She was a nurse, after all. Plenty of belligerent patients and grumpy doctors growled at her, and she took them in her stride. She smiled. "Yup, Donna's my mom. Axel and Kurt are in the back room. I'll show you to them."

"I know the way."

"Then be my guest."

The woman stalked past her. "I ain't no guest. This is my home."

It used to be. Karli followed behind. She didn't give a crap about Sylvie, but she did want to see Axel's reaction to her.

Sylvie walked to the middle of the three-season room and propped her hands on her hips. "You're a freakin' mess, both of you, and so is this room. It's a good thing I came to take care of you."

Axel's eyes narrowed. "I'm doing just fine. Karli cooks for us and Keagan wheels me in for plenty of showers."

Sylvie was unimpressed. "I can get you in and out of the tub, and I'll cut your hair and beard, too."

"To hell with that." Axel crossed his arms. "You're my daughter. I'm not undressing for you."

"You're too old to worry about that, nothin' much to see."

"Doesn't matter. No woman's washing me."

"We'll see about that." Sylvie turned on Kurt. "Why ain't you givin' him showers?"

"I have a bad back."

She barked a laugh. "Sure you do, but at least you've been fixin' the place up."

Axel shook his head. "Kurt hasn't lifted a finger. Karli's done all the painting and cleaning around here."

"Nice of her. She's done a good job. She and Kurt can leave now."

"I invited them to stay." Axel glared at her.

"And I'm tellin' 'em to go." Sylvie glared back.

Axel gave a thin smile. "As far as I know, this is still my house, so if I say they stay, they stay."

Sylvie nodded at Karli. "That girl ain't gonna hang around till you croak. I will, so you'd better start doin' what I tell you."

"You'd better start listening to *me*," Axel said, "or I'll sign Karli up for power of attorney."

Like she wanted *that* responsibility. Karli shook her head, but Axel ignored her.

Sylvie straightened her back. "Okay, we'll play it your way and see where it goes."

Axel turned his attention back to the TV. "There are plenty of bedrooms upstairs. Pick one."

Kurt was on his feet, hurrying ahead of her. "I got Mom and Dad's old room. It's mine."

When they left, Axel reached for his cell phone.

"Are you calling the sheriff to have them evicted?" Karli asked.

Axel shot her a dirty look. "Nope, I'm calling the rest of the kids. Charlie was a good boy. He'll come to help me."

"Good luck with that." She started to turn away.

"One of them will."

"I'm not holding my breath." And when she heard him rant, *After I kept a roof over your head and food in your belly*, she assumed it wasn't going well. When he called for a glass of water later and she took it to him, he sat hunched against his pillow, pouting. He glared at her. "Damn ingrates, they owe me."

She shook her head at him. "They think they owe you, too, but they're too nice to give you what they think you deserve."

He grunted. "Full of snappy answers, aren't you?"

"I'm just waiting for the truth to sink in. You'd better come up with a game plan. I can still get in-home care for you and Meals on Wheels, or you can hope Kurt and Sylvie take good care of you."

He sighed. "Give me one more week and I'll give you an answer."

"Promise?"

"Boy Scout's honor."

She rolled her eyes. "Were you ever a Scout?"

He smiled.

Damn old man! "One week, but that's it. I have a life, and it's a lot more fun than spending time with you."

"Is that so?" He leaned forward. "Does Keagan live wherever that life takes you?"

"No, but Keagan won't leave Mill Pond. You know that."

He sniggered. "That boy's worth some bother."

She narrowed her eyes at him. "He's one person you're actually nice to."

"Have to be. The boy's nice, but he won't take no crap off anyone. Not even me."

"I noticed."

"You don't either." Axel studied her. "You two have some things in common."

She liked that thought.

Axel pulled on his grizzled beard. "Are you still going to cook for me now that Sylvie's come?"

Karli hadn't thought about that. "Maybe we can take turns. I didn't come here to run a bed and breakfast."

"I'm betting she sucks as a cook."

"You've just gotten spoiled. She might surprise you."

They heard Sylvie's steps on the stairs. "Let's find out." When his daughter came back in the room, Axel said, "Karli fixed stew today. Are you going to cook for me, too?"

"I'll cook for you, but I'll be damned if I'll cook for Kurt and Donna's kid."

"Then forget it." Axel turned to Karli. "What's the point of everyone fixing separate meals?"

"I don't mind. I'll run into town to eat. She can take care of you fulltime."

"What about Kurt?"

Karli shrugged. "I didn't come here to take care of Kurt."

"But I like your food! You can cook for me, and Sylvie and Kurt can run into town together and pay for their own meals."

Sylvie's hands went to her hips again. "You haven't even tasted my food. What do you have in the refrigerator?"

"Karli bought everything in there. We have a grocery store in town, remember?"

Sylvie scowled. "You expect me to pay for your food?"

"Karli does."

"Karli's crazy then. We came to help you, not support you."

Axel turned to Karli with a smirk. "See. What did I tell you?"

Karli was tired of both of them. "You two figure it out. I'm going to grab a sausage sandwich at Joel's microbrewery. You're on your own." She'd had as much of Axel's family as she could stand.

Sylvie went to scrounge through the refrigerator. "Looks like fried potatoes and eggs to me."

"Too much grease makes me sick."

"Get used to it, old man. I fry everything."

Karli headed to get her coat. She might need to find a permanent table at Ralph's every other night.

Chapter 31

Axel didn't feel good when Karli got home. "My stomach's off."

No kidding. From all the splatters on the stove, she'd guess he'd ingested more grease than any human being should. She brought him two antacids and a glass of water.

She'd had a nice night. Harley and Kathy were at Joel's, and she'd sat with them. They'd filled her in on all of the recent couplings in Mill Pond, told her how Ian had met Tessa, Paula had fallen for Chase, and Joel had snagged Miriam.

"I'd better be careful then." Karli laughed. "I'm not looking for anything permanent."

Kathy raised a warning eyebrow. "Neither were they."

"The bumpiest was Tyne and Daphne," Harley said. "That one was fun to watch."

"How did you two meet?" Karli asked them.

Kathy smiled. "In a graveyard." And then she told her the whole story, how her car had broken down and she pulled into a cemetery to call for a tow truck and Harley found her and rescued her. Her car. Her heart. All of her.

Harley smiled, listening to his wife. "When you meet a stranded beauty at your mother's grave, it's a sign, right?"

"A gift from the gods," Karli said.

Without her asking, Harley told her about Keagan and Cecily. "Talk about two people who were wrong for each other. Keagan's a homebody, loves Mill Pond and his family; loves his job and his art. Cecily wanted to be on the go every waking hour. They had nothing in common."

Was he hinting at something? Warning her off? Did she have any common goals or passions with Keagan?

After the three of them finished their meals and said their goodbyes, Karli fussed on the drive home. Was she right for Keagan? When she reached the house, though, anger pushed everything else out of her mind. Dusty ran from the barn when he heard her footsteps. It was a cold night. What the hell was her cat doing outdoors? She scooped him into her arms and carried him inside. Purrs greeted her.

Sylvie was in the dining room, watching something on YouTube on Karli's laptop.

Karli stopped short and stared. "That's mine. It was in my room."

Sylvie shrugged. "You weren't usin' it."

"Doesn't matter. It's mine. Hands off." She glared. "What was my cat doing outside?"

"Cats don't belong in a house. I don't like pets."

"Tough. Dusty's mine. He stays with me." As she spoke the words, she knew they were true. When she left Mill Pond, the cat was coming with her.

"Don't get your shorts in a twist," Sylvie barked. "I brought my TV with me. I just ain't got it hooked up yet. I called and someone's comin' tomorrow."

Karli nodded, then looked out at the kitchen. Dirty pots and pans covered the stove. Food dried on dishes in the sink. "You didn't clean your mess."

"I'll get to it tomorrow . . . when I damned well feel like it."

"Good, then you go to town when the mood strikes you and buy the food to fix meals, because I'm not working in there."

Sylvie's expression hardened more than usual. "You're a real pain in the ass, ain't you?"

Karli had heard that before. "I can be, but I'd guess you're better at it."

Sylvie bit her bottom lip. "How long you stayin'?"

"I promised Axel I'd stay another week."

Sylvie's shoulders relaxed and she smiled. "A week ain't that long. You can have the kitchen. Cook everythin' the old man likes and make him happy."

It was better than degreasing every day from top to bottom. "Deal."

Sylvie nodded and stood, pushing Karli's laptop toward her. "Guess you never learned to share."

"Not with people I don't know." Karli took it and carried it to her room. By the time she went to the kitchen, Sylvie had crammed every dirty pot and dish in the dishwasher and started it. Karli sighed and reached for the multi-purpose spray. She was cleaning the counter top and stove when Axel called, "I still don't feel so good."

Karli made him a cup of tea. "I'm going to cook until I leave here. I'll try to keep you healthy for as long as I can."

He took a sip of tea and sighed. "I asked for cottage cheese, but she wouldn't bring me any."

Karli patted his hand. "Give the pills a little more time to work, then you'll feel better." She looked at the empty chair where Kurt usually sat. "No Kurt?"

"He didn't feel so good either, had to keep making runs to the bathroom. Went to bed early."

"Maybe you'll both get more tolerant of fried food."

"Don't want to." Axel glanced away from the TV screen when his show went to a commercial. "I called Keagan. He's coming tomorrow after work to clean me up and cut my hair and beard again. Doesn't do a half bad job of it."

Karli tucked his blankets higher around him. "It's getting uncomfortable out here. When do you usually move inside the house?"

"Keagan's bringing me some kind of fancy heater, takes pellets. I like looking out the windows."

Karli pulled the drapes closed around Axel's bed. "That might help a little. Keagan's sure nice to you."

"He's a good boy. Should have kept his money, but he's all hot and bothered about his family."

Karli nodded. In the future, if she wanted to see him, she'd have to come here. She'd be happy to make the trip as often as she could, as long as Keagan would keep spending time with her. When she had Axel comfortable, she went through the house, turning off lights. She felt more tired than she expected. She fed Dusty, then changed into her pajamas. As soon as her head hit the pillow on her air mattress, she was asleep.

Voices woke her in the morning. Dusty stretched and yawned beside her. Karli pulled her pillow over her head when she recognized Sylvie's strident tone.

"What did you do? Leave your TV on all night? What are you—rich? You can afford to pay for that much electricity?"

"It's seven." Axel's voice sounded slurred with sleep. "Turn the damn thing off and leave me alone."

"Nope, time to get you in your wheelchair and roll you into the bathroom. You don't need those diapers. You're just too lazy to hoof it to the toilet in time."

Had Sylvie ever worked with old people with weak bladders? Karli listened for an answer.

"Too late. My diaper's already wet."

"You think that's funny, don't you? But if I have to set my alarm for five a.m., I'm getting you up and moving in time."

"Go away and let me get more sleep."

"Nope, I'm getting you up and walking. We're going to build up your strength."

The woman was a sadist. Karli rolled her eyes. Poor Axel's frame was fragile. He probably suffered every time he rolled from one side to the other.

"Come on," Sylvie demanded. "Let's get you moving."

"Karli!" Axel roared.

Oh, damn. He was pissed. She pushed off the air mattress, pulled on her robe, and went to rescue him. When she got to the sun-room, Sylvie was pulling on him, trying to yank him to his feet.

"His legs won't hold him," Karli said.

Sylvie whirled on her. "How do you know?"

Should she state the obvious? *I'm a nurse.* Sylvie probably wouldn't believe that. So she said, "I've been wheeling him to the bathroom to brush his teeth every night. He's not strong enough to stand."

Sylvie didn't look happy. "You didn't take care of yourself, did you, old man? You expected us to do everything for you."

"He's old," Karli said. "And he's worked hard all his life. It takes its toll."

Sylvie wrinkled her nose. "When was the last time anyone cleaned his sheets?"

"They're clean. Every time Keagan gives him a shower, I change them. I change the waterproof mats under him once a day, but if you think he needs more, go for it." Karli motioned to Axel's bed.

"Why should I be the one to do it? Why doesn't he hire someone?"

Karli snorted. "Let me know how that works out. I'm going back to bed." As she walked to her room, she heard them bickering again. She didn't care if Sylvie made Axel miserable. It served him right, but she couldn't try to make him stand and cause him physical damage.

At nine, when she woke for the second time, they were still going at it. Axel had to be about whipped. He usually slept later than Karli did.

Karli went to the kitchen and started the coffeepot. Maybe Sylvie didn't like caffeine? But the minute the pot finished gurgling and the aroma of coffee filled the house, Sylvie was there with a mug. Karli watched her carry it upstairs and then poured a cup for Axel and her.

"Has she been at you all morning?" Karli asked.

Axel looked exhausted. "After breakfast, I'm taking a nap."

"I don't blame you." She made him eggs and toast. He was asleep soon after she removed his dirty dishes. Sylvie was nowhere in sight, and she suspected she'd fallen asleep, too. Had the woman gotten up just to annoy Axel?

Karli had meant to start work on the cupboards, but she'd never finished the floor last night. She didn't expect to see anyone soon—it was common for Kurt to sleep until noon—so she put on her oldest jeans, got on her hands and knees, and stained half of the kitchen floor. Meg had told her that it took twenty-four hours before you could walk on it in socks, no shoes. She could get to the refrigerator but not to the sink and stove. No worries. She'd carried paper plates and her slow cooker into the dining room, but tomorrow, after she finished the second half of the floor, she'd have to bring food in and come in the back-porch door to deliver it. A bother, but worth it.

She didn't hear any movement until lunch time. By then, the sloppy joes were already simmering in the slow cooker for supper tonight. She'd bought deli meat to make sandwiches for lunch. Kurt came into the kitchen and stopped at the halfway mark. He studied the floor and said, "It looks like a perfect match."

She blinked, surprised. Kurt hardly ever complimented her. "Thanks. You hungry?"

He looked at the stack of sandwiches she'd made and covered with plastic wrap. "I could eat a couple."

She dished him up two sandwiches. "Throw your plate away when you're done. Sylvie got Axel up early this morning. He might sleep for a while."

"Can I use the remote until he wakes up?"

She shrugged. "Why not?"

He went to the back room, slumped into his chair, and looked happier than usual. She wondered what it would feel like to live off the scraps of someone else for your needs in life. That alone would motivate her to work, but not Kurt.

Axel and Sylvie woke an hour later, and she gave them sandwiches, too. Before Sylvie finished hers, the cable man came to connect her TV upstairs, and she disappeared with him.

"Will the connection only work in Sylvie's room?" Kurt asked.

"Beats me. I don't know how things work in the country." Karli was just glad Sylvie might spend more time in her room.

Kurt disappeared. Karli suspected he was sitting upstairs, in his room, listening to what the cable man told Sylvie. Dusty wove around her ankles, and she realized that the cat had emptied his food bowls and was begging for scraps of deli meat. She tossed him a few. She couldn't really do anything else at the moment, so she went in her room and turned on her Kindle. She'd enjoy herself for a few hours.

She was startled when someone knocked on the front door later in the afternoon. Cripes! It was after five, and she'd gotten lost in her book. The door opened and she heard Keagan call, "Hello?"

She hurried to greet him. "Sorry, we're off schedule today. Sylvie tried to get Axel up early this morning, and everyone's tired."

He stopped in the dining room and smiled at her. "You look pretty. You've been working in the kitchen, haven't you?"

Yup, the man liked the natural look, and that was being generous. Her old jeans had holes in them now and were stained. She touched a hand to her hair—a bushy mess. "Are you hungry? I made a pot of sloppy joes. There are paper plates and buns on the dining room table."

"Let me clean Axel first." When he got to the kitchen, he examined the half that was stained. "A good match."

She smiled, pleased.

When he stepped into the back room, he stopped and frowned. Axel and Sylvie faced each other, arms crossed, glaring. Karli hadn't heard them argue. What were they going on about now? Sylvie glanced at Keagan. "He's not getting a shower until he drinks his V-8."

Keagan looked at Axel. "You like V-8. What's the problem?"

"She's not my boss. She's in my house. I'll do what I want."

Karli looked from one of them to the other. "Why didn't you call me, Axel? I didn't hear Sylvie come downstairs."

"She wore her socks and tiptoed." Axel didn't break eye contact with his daughter. "But I can handle her. I don't need any help."

Like hell, he didn't. Karli wasn't going to argue about it, though, so leaned against the doorframe to watch the fireworks.

Sylvie poked a finger at Keagan. "That old man's sitting there until he drinks his V-8."

Keagan ignored her. He pushed Axel's wheelchair closer to his bed and said, "Need some help getting in?"

Sylvie came to stand behind the chair. "You're a neighbor. I'm his daughter. He'll do what I say."

Keagan turned and towered over her. "It's like this. It's Axel's house. He hasn't been declared incompetent yet, and it won't happen. He's plenty sharp. If you were trying to help him, I'd side with you. But you're just trying to bully him, so go away."

Sylvie straightened her shoulders with a smirk. "I just might challenge all of you. I get to weigh in, or I'm thinkin' of callin' the authorities."

"Here." Keagan offered her a phone. "Let's see where that gets you."

"The old man's a fool. He can't manage on his own."

"No arguments there, but you're supposed to care for him, not make him miserable."

"He deserves it. He made us miserable, and there was nothin' we could do about it."

"I get it. This is your chance for payback, but that's not the way it's going to work."

Sylvie turned on her heel and stomped upstairs.

Keagan leveled a gaze on Axel. "Do you have to antagonize her? You're the one who called and invited her here. Mind your manners or I'm going to be too busy for a few days to check on you."

Axel looked at Kurt. "Having my kids here hasn't turned out so hot."

"Anyone could have told you that. You were a crappy dad. Now, come on. Get in the chair. I can't stay here all night."

Karli expected bluster from the old man, but he did as Keagan asked. Keagan didn't sweet coat anything for him, and he didn't mind.

While Keagan washed and scrubbed him, Karli changed Axel's sheets and laid out clean clothes for him. By the time Keagan was finished trimming his hair and beard, Karli had potato chips and deli coleslaw on the dining room table. Axel enjoyed sitting at the table with them to eat. So did Kurt. Even Sylvie came downstairs.

When they finally got Axel settled back in his bed, Karli walked Keagan to the door. "Thanks for everything. I have neighbors in Indy, but they aren't like the people around here."

Keagan laughed. "There are too many people in big cities. They can't be like Mill Pond. That's why I love it here."

She loved *Keagan*. No, wait. She wasn't the type to fall in love, but she *did* like him a lot. More than she'd ever liked any man. Would she be happy living in a small town? What the hell was she thinking? She loved her independence. She'd feel stuck here. Wouldn't she?

Chapter 32

The next morning, another daughter knocked on the door. Karli invited her in and stared. Prim and proper wouldn't even begin to describe her. Her graying hair was scraped back in a tight bun. No makeup. She wore a long, black skirt and black top.

"I'm Ida, the eleventh child of Axel and Eloise Crupe."

Karli tried to remember her manners, even though she was certain Ida wouldn't make her life any easier. "I'm Donna's daughter." Ida was probably in her mid-forties, about five years younger than Karli's mom. Eloise had miscarried after her mom was born, but was determined to have another baby. She miscarried twice after Ida until she had Charlie, her last child.

Pale gray eyes studied her. "How is your mother?"

"Fine. Happy. You?" Karli couldn't recall seeing her mom's sister before. Where had Ida been when they'd returned to check on Charlie? Had she run away from home at an early age? Or did she hide every time their family came to visit? She and Mom were close in age, but opposites in personality.

Ida drew herself up. "I'm happy enough. I've been blessed with a job that's let me support myself. When I heard about Father, though, I took a leave of absence to do my duty."

"Your duty?"

"To care for him, of course. How ill is he?"

"He's old and can't walk. He has good days and bad days, but he might last a long time."

Ida frowned. "My leave won't extend past three months."

Three months? "Axel's in the sun-room. We'll have to use the living room to reach it. I stained the kitchen floor last night." She'd decided not to take a chance and stayed up late, finishing it. She'd used duct tape to put up sheets of cardboard at each doorway to keep Dusty out of the kitchen. The floor wasn't dry enough to walk on yet, but it wasn't sticky either. If Kurt snuck in, lured by leftovers, she should be able to sand out his footprints and re-stain. She'd put deli roast beef and bread in the cooler before she'd started and set it outside. It was cold enough to keep the food safe. They could eat sandwiches for supper tonight. She'd already phoned Ralph's diner and ordered four of his specials for lunch. She'd have to grab another corned beef dinner for Ida, but it was time to set some limits. She didn't mind feeding Axel. If he ate well and moved around more, she was helping him. When Kurt came, she didn't think he had any money, so she didn't push for him to chip in. Sylvie was another story, but Karli hadn't expected to stay long once she showed up. And now there was another Crupe.

She led Ida to Axel. He stared at her and let out a long breath. "You look just like your mother at that age. What's wrong with you? You used to be pretty. Still could be."

Ida shrugged. "Vanity is a sin."

"No man in your life, huh?" His words stung. They were cruel, even for Axel.

"That's rude!" Karli snapped.

Axel studied his daughter. "She packed a bag and snuck out of here to run away with some tourist when she was fifteen. She was always boy crazy. Now I'm supposed to believe she's a saint?"

Karli felt sorry for Ida and turned to offer her sympathy, but Ida looked unaffected.

"I found out, like most women, that I was better off without men."

Ouch!

Ida walked closer to stare down at Axel. "I have a three-month leave of absence. You have to die before then, or I can't help you."

Axel threw back his head and laughed. "I plan to be inconvenient."

"Your choice." Ida looked at Karli. "My father's never been easy to deal with. You must have a beautiful soul to have tolerated him this long, but I can look after him now."

"You'll be havin' plenty of help." Sylvie walked into the room. "Should we be honored that you've finally come to our rescue?"

Ida looked Sylvie up and down. "I see you haven't defeated your dark side yet. You're just as unpleasant as always."

Kurt coughed from his corner of the room, and Ida finally noticed him. She shook her head. "Still lazy. Idle hands are of no use in this house."

Axel interrupted. "Enough already. I listened to you three bicker the whole time you were growing up. I don't have to listen to it now. I'd rather go to a home."

"No!" all three of them said together.

Karli frowned. "What's wrong with a home? He'd get three meals a day and twenty-four-hour care."

"They'd take all his money," Kurt blurted.

Axel gave a sly smile. "Damn right, they would. You three wouldn't like that, would you? And I'll make sure to live long enough that it's all gone."

They exchanged glances, and Karli realized even Ida had come for the cash. Well, that was their problem. Thankfully, she needed to drive to town to pick up their meals, and she couldn't wait to get out of this house.

"The toaster and bread are in the dining room, if you're hungry. There's peanut butter and jam, too. We can't use the kitchen until the floor dries, so I ordered food from Ralph's. I need to go get it. I'll be back in less than an hour."

Ida's gaze shot daggers at her siblings. "I'll get my things and take them upstairs. I don't expect anyone to enter my room once I get settled."

Sylvie rolled her eyes. "You haven't changed. You'd scream if one of us touched your doll when you were little."

Karli was tired of listening to them. She turned on her heel to get her coat and purse. She didn't turn on the radio on the drive to town. Silence felt like a blessing. No more squabbling. She decided the three worst Crupe kids had come like vultures to hover over Axel. She almost felt sorry for him.

She was passing a harvested field when she noticed movement in it near the tree line. A dozen wild turkeys pecked for corn that had fallen. She slowed to get a better view. It was a first for her. She loved the mix of shops, fields, and lakes around here. Indy had more restaurants and activities on offer, but Mill Pond had more charm. She sighed. She loved this town and its people.

When she ducked into Ralph's, the diner was crowded, as usual. Brad was sharing a table with a woman she hadn't met. Karli's order was waiting, but Ralph's wife, Jules, told her it would take a minute to make up another one. Brad waved her over in the meantime.

"Have you met Steph? She makes bread with Maxwell, and they do catering together."

"You sent Axel pumpkin and zucchini bread," Karli said. "They were delicious."

"Thanks." Steph grinned. "I've gotten really lucky. First, I got to work with Paula and Tyne at the inn, then Tyne introduced me to Maxwell, and Max has taught me all about breads. Sometimes, I think about what I'd have learned if I'd gone to culinary school, like Paula wanted me to, but I'm doing what I want to now."

Karli frowned. There was a whole history here she didn't know. "You don't think you'd have liked culinary school?"

"I'd have loved it," Steph's expression softened, "but I love being married to Ben more, and I'm still cooking and baking. I have the best of both worlds."

She'd chosen a man over school. Karli was intrigued. "I don't want to pry, but do you ever regret not leaving?"

Steph didn't hesitate. "Never. For me, life's about being surrounded by people I love who love me back. A job comes second."

Jules motioned Karli to the counter to collect her order, so Karli said her goodbyes. On the drive back to the farm, she thought about what Steph had said. She loved her mom and dad, but she really enjoyed traveling. Her jobs were so temporary, though, she didn't make deep friendships. Even her affairs were casual, and that was beginning to wear a little thin.

How much more did she want? Would Keagan be satisfied if she drove to Mill Pond every other week? She didn't think so. When she left here, he'd move on. Would she regret losing him? Yes. The question was: How much?

Chapter 33

Karli took down the cardboard at the kitchen doors before she went to bed. The wood floors looked wonderful. She'd have liked to give them another clear coat to protect them, but not with three extra people milling around the house. She fed Dusty, then went to her room for the night and called her mom before it got too late.

"Ida came today. Kurt and Sylvie don't seem to like her any more than they like each other."

"She made it hard to like her," Mom said. "Charlie, Ida, and I were the last three kids Mom had. Charlie and I stuck together, and we'd have included her, but she always made us feel like competition. If we got something, she made us feel that it was at her expense. Our oldest brother, Jackson, left Mill Pond before Ida was born. Three years later, Ronnie left, and three years after him, Kurt moved away. Each time a brother or sister left, there was more room and more food at the table—Ida's slice of the pie got a little bit bigger, but she wanted it all."

"That's sad."

"It was her choice. According to her, she was always wronged. She became the grand manipulator, trying to think of ways to use people, especially boys."

It was hard to imagine Ida attracting boys, but Karli remembered that Axel had been surprised when he saw her. He'd said that she used to be pretty. "She's dowdy now," Karli told her mom. "I think she could be attractive, but she chooses not to."

"She never picked the best men, probably got burned too many times." Her mom sighed. "I always hoped she'd get smart, be more open to real love that was mutual, but it must not have happened."

"I don't remember her at all."

"She ran off with a guy in his late thirties when she was fifteen, thought she'd hit pay dirt."

"I kind of feel sorry for her."

"So do I, but be careful. She's not all that likeable."

Karli had already decided that. They talked about Axel and the town a little longer, then Mom gave a long yawn. "Sorry, but it's been busy at the office lately. I come home wiped out."

"Then go find Dad and get some sleep." Karli worked twelve-hour shifts when she was on duty. She knew how tiring work could be. She glanced at the clock—too early to sleep, so she pulled her blankets around her and reached for her Kindle. She'd finished her Regency and decided to try a mystery this time. Why not go classic? She bought an Agatha Christie and was trying to keep up with Hercule Poirot when she looked at the clock and was surprised to see it was eleven. How did that happen? Too many clues and red herrings, but it was time to call it quits.

When she curled on her side, Dusty snuggled close, purring loudly. She slept until Dusty jumped off the bed to check out sounds in the kitchen. Someone was moving around in there. It was still dark outside. The cat could fend for himself, so Karli turned over and went back to sleep.

She woke at eight-thirty to the aroma of garlic, onions, and tarragon. She dressed quickly and went to the kitchen. Perfectly sliced egg noodles draped from every open cupboard door to dry. Karli cussed under her breath. She'd scrubbed every one of those, and now they'd need to be cleaned again.

Ida glanced at her. "I'm making chicken and noodle soup for Father. Everyone else can eat something else."

"Good. I was going to bring that up. We can all pay for our own food." Ida could do her own thing. No skin off her nose. She shrugged and started the coffeepot. When the coffee was brewed, she poured herself a cup and lifted an empty mug in a question to Ida.

Ida shook her head. "I gave up caffeine a year ago. I only drink water now."

Whatever. Karli carried her coffee into the dining room and scanned the headlines on her laptop as she sipped it. She'd almost finished when Axel called, "Whatever you're cooking has made me hungry. What's for breakfast?"

"Eggs?" Karli asked.

"And two pieces of toast," he yelled back.

When Karli carried his food into his room, he asked, "What smells so good?"

"Ida's making chicken and noodle soup for you. Homemade noodles. She got up early to make everything from scratch."

"What are you making?"

Karli blinked. "Maybe nothing. I might go out to eat. There are too many people for me to keep paying for everyone's groceries."

He grunted and dug into his eggs. Kurt drifted down a little later. He sniffed appreciatively and followed the aromas into the kitchen.

"It's not for you," Ida said. "Only for Dad and me."

"When Karli cooks, it's for all of us." Kurt bent over the pot and smiled at the whole chicken simmering in the broth.

"She didn't have to live with you like I did. You'll have to fend for yourself." Ida finished peeling potatoes to put in a pan of cold water.

"Karli bought all the food you're cooking," Kurt said. "She should get a vote."

Karli came into the kitchen to make herself some toast. "Ida just got here. I'll donate all of the ingredients to her today. From now on, she'll have to buy her own."

Ida frowned. "Why isn't Dad buying the groceries?"

"He doesn't want to." Karli buttered her toast and reached for the cherry preserves.

"That's going to change." Ida raised an eyebrow at the bread. "Am I allowed a piece of toast?"

Karli nodded. "Be my guest. Today."

Kurt snickered and opened the refrigerator. He grabbed three pieces of deli meat and pressed them between two slices of bread, then went to join Axel on the sun porch.

Ida turned to stare at Karli. "Don't think we're reimbursing you for the food you cooked Dad."

Karli poured herself another cup of coffee. Ida made Sylvie look like a pussycat. She smiled. "I didn't come for Axel's money. I wanted to set up health care options for him. He's not cooperating."

"He doesn't need options. He has us."

"Yeah, I feel sorry for him." Karli heard a chuckle from the back room. Axel had heard her.

Ida's expression turned nasty. "What's your game? What do you want?"

"I want Axel to make up his mind one way or another by the end of the week. Whatever he decides is fine with me."

"No one's that damn Goody-Two-shoes," Ida snapped. "You just came to help?"

Karli pursed her lips, considering, then nodded. "That's about it. Mom was worried, and I knew she'd come, even though she didn't want to. I had time off between jobs, so I could spare her any unpleasantness."

"Aren't you the good little girl?"

Karli laughed. "Not really, but I figured I could handle this."

"She's a nurse!" Axel called from the back room.

Ida blinked, surprised. "You're a nurse?"

"Yup, I could help Axel, but he won't let me."

That statement was followed by a long silence. Finally, Ida asked, "You're leaving at the end of the week?"

"That's the plan."

Ida looked as happy as Sylvie had. Karli wasn't going to get any awards from them for how to win friends and influence people. Not that she cared.

Ida's shoulders relaxed. "You still don't get any of my soup. I cook for Dad and me from now on. Got that?"

"Knock yourself out." Karli cleaned up her mess and went back to the dining room table and her laptop. Ida had rubbed her the wrong way. She'd thrown down the gauntlet for the wrong person. It was on! Out of spite, she typed *one-dish meal recipes* in the search engine. Karli might smile and nod to Ida, but the dumb ass was going down. She wasn't going to be here that much longer and it would be worth the money to mess with her.

She'd saved a dozen recipes to a file and made a long grocery list before Keagan knocked on the door with mail. He licked his lips when he stepped inside the house. "Smells good."

"Ida's making soup for Axel and her."

He frowned. "Five people live here."

"Tell her that. She doesn't share."

He caught something in her voice and smiled. "It's like that, is it?"

"She can cook for Axel. I'll cook for Kurt and me."

Blue eyes sparkling, Keagan held up a nine-by-thirteen envelope. "Axel has to sign for this. Something official."

As he walked through the house to the back room, Sylvie and Ida lined up to follow him. Kurt stood when he took the envelope to Axel.

"What is that?" Kurt asked.

"Don't know. It's for Axel."

Axel muted the TV and signed for it. He opened it and smiled.

"What is it?" Kurt repeated.

Sylvie's hands went to her hips. "Did you make out a will, old man, tryin' to cut us out of your money to leave it to charity? You'd do somethin' like that, wouldn't you? But we'll contest it."

Ida demanded, "Do you have a will?"

Axel held up a stock statement. "I cashed everything in and had it put in the bank."

The three of them looked at the numbers and their eyes gleamed with greed. "You don't have to wait till you're dead to give us money," Ida said.

Axel waved the paper in front of Karli. "What do you have to say, girlie?"

"You're an idiot. Why don't you use some of that to hire some help and live better?"

He snorted. "I'm happy doing what I do, but maybe I'll buy myself a fancy car and hire a chauffeur."

"I'll drive you," Kurt said.

"So will I," said Sylvie.

Keagan shook his head and turned to Karli. "I'll come tomorrow night to help you with the cupboards if you're still doing them. You're going to have to clean them again since somebody with no brains hung noodles over them."

Ida's eyes narrowed, she opened her lips to bitch Keagan out, but gave him a closer look and decided to keep quiet. Keagan had a certain aura about him that warned people off.

"I've got to finish my route," he said, starting for the door. "See you tomorrow, Karli. Congrats on your money, Axel."

Axel shot back, "At least I don't give mine away like some people do!"

"Yeah, and look what you ended up with." Keagan nodded toward Kurt, Sylvie, and Ida. "Sometimes you get what you pay for."

After Keagan left, Karli grabbed her grocery list and started to leave, too. "I need to stock up." Kurt grimaced and she took pity on him. "I'll buy you some beer."

He stared, surprised. "Why?"

She looked at Sylvie and Ida. "Just because."

On her drive to Art's, she felt happier than she should. And it was for the wrong reasons. She was being petty, but she intended to enjoy it. Let's just see how Ida's chicken and noodles stacked up against smothered pork chops! She bought more groceries than usual, stuff she'd never bothered with before.

When she got home and carried all of the bags into the kitchen, she had to laugh at herself. All this work to prove what? Then she frowned at the stove. Where was Ida's big pot? Every noodle had disappeared, but flour smeared each cupboard door. Had Axel annoyed Ida, and he was being punished? No soup for him either?

When she opened the refrigerator to put away groceries, the pot was on the top shelf. Two empty bowls were rinsed in the sink. Had they already eaten?

Ida came to stare at what Karli had bought. "The old goat wouldn't even taste my food, but he'll be hungry by tomorrow."

It had to half kill Axel not to wolf down chicken and noodles, but he didn't like anyone telling him what he could or couldn't do, and Ida must have pushed it.

Karli shrugged as she started to put things away. "We usually don't eat this early."

"No one's feeding me!" Axel called from the back room.

Karli blinked. "You tried to feed him?"

"He kept dripping broth on his shirt. I tried to spoon soup into his mouth, and he slapped the spoon away."

Yeah, Karli could see that. Axel liked his independence.

The man wasn't done complaining yet. "I'm not eating supper at four either. And I'm not going to bed at nine. What are you making for supper, Karli?"

"Smothered pork chops." And she hoped they'd taste good. She'd never cooked them before.

"Hurry up! I'm starving."

Ida shook her head. "He's not allowed to have any. He'll get hungry eventually and do what I tell him."

"Not gonna happen," Karli said. "While I'm here, he gets a plate of whatever I cook."

Ida's pale eyes grew a shade colder, then she smiled. "But you're only going to be here one more week. Then we'll see how the old goat likes refusing my food." She looked pissed. Axel had won this round, but only because she was here, Karli decided. When she left, heaven help him.

Chapter 34

The next day, when Keagan stopped to deliver their mail, he brought a chocolate sheet cake from Iris Clinger—their local real estate agent. Sylvie let him in the house.

"Where's Karli?" He handed Sylvie the cake.

She nodded toward the kitchen, and he saw Karli balancing on a kitchen chair, scrubbing down the cupboards again. Lord, she had a great ass. He called, "How's it going?"

She turned when she heard his voice. "I'm getting there. They'll be clean by the time you come tonight. Want to stop for supper? I'm making roast chickens, found a recipe where you stuff the cavity with quartered onions and oranges."

He laughed. "Since when did you turn into super cook? You told me you only cooked when the mood struck you."

She raised her eyebrows, surprised. "I guess when I have someone to cook for, it's more fun."

He'd love to eat supper with her, but not enough to brave Axel and his offspring. "Can't tonight," he lied. "I'm meeting Harley at Chase's bar." That much was true, but if Keagan called off to spend time with Karli, his friends would celebrate. They were ready for him to womanize.

Karli nodded. "When do you think you'll get here?"

"About seven? It might take me more than an hour to remove all the cupboard doors. I don't want to run too late."

She gave him a thumbs-up. "I'll be ready."

Hopefully, she'd get on a ladder and he could stare at her ass some more. Better yet . . . He let that thought pass. Maybe sex was like sugar. Experts claimed they were both addictive. When you had them, you wanted more. He gave her a wave. "Have fun!"

She snorted. "Yeah, right. This is the easy part, right?"

Nothing about renovation was easy, but she was learning that. She was a trooper, he had to give her that. She was putting in blood, sweat, and tears fixing a house that wasn't even hers.

He thought about Karli for the rest of his route. Fun. Pretty. And great in the sack. He'd fallen for Cecily because of those three things. Karli was *more* than that, but Cecily hadn't been. He realized that now. Karli had ambition and grit. She was loyal to her family. She cared about people. Cecily never stopped to see her mom and dad. Didn't pitch in to help her brother when he needed it. That should have told Keagan something, but he was too in lust to notice.

He'd delivered the majority of the mail before he reached his last stretch of road. When he got to Libby Jordan's Cape Cod on the edge of town, there was a package to deliver. It was only the second package he'd ever brought to her. The first time, she'd acted so frightened when he knocked on her door, he'd wondered if she thought it was just a scam for him to push his way into her house and have his way with her. Hopefully, this time, he wouldn't scare her so much.

He knocked on the door and it immediately opened, as if she'd been waiting for him. She forced a smile on her lips. Nervous, as always. Her hair, usually pulled back in a tight knot at the back of her neck, fell in rich, brown waves around her shoulders. Usually makeup free, she wore mascara and lip gloss. He'd never realized how pretty she was. He smiled. "Going out? You look nice." Come to think of it, though, he'd never seen her around town unless it was at Art's grocery store.

A blush rose all the way to her hairline. She couldn't make eye contact with him. "Thanks."

He motioned for her to sign for the package. "Looks like you're anxious for this."

She signed and tossed the package on a nearby chair. She didn't even give it a glance. Pushing her glasses higher on her nose, she turned to him, a determined look on her face. "I only ordered it so that I could see you again."

Oh shit. He hadn't seen this coming. She was one of the nice, demure girls he told himself he was interested in. Except he wasn't. He tried to choose his words carefully. He was guessing this was the first time Libby had worked up her courage to flirt—if you could call it that.

He smiled. "If I were on the market, I'd be tempted." Not really, but he wanted to encourage her.

She frowned. "But you broke up with Cecily three years ago."

How to word this to encourage her to try again? With someone else? "Cecily dumped me to run off with another guy. I've licked my wounds a long time, but I finally got brave enough to try again. I don't know if it will work out, but I hope it does."

Her eyes filled with concern. "*She* dumped *you*? That had to be awful. I don't think I could survive it."

"Sure, you can. The pain goes away after a while, and you learn from your mistakes. The trick is to find someone who has something in common with you."

She frowned, confused. "You mean, I should look for another bank teller?"

This was going to be harder than he thought. "No, I'm talking about common interests, how you approach life, what's important to you."

"How do you figure that out?" She reached for a pencil and a notebook. Oh, Lord, was she going to take notes?

He held back a sigh. "You have to put yourself out there and meet some people. It's easier to do it in a group setting if you can. Join something. Go places."

Her expression turned thoughtful. "I've always wanted to take photography classes. I love birding."

"There you go! Sign up for some classes. Join a bird-watching group."

She pursed her lips and squinted up at him. "If I can't make myself do it, could I talk to you once in a while? Would you help me, give me pointers?"

Him? A matchmaker? Advice giver? He'd screwed up pretty well. But Libby was too shy to approach someone else. He nodded. "When you need me, put the red flag up on your mailbox and I'll do my best."

She bit her bottom lip, unsure of herself. "I'll try to meet people, but I get so nervous. Maybe you could write down things for me to say."

"You'll do better if you're just yourself. Don't try to be something you're not. If you need it, I'll talk you through this."

She jerked a quick nod. "You were so nice to me before, I didn't think you'd laugh at me if I tried to flirt with you. Some men will, though."

"You don't need men like that in your life. If they laugh at you, forget them and move on."

She gave a frustrated sigh. "I'll try. I really will. Everyone I work with is married. I want to meet someone."

She was growing desperate, and he felt sorry for her. She'd cave the minute something went wrong, though. She needed a deadline and encouragement or she wouldn't do this. "I'm stopping and knocking on your door two weeks from now for a report."

Her hazel eyes went huge behind her glasses. "Two weeks isn't very long."

"I won't expect you to be engaged or married. I just want to know you've taken some first steps."

She wrung her hands together, then straightened her shoulders. "I'll do it."

He grinned. "Good. I'll see you two weeks from now."

She shut her eyes, took a deep breath, and then nodded again.

"Good luck, Libby." He really did wish her success. Then he turned and went back to his truck. He had to meet Harley at Chase's, then hurry to Karli's house to help with her cupboards.

Libby was a sweet girl, but too timid for him. She needed to find someone as quiet and cerebral as she was. Karli was everything he wanted, but she wasn't going to stick around. He tried to think of all the single women he'd met. Mill Pond wasn't that big, and when he ran through the list, he didn't find anyone who tugged at him like Karli did. He was going to have to expand his search. There were plenty of small towns close by. Maybe Karli's double was hidden in one of them.

He hurried home, changed into old jeans, and rushed to meet Harley. As always, Chase's was doing a booming business. Harley had saved him a seat at the bar, and Keagan slipped onto the stool.

Harley turned to study him. "You look serious."

Keagan told him about Libby. "She's a really nice person, but she's so quiet, men won't notice her. I hope someone takes the time to talk to her and *see* her."

Harley shook his head. "Can't think of a good match for her around here. But then, I can't think of anyone like Karli around here either." He gave Keagan a meaningful stare.

"Neither can I, but I'm not following her to Indy and then to wherever her next job takes her and the one after that. I like roots." It hurt to think about her leaving, though. He'd have to give himself a set time to get over it and move on. He wasn't going to lose three years again, moping.

Harley sighed and clinked his bottle of beer against Keagan's. "It sucks, man."

"Tell me about it."

When Chase came to take their order, Keagan decided to break tradition and ordered a pork tenderloin deluxe instead of his usual burger. Chase raised his eyebrows. "Somebody's feeling a little frisky tonight."

Harley laughed. "He's going to help Karli with her cupboards when he leaves here."

"No wonder he's a happy man." Chase grinned. "Be back in a minute with your food."

Harley and Keagan concentrated on their meals when Chase returned, only talking now and then. "Where's Kathy tonight?" Keagan asked. "How did you end up on your own?"

"She has to take classes once a year to keep up with new accounting laws. She drove to Bloomington for a four-day course."

"I'm glad mailmen don't have to stay current." Keagan drained his beer and reached for his wallet. "Is she staying on campus?"

Harley nodded and dug for his money, too. "She got a good rate on a room at the student union building. An old friend of hers is taking the course, too, so they're staying together."

"A female friend?"

Harley gave him a look. "Yeah. What are you trying to do—worry me?"

"It's not safe to take a wife as pretty as yours for granted."

"Thanks, pal, I'll keep that in mind, but that's one of the perks of marriage, isn't it? A sense of trust?"

Keagan wouldn't know. He'd never felt secure with Cecily.

They paid their bills, then walked to their vehicles together. Harley called, "Try to get some work done tonight and not stare at Karli the whole time."

"Will do." Harley knew him too well. Keagan gave a wave and headed to Axel's farm.

Karli welcomed him and led him to the kitchen. She waved a hand with pride. "Sparkling," she said.

Dusty came to weave between his feet, and Keagan bent to pet him. "Your cat has the softest fur I've ever felt."

"I'm keeping him." Karli rubbed his chin. "He's special. I can't leave him behind."

Keagan felt a quick stab of jealousy. She'd leave him. "If I let you pet me, will you stay because I'm special?"

She blinked. "I've already signed a contract, but I'd take you with me."

Keagan reached for his cordless screwdriver. "I like my job here, and I'll have early retirement. But it was worth a shot." He hadn't meant to bug her about leaving. The words had just popped out. He looked at her clean cupboards and smiled. "These are ready to go." He didn't want to talk about when she left anymore, so started taking down doors.

He removed them and she carried them to the barn. Working together, they moved them all in an hour and a half.

"I can come back tomorrow night to help you sand them," Keagan said. "They're in good shape. They'll go pretty fast."

"Come for supper, then we'll get an earlier start."

He gave a lopsided grin. Free food was a great incentive. "What are you making?"

"It's Friday. Fried catfish."

Keagan wrinkled his nose. "Sorry, not my thing."

"Do you like any fish?"

"Tilapia, cod—any fish that doesn't taste too fishy."

"I'd change my menu, but I already bought everything to cook."

"No biggie, I'll live. I still have some leftovers Mom sent home with me."

"Would you rather wait till Saturday to sand the cupboards?"

"I thought we could paint on Saturday. We can work all day if we have to. Want me to bring donuts when I come Saturday morning?"

"Just your long, lean, wonderful bod." She licked her lips.

Lord, he hoped Axel wasn't listening. And he wished the inside of the barn was more than a dirt floor. There was not only no hay to roll in, there was nothing comfortable in sight. "You're a tease. All you want is a pretty kitchen."

She laughed. "Once this kitchen is done, I'd be happy if you'd show me the sights again, maybe take me to the national forest. I figure I won't be here that much longer."

"Are you leaving right after Thanksgiving?"

"Probably."

He'd better enjoy her while he could. The national forest. He'd thought about their time there every hour or two, probably more. "I think I can work you into my schedule. We didn't make it to the lodge. It's worth seeing."

She raised her eyebrows. "I want to see it all. I don't want to miss anything."

He didn't think she was just talking about the scenery. "On Sunday? We could pack a picnic. I'm not eating at my parents' house. Mom's already hyping up for Thanksgiving."

"Thanksgiving! I can't believe I've been here this long."

It had gone too fast for him. He could hardly wait for Sunday. He'd pack a picnic, and they could eat in his SUV. And then . . . he'd show her new things. They'd make it special, because she'd be gone soon after that.

He was playing with ideas of what to pack when he passed the Yeagers' place with the SOLD sign in the front yard. He pulled to the side of the road to stare at it. He shouldn't have. He should have just kept going, but it hurt more knowing the house was off the market than he'd expected. An ache settled in his stomach. The perfect property for his studio. Gone.

It was his own fault. No one would have blamed him if he'd used his money for a down payment on it. But he'd feel guilty every time he threw clay on his pottery wheel and knew his parents were in trouble and he didn't help them. He sighed. He wouldn't drive this way again for a while. He'd take a longer route to avoid it.

As he pulled away, he couldn't get his good mood back. He'd lost his house and property, and soon, he'd lose Karli, too. When she left town, he'd have to get busy and come up with some new designs for his dinnerware. He was going to have work long hours to get through this.

Chapter 35

On Friday, Karli carried the slow cooker into the dining room again. She stretched plastic over each door-less cupboard and taped it in place.

Ida raised an eyebrow. "What now? Can't you ever leave things alone?"

"I want to finish the kitchen before I leave here. I want to sand all the frames and paint them before we refinish and install the doors."

Ida glanced at the slow cooker on the dining room table. "What are you making for lunch?"

"I'm melting canned chili and a block of cheese together for a dip. I bought chips."

"I can do that for you. Dad can't fuss about me messing that up."

Karli stared at her, surprised. "Thanks for the help. I appreciate it."

"Idle hands are the devil's plaything. Besides, if it gets you out of here faster, I'm a volunteer."

Karli rolled her eyes. She should have known. While Ida fiddled with lunch, Karli got her wood block, wrapped in rough sandpaper, and got busy. By noon, she'd made a lot of headway.

When they carried Axel's lunch to him, he eyed it warily. "What the hell is it?"

"A Mexican dip and chips," Karli told him. "We have celery and carrot sticks, too."

He grunted, but managed to eat everything on his tray. "Are you making real food for supper, or will we get party food for that, too?"

"Don't push it, old man. I already told you we were having catfish."

His face brightened. "My mom always fixed grits with fish."

"Grits?" He was out of luck. "I've never made those."

Ida let out a long-suffering sigh and came to stand in the doorway. "I can make them if you'd eat them, Dad."

Axel struggled for a minute, then nodded. He must really love grits. "Enough for everybody?"

Ida shook her head in disgust, but didn't argue with him.

By suppertime, Karli had finished sanding the cupboards and cleaning the kitchen. Then she cooked the fish while Ida stirred the grits. Axel was excited enough, she even wheeled him to the dining room for supper. When the five of them finished eating, he leaned back in his chair and grinned. "Just as good as my mom's. This was a meal to remember."

Sylvie raised a warning eyebrow to her sister. "I'll cook for Dad tomorrow night." She glanced across the table at him. "What do you wanna eat on Saturday, old man?"

"Why? Are you ready to kill me off?"

Axel was back to normal form. Karli wasn't completely comfortable with the happy man who lavished them with compliments. She looked at him. "What are some of your favorite meals?" She'd have never thought of grits. She wondered what his mom had cooked for him.

"Sausages, potatoes, and green beans in a pot. Ham. Tuna casserole. Vegetable soup, fried chicken, and chicken à la king."

"I can make tuna casserole," Sylvie said. "I'll do that."

"Can you add grease to it somehow?"

She scowled. "No, so you might survive."

He rubbed his forehead, and Karli realized he must be getting tired. "I'll get you back to your bed, then you can relax."

Kurt stood. "That was a great meal. I can take him back and get him settled."

Karli stared. Had a fairy sprinkled Axel's kids with *nice* dust tonight? "Thanks."

While Kurt wheeled Axel to the back room, Karli got busy with clean up. Ida stayed to pitch in, but Sylvie disappeared upstairs to her room and TV, as usual.

"Did you bring a TV here, too?" Karli asked Ida as she washed the dishes and passed them to Ida to rinse and dry.

Ida nodded. "You weren't here when I carried everything in, but I brought lots of books, too. I don't believe either my sister or Kurt read. I'd be lost without my daily devotionals." She arched an eyebrow at Karli. "You read, but it's all drivel."

"I read to relax and unwind." Karli handed Ida the last plate.

"Our minds need to be constantly challenged and improved upon. That doesn't happen with mysteries and romances." Ida quickly washed her hands and dried them, then gave the kitchen one more critical scan. "We're finished. I'm going upstairs. I don't like seeing your friend Keagan. He coddles Dad too much."

"Keagan's the person who called to tell us that Axel needed help, that he couldn't take care of himself anymore."

"He's a mailman. That's what they do." Ida straightened the towel before she left the kitchen. Karli stared after her. Sometimes it felt as if there was a nice person buried in her somewhere, but Karli couldn't be sure.

Keagan knocked on the door a half hour later, and Karli pulled on her heavy jacket. They walked to the barn together, and Keagan showed her how to work the sander. He'd brought his dad's with him, so they could both work at the same time.

They made small talk between working on the doors. She asked, "How's your family? Did they get the fields plowed they wanted to?"

He nodded. "Marcia's twins got sick, and then Stuart caught it, so Dad had to do most of the work, but they finished them."

"The flu?" At the hospital, the patients usually swarmed in later than this—usually in late January and February. She'd worked with sick patients a long time, but if it was a new strain of flu, she still caught the damn stuff, and it made its way through the floor until most nurses had suffered through it.

He nodded. "Mom always says kids are little germ breeders. When they get sick, their loved ones catch it. I've been staying away. I love them, but not enough to risk losing vacation days."

She laughed. There was a lot of truth to that. "How's Brad?"

Keagan grinned. "He went to Chase's bar tonight to meet Kendall. We should double with them sometime. Kendall's a nurse, too, in Bloomington. Works ER. She grew up in Mill Pond, but she was younger than us. Her parents live here."

Karli stopped sanding to glance up at him. He was studying her. "There's a hospital in Bloomington?"

"A small one, not as exciting as the patients you see in Indy."

He was throwing this out to gauge her reaction, but she didn't know how she felt about it. She loved the rush of big hospitals. Would she be bored if she only had three patients with mundane health problems? She bit her bottom lip. "I don't know if I'd like working in a Band-Aid hospital."

"Band-Aid?"

"You know, common ailments and health issues. On my floor, if a patient doesn't have at least three tubes, he's moved out."

Keagan nodded. "I get it. You like the adrenaline. I wondered about that." He turned his attention back to sanding.

She had the definite feeling he'd thrown her some bait, and he didn't think she'd taken it. She hadn't. She didn't want to face this yet, didn't know what she'd do when she had to make a decision.

Chapter 36

Keagan came early on Saturday morning, and as promised, he brought donuts—enough for everybody. Kurt grabbed three out of the box before anyone else even had a chance to pick one. Karli carried the box back to Axel, and he took a bear claw, looking happy with himself. She gave him a small carton of cottage cheese, too, in case the donut didn't satisfy him very long.

She and Keagan each drank a cup of coffee while they ate theirs, then they bundled up and headed to the barn. Karli had never used a spray gun before, and it took her a while to feel comfortable with it. Too much spray, and the paint ran. Too little, and the coverage was spotty. But once she got the hang of it, she was happy with the results. The doors were a gleaming white. Once they dried, she'd bought new hardware for them. Keagan volunteered to put them on later.

"We can paint the cupboards indoors while these dry," he told her.

"Inside and out?"

"It looks better if the interior and exterior match, but I vote we wait on that. It's a serious undertaking."

They decided to stop for lunch. Karli gave Kurt the keys to her Dodge and enough money to buy pizza. Once again, they collected around the dining room table. Keagan got Axel into his wheelchair and brought him to join everyone else while Karli put out paper plates and napkins. Ida and Sylvie helped with drinks. When Kurt walked in the house, carrying four stacked boxes, he looked happier than usual.

"You even ordered bread sticks. Three large pizzas *and* bread sticks."

It didn't take much to make Kurt happy.

"I haven't been out of this place since my car died. It felt good to go to town."

Karli stared at him. "Your car died? Like in dead?"

He nodded. "I haven't had the money to keep it up. It wasn't great when I bought it, but it got me here."

Ida stared at him. "How are you going to get home?"

"I'm not leaving till Dad dies. I'll have money then."

Karli glanced at Axel, wondering how he'd take that, but he seemed fine.

Keagan took a seat and sighed. He tossed a telling glance at Karli.

Ida caught the look and her lip curled. "Don't be so full of yourself. If you could collect on your parents' cash, wouldn't you?"

Axel reached for a slice of pepperoni pizza and grimaced. "He just gave his parents all his savings. You're preaching to the wrong person."

"How much?" Ida asked.

"Fifty thousand." Axel waited for her reaction.

Her eyes went wide. She looked at Keagan as if he were an alien life-form. "You gave your parents *your* money?"

"They'll pay me back." He chose a slice of chicken club.

She shook her head.

Axel tried to look innocent, but failed, when he asked her, "You spend a lot of time with the scriptures. Isn't it better to give than to receive?"

Her eyes narrowed. "Didn't know you'd ever cracked open a Bible."

"There's lots that you don't know, and let's keep it that way."

Her glare turned frosty, but Sylvie shook her head, bored by the whole conversation. "Quit with the drama already. I got my tuna casserole done this morning like you asked me to, so you can have the kitchen now."

Karli jumped on that, anxious to move to a new topic. "No one will want to be in there while we paint. I'll crack a window so the smell isn't so bad. We'll wait till you put the casserole in the oven to put the doors back up."

Ida snorted. "Why not wait till Sunday?"

"Keagan's going to take me out tomorrow, show me more of Mill Pond."

"Lucky you. It's one boring, little town." Ida's tone was flat, unimpressed. "Do we have plans for Thanksgiving? Are you cooking it all?"

"Keagan's family invited me to their place. I was going to make a small turkey and buy a box of Stove Top stuffing mix for you guys. Nothing fancy."

"How thoughtful." Ida looked at her dad. "Sylvie and I are here. Want a traditional meal?"

"Are you paying?"

Ida shrugged. "If Karli's buying a turkey, she won't mind tossing in a few more things."

"This was your idea. You can fork out money for the extras." What was it with this family? No one wanted to spend a penny on the person sitting next to him.

Axel surprised her by saying, "I'll pay if you cook."

Karli stared. "Should I faint now or later?"

Axel laughed. "I have a little money tucked away. Tell me how much you need, and I'll get it to you."

Ida and Sylvie tossed ideas around until Kurt said, "We have to have pumpkin pie. Mom always made that."

Axel looked at him. "You remember that?"

Kurt nodded. "Mom was no great cook, but she always went all out for the holidays."

Ida gave a derisive sniff. "I wouldn't call it *all out*, but she at least made a real meal."

They made a menu while they talked.

By the time Keagan got Axel back to his bed, the three siblings were writing out a grocery list. Karli left them to it and went to the kitchen to start painting. She and Keagan worked on the upper cupboards together, then he left to put the hardware on the doors while she finished painting the base units.

Sylvie stepped into the kitchen at five. "It's my turn. I need to cook."

"Be careful. The paint's still wet."

Keagan helped her grab their gear and carted it to the barn to clean. Karli shot Keagan an enticing smile. "Sylvie's making tuna casserole for supper. Want to stay?"

He blanched. "That's the one thing my mom makes that I avoid. It got too late to hang the doors tonight, so I think I'll go home for a shower and change. How about you? Do want to stay for the casserole, or would you like to eat with me?"

More time with Keagan? "Where are you taking me?"

He caught her gaze and held it. "Name it, and we'll go, but Brad's meeting Kendall again tonight. I thought maybe I'd cook for you and we could stay in."

They'd have some alone time? Close to a bed? "When do you want me? Give me your address and I'll be there."

"Brad leaves the house at seven. Does that work? I'm great at steaks."

"Steaks?" came a voice from the back room. Did Axel listen to *everything* they said? The old man sure hadn't lost his hearing, even with a TV blaring in front of him.

Keagan chuckled and called, "Can you even chew steaks?"

"I'd gum them to death if I had to."

Karli shook her head. "Maybe I'll make those the last night I'm here—a going away present."

"I'm an old man," he told her. "Who knows how much longer I'll be here?"

"Good try." But she'd already decided to buy the old fart some rib eyes, and he knew it.

Keagan left, and while the others ate Sylvie's casserole, Karli took a shower and dressed in clean jeans and a low-cut top. She took special care to wear a matching bra and panties, then applied makeup, but subtly.

When she went to say her goodbyes, Ida was upstairs reading her devotionals and Sylvie was watching TV with Axel.

"Where's Kurt?" Had he decided to take a shower, too? Miracles did happen.

Sylvie nodded toward the barn. Its double doors stood open. "He took Dad's pickup to drive to town for beer. He's getting me some, too."

Karli turned to Axel. "When did you stop driving?"

"When they took away my damn license. That truck was six years old when I bought it, hardly any miles on it. Had a stroke five months after I got it."

A stroke. New information. "Have you had any more strokes?"

"A few small ones, but I take my meds. Get poked for lab draws when the guy shows up. I'm doing better, but I have a bad ticker. The doc still won't let me drive."

"Then it's probably good somebody's using the truck. It's not good for a car to sit too long." She frowned. "I'm surprised Keagan didn't tell me you'd had strokes."

"Boy doesn't know. Never told him. He'd have fussed at me more. Don't need that."

"Everyone knows everything in Mill Pond."

He grinned. "I told him the doc wanted to check me out because I was losing weight and couldn't keep food down. I was doing okay back then. That satisfied him."

Karli frowned. "I called your doctor and asked about your meds and health, and he didn't say anything."

"Can't. Health records are private, and I signed that I wanted complete privacy."

He would. Could there be a worse patient than Axel? Karli sighed. "Well, I'm glad Kurt's driving your truck for now. It'll be good for both of them."

Axel snorted. "Like he cares about that."

Okay, he had her there. She'd guess Kurt was just overjoyed to find a vehicle he could use. She frowned. The last she'd known he was broke. He must have scraped up enough money for beer, or maybe Sylvie had pitched in.

"You'd better get movin' if you're goin' to have a hot steak," Sylvie said. "But I make a mean tuna casserole. You'd have liked it."

Maybe. Karli reached for her jacket and started to the door. "I'll be home at a decent time."

On the drive to Keagan's, she replayed their conversation. Sylvie had been anxious to get rid of her. Was she missing something? Was something going on Sylvie didn't want her to know about? She shrugged. She wasn't a caregiver for any of them. Not even Axel, really. He wouldn't listen to her.

It was ten after seven when she knocked on Keagan's door. He lived in a nondescript, tall, narrow two-story. When he called for her to come in, she opened the door and followed his voice to the kitchen. Finally. Some time alone with him. Her stomach fluttered.

A round, wooden table was set with dishes from his winter collection. A tossed salad sat in the center of the table in a beautiful bowl embossed with snowmen. She looked around, frowning. Where was Keagan?

Her body quivered in anticipation.

And then he stepped out of the pantry, wearing nothing but a long chef's apron. His gorgeous, tight ass came in full view when he turned to open a can of black olives.

She whooped out a laugh. "Aren't you chilly?"

"Thoughts of you kept me warm." Thoughts of him sent heat through her veins. He put the olives on the table and stepped toward her. "Which do you want first? Steak or me?"

She snorted. "Hard choice. You." The way his apron was poking out in a certain spot made it easy to decide.

His crooked smile made her heart lurch. Taking her hand, he led her upstairs and turned into the bedroom on the left. It was tidy. Period. She'd expected pictures on the wall, artistic touches. Nothing.

He went to pull the blinds, and she stared at his perfect fanny. The man's body was a thing of beauty. He came to her and pulled her close. He bent his head and his lips brushed hers. "You're overdressed. Here. Let me help you out of those."

His fingers gripped the bottom of her knit top and lifted it over her head. His lips skimmed her neck, the hollow at the base of her throat, and lowered to sprinkle kisses above her bra. Pricks of pleasure burst through her, and he pushed her against the wall. He reached to unhook her bra and drop it to the floor, then his mouth took her breast so his tongue could play with her nipple. She couldn't breathe.

His hand slid under the waistline of her jeans. He unzipped them and lowered them to her ankles. His fingers trailed from her breasts to between her thighs. Her body tensed, and . . . her cellphone came to life.

Ignore it! Ignore it! Keagan raised an eyebrow in question and she shook her head *no*. He returned to playing with her nipple. A gentle nip made her insides quiver. The cell rang again. He looked up, and she threw her arms around his neck, raised her face so she could taste his lips. Their kiss lengthened. Heat built. And the cell rang again. This time, Keagan pushed away from her, took it out of her jeans pocket, and handed it to her. She frowned at the I.D. *Caller unknown.* But he was waiting, watching, so she punched the button. Sylvie rushed into speech.

"Dad's sick. He doesn't look good. You're a nurse. What should we do?"

"How sick?"

"He's gripping his left arm. He's in pain. His face looks pretty white."

Oh, damn. His heart. "I'm on my way. Call 911."

"Hurry!" Sylvie hung up.

Keagan stepped back, looking worried.

Karli tugged up her pants, yanked on her shirt. "Axel's sick, maybe a heart attack."

"I'll follow you there." Keagan went to his closet, started pulling on clothes. While Karli raced to her car, he ran to the kitchen to turn everything off.

As she sped to Axel's farm, Keagan followed close behind her.

Please, let him make it, Karli repeated over and over in her mind. The man was a pain in the ass, but she wasn't ready to lose him yet.

Chapter 37

The EMS was at the door when she arrived, two men carrying Axel to it on a stretcher. She ran to see him. When she stood close enough, he winked at her. He looked weak and tired, but he still had plenty of vinegar.

"What's his blood pressure and pain level?" she asked one of the medics.

"He's more stable. We gave him nitroglycerin. The doctors will decide from there."

She nodded. She should have known the medics were only allowed to tell her limited information. When Keagan came to stand beside her, Axel winced. "I ruined your night."

"No problem." Keagan smiled. "We'll see you soon."

Sylvie started to climb in the ambulance with him, and Axel shook his head. The medic shrugged. "Sorry. We don't want him upset."

Everyone climbed in cars to follow Axel to the hospital.

"Why don't you ride with me?" Keagan asked Karli. "It takes a while to reach Bloomington."

She settled onto the passenger seat next to him, and Axel's kids climbed in Axel's pickup with Kurt behind the wheel. Keagan's lips pressed into a tight line, but he didn't comment.

They didn't talk on the drive, going as fast as possible to trail the ambulance while still driving safely, Kurt not far behind them. The ambulance pulled ahead, its lights flashing, and it was sitting at the emergency room doors when they reached the hospital. They parked next to each other in the lot and walked in together.

There was no one behind the desk, but when a nurse hurried into the room and saw Keagan, she came to talk to him. "He's already been taken to the cardiac doctor, floor three. You can wait for news in its waiting room."

The girl had shoulder-length, shiny brown hair, intelligent hazel eyes, and cupid-bow lips. Her creamy complexion glowed. She looked thin, but Karli would bet she was strong enough to hoist bodies in and out of beds.

"Thanks." He turned to Karli. "This is Kendall, Brad's friend, and Kendall, this is Karli, my friend."

She smiled. "Nice to meet you."

A family came in and half-carried a teenager to the desk. He couldn't put any weight on his leg. Kendall turned. "Have to go." She hurried to take their information.

Karli admired how cool and efficient she was while still making the family feel well cared for. "If Brad lets her slip away, he's going to kick himself later."

Keagan started down the hallway, motioning for them to follow. "The elevator's this way." Karli studied the hospital as they passed through it. It was bigger than she'd thought, and it was busy. Could she be happy working here?

He led them to the third floor waiting room. Sylvie reached for her pack of cigarettes, frowned, and plopped onto a chair, crossing her arms over her chest. Ida took a daily devotional out of her coat pocket, and Kurt stretched his legs in front of him and turned his attention to the TV in the corner. Keagan reached for Karli's hand and gave it a squeeze.

His touch grounded her. Her mind had been filled with scattered thoughts and worries, but he looked so calm, so able to deal with anything, she felt her emotions settle, too. She glanced sideways at him, and he gave her an encouraging smile. What would it be like to wake to a man like Keagan every morning? To go to bed with him every night?

They settled in for the long wait. Hours later, the doctor swung into the room and asked, "The Crupe family?" When they nodded, he looked at his notes. "Axel's not in good shape. We're going to keep him here until he's a little stronger, but then he wants to go home." He smiled. "He has strong opinions, doesn't he?"

They nodded in unison.

The doctor took a deep breath. "Look, I gave him the okay to go home when he leaves here. He might as well. In my opinion, he doesn't have a lot more time. He said he wants to die at home."

Die? At home? Karli gripped Keagan's hand tighter. She'd been trying to decide between in-home care and a nursing home. She hadn't thought about death.

The doctor studied her. He must have seen her surprise. He started to say something else, but Kurt interrupted him.

"I get his truck. It's mine."

The doctor stared.

"That's all you get," Sylvie said. "The rest, we split between the three of us."

"Why should he get the truck?" Ida argued. "My car's in bad shape, too."

The doctor talked over their bickering. "We've moved him to a private room. You can see him for a few minutes, but don't upset him. Then you have to leave. He needs to rest."

Sylvie, Ida, and Kurt rushed out of the room. Keagan pulled Karli close and hugged her to him. "Are you okay?"

She nodded. "I didn't realize how bad he was. He was taking heart meds, but I didn't think he'd have heart failure. I thought I was just finding him better health care for his final years."

The doctor looked sympathetic. "He's a stubborn, old man. He might last longer than we think, but his heart's in bad shape. I'd make sure everything's in order, in case."

She nodded, and he left. Keagan asked again, "Are you okay?"

"My mom needs to know. I'll call her when I get home."

Keagan shifted so that his arm spanned her back. "Come on. Let's go see him before he's worn out by the others."

He was right about that. When they got to Axel's room, the nurse on duty looked like she'd like to throttle Kurt, Ida, and Sylvie.

"No one else came," Sylvie was saying. "We're the ones who deserve your inheritance. You should put that in writing."

Karli blocked them out. She went to the bed and took Axel's hand. "How you doing, old coot?"

He smiled, but he looked wiped-out; spent.

"Are you in pain? Uncomfortable? The nurse is here. She can help you."

He turned his head, upset, until he saw Keagan. Then he relaxed. "Karli promised me a rib eye. You should come when she cooks it for me."

Keagan grinned. "You don't have to ask me twice. I'll be there. You look a little worn-out."

Axel raised an eyebrow. "I can still give you a run for your money."

"Nope, you're all spit and vinegar. If you plan to pester me, you'd better get some rest. I've got the advantage right now."

Axel chuckled, but his eyes drooped. "Take Donna's vixen home and keep an eye on things for me. I'll be back soon."

"Got you." Keagan looked at the nurse.

She raised her arms and said, "Everyone out. You need your rest, and so does Axel."

On the drive home, both Karli and Keagan were rattled. They held hands until they reached Axel's farmhouse. It was nearly midnight. Before Karli stepped out of the SUV, she leaned forward and kissed Keagan's cheek. "Thank you for being there. I needed it."

"Mutual," he said. "If you need anything or his condition changes, call."

Lord, she loved this man. Yes, loved him, she thought as she walked into the house. Thankfully, the others weren't back yet. She walked into her room and closed the door. Dusty scratched at it, and she realized she hadn't fed him. She hurried through her evening chores, then rushed to her room when she heard Kurt pull into the driveway. She left the door cracked for the cat, but she didn't want to see them. Right at the moment, she'd like to hurt all of them. She turned off the light. Moonbeams spilled through the long, narrow windows, and she went to sink onto her air mattress.

She listened to the others spill into the house. They went to the kitchen and then sat around the worktable, arguing back and forth. Who should get this? Who should get that? She could spit on them all. Axel could be dying, and they were dividing up the loot. They disgusted her.

Dusty jumped up to cuddle next to her. He'd disappeared during all the commotion, probably hiding out in the basement, but he'd returned. She stroked his smooth fur and called her mom.

"Karli? Are you all right? It's late."

"We had to call the EMS for Axel," she said. "Your dad's heart problems have gotten a lot worse."

After a brief hesitation, Mom said, "I'm coming there. I'll take off work. I didn't realize Dad was so bad."

"Neither did I. How's your project at work?"

"We're through the hard stuff. Other people can handle the rest. Your dad will take care of the house and everything else. He can go to Milwaukee without me."

"You're sure? Axel won't be nice to you if you come."

Her mom gave a sharp laugh. "What's new? He was never nice to us. But if he dies before I get there, I'll always be mad at myself."

That's what Karli suspected. That's why she'd called. "The fab three will take care of him until he croaks." Her voice sounded bitter. She hadn't meant for it to.

Her mom laughed. "The fab three—I like that! They can do what they will, but I want to say goodbye to Dad. I need closure."

"Okay, then. I'll see you soon." Karli reached to pet Dusty. She felt better. Keagan would be there for her, she knew. And Mom was coming. She'd clean a room for her upstairs.

"Thanks for doing this, Karli," her mom said.

"Anything for you, Mom." And when she hung up, Karli knew that if her parents needed her life savings, she'd give it to them. She loved Keagan all the more for doing that.

Chapter 38

Without Axel to cook for, Karli made herself a peanut butter sandwich before driving to Bloomington to check on him. Kurt, Ida, and Sylvie could fend for themselves.

"Are you going to the hospital to visit your dad today?" she asked them. They were rummaging through the refrigerator and didn't look happy. None of the leftovers must have pleased them.

Sylvie shrugged. "Seein' us isn't goin' to make his day. We thought we'd stay here and wait for him."

Why didn't that surprise her? If there wasn't some incentive, they didn't put themselves out.

"Are you goin'?" Sylvie waited for her answer.

"I'm getting ready now." Something was up, but Karli couldn't put her finger on it. She studied the three of them, but they all did their best to look innocent. Finally, she shook her head and went to get her coat. "My mom will be here later tonight. I told her about Axel."

Ida grimaced. "You mostly leave us alone. I don't suppose your mom will."

"She'll probably be excited to see you."

Sylvie snorted. "Yeah, right."

Her mom was probably dreading it, but she wasn't about to say that. "Axel gave me the money to get what you need for Thanksgiving." He'd given her more than she'd probably need. "Mom will be here, too. If I buy now, you can make things ahead. Need anything else?"

"We're fine." Ida looked hopeful. "You're going to be gone a while, aren't you?"

Karli stared at her. Did she bother them that much? "Is there something you need right now?"

"No!" Sylvie glanced at her sister, then forced a smile. "Tell Dad we love him."

That couldn't sound more fake. Karli glanced at each of them again, but gave up. She was wasting time. "Well, see you later."

She could almost hear their sigh of relief when she left the house. What was their game? Were they going to go through the house and put their names on each thing they wanted? Start carrying things to their cars? It wouldn't surprise her. Which one of them would want the fine china and silverware in the built-in dining room cupboards? They'd been covered in dust. She didn't think anyone had touched them since Axel's mom died.

With a sigh, she pushed the fab three out of her mind and concentrated on the drive to Bloomington. She turned on the radio and let music distract her. By the time she reached the hospital, she'd mentally ticked off everything she wanted to get done for the day.

As she exited the elevator on Axel's floor, she saw a man leaving his room, a man she'd never seen before. He looked serious. A doctor maybe? No, he wasn't dressed like a doctor. A minister? Would Axel want to make amends before his last breath? If he did, he wouldn't want her poking into his business, so she decided to keep quiet.

She knocked before entering his room. When he looked up and saw her, he grinned.

"Coming to see if I'm still alive?" He pointed to the hospital menu. "Guess what? They're bringing me a steak for supper."

She shook her head. "That's great for cholesterol." But why not? He might as well enjoy whatever he wanted. If he became a vegan now, it wouldn't make much difference.

Axel scowled at her. "You're not going to leave now that you think I won't be around much longer, will you?"

His question startled her. She could tell by his tone he wanted her to stick around. "I have a job starting the second week of December, have to start work then. I signed a contract."

"But you'll stay until then?"

She frowned. Where was the man who grumped at her day in and day out? "You're not thinking of kicking off that soon, are you?"

"You'll stay?" he repeated.

She nodded. "I'll stay until I have to start work."

His shoulders relaxed.

She wanted to make him feel better. "My mom's coming to visit you. She'll get here tonight."

He rolled his eyes toward the ceiling. "If she has to."

And there was the true Axel—a pain in the ass. "I thought you'd like that, that you wanted your kids to bicker over you."

"I guess." He gave her a shrewd look. "You kind of like my mailman, don't you? Why haven't you made a move on him?"

"Like it's any of your business."

"Do you have a guy on the stringer at home?"

Where was he going with this? "Do you have a point, or are you just pushing buttons, as usual?"

Axel grinned. "Keagan's quiet but stubborn. Once he makes up his mind, a mule would have to kick him in the head to knock some sense into him. You'd be good for him."

"Now I'm a mule handler?" she asked.

"That boy's a keeper."

She shook her head, ready to argue, when a nurse poked her head into the room. "Sorry. I need to take Axel down for some tests."

Axel let out a loud breath. "More poking and prodding."

Karli slanted him a look. "Isn't that what you were just doing?"

"Why don't you give him a shot?"

She put her hands on her hips. He wasn't going to let it go. "Who says I haven't?"

His whole face burst into a smile. "That's my girl!"

The nurse started fussing with tubes, and Karli started to the door. "Do you need anything?"

"I wouldn't mind coming home to a pot of your white bean chili and a fancy chocolate cake."

"Homemade or bought?"

"How good are you at cakes?"

She flicked her middle finger at him. "It's a good thing you're an invalid. I'll look for some recipes."

He laughed. "Tell Keagan *hi* for me."

She bit her bottom lip, so she couldn't say the words ready to spill out. The nurse watched her, her eyes twinkling.

On the drive back to Mill Pond, she was convinced the old coot was so mean, he'd live forever. When had he decided he was Mr. Matchmaker? As she walked through the aisles of Art's grocery, though, she piled the cart high with anything she thought he might like, including rib eyes. The old fool hadn't taken care of himself. No wonder he was in such bad shape. She'd only be around him for a couple more weeks. Then what? She might as well make those weeks special.

When she got home, she stared at the fresh tire tracks that led to the barn. Kurt had taken the pickup somewhere. She went to the front door and called, "I could use some help! I've brought groceries!"

She heard people scrambling while bottles clunked and papers crumpled. She headed into the kitchen, and her jaw dropped in surprise. "What the hell?"

Kurt couldn't meet her gaze. Ida glared, and Sylvie crossed her arms over her chest. A half bottle of Johnnie Walker Gold sat on the table and discarded, eaten lobster tails filled the waste basket.

Karli's fingers curled into fists. "Which one of you won the lottery and didn't tell me?"

No one said a thing.

"All right, I'm calling Axel to try to figure out what's going on."

Kurt blurted, "When he gave you grocery money, I knew he had cash stashed somewhere. I found it in his sock drawer in the bathroom."

How original. She thought Axel was smarter than that. "So you decided to have a party on your dad?"

"It's not like he's volunteered to buy us anything!" Ida snapped. "If you didn't pay for groceries, we'd go hungry."

Okay, she had a point. "How much?" Karli asked.

"A thousand dollars," Kurt said.

Karli shrugged. "Have fun. I need help with groceries, though, and since I paid for them, and you didn't contribute anything, you can put them away."

Sylvie opened her mouth to argue, but Kurt gave her a sharp shove. "Just shut up for once."

While they carried everything into the house and put it away, Karli went upstairs and cleaned a bedroom for her mom. When she was finished, it was dust free and the bed had fresh sheets and a clean blanket. Then she went downstairs to start a chicken-rice casserole for supper, one of Mom's favorites. She was starting work on a tossed salad when she glanced out the kitchen window and looked across the fields to the white house in the distance.

Tomorrow was Sunday, and Keagan wouldn't be going to his parents' house. They'd planned on having a picnic and hopefully make love, but everything had changed. She reached for her phone and texted him. *My mom's coming tonight. Can't leave the house tomorrow. Want to come here to eat?*

He returned a message almost immediately. *No worries. Enjoy your mom. Can you still make Thanksgiving?*

Lord, I hope so. She'd written the text and sent it before she stopped to think about it. It surprised her. Would she really leave her mom with the fab three and take off to see Keagan? *Hell, yes.*

Her phone beeped. She read, *I hope so, too. Love you. K*

Love you? Her heart sped up. He loved her! Without thinking, she texted back, *Love you, too. Thanks for everything.* She did love him. But as she told her friend, who had a knack for always picking the wrong man, love wasn't always enough. She and Keagan were going in different directions. It sucked.

Chapter 39

Her mom pulled in the driveway early in the afternoon. Karli ran out to the front porch to meet her. Mom got out of the car, looked at the house, stopped and stared, and then burst out crying.

"Mom?" Karli ran to her. "Are you okay?"

Wiping her eyes, her mom took a deep breath. "It's just so beautiful. I always knew it could be."

Karli had thought fixing the house would make her mom happy, but she'd never expected this much emotion. "I painted inside, too."

More tears fell.

Karli wrapped her arms around her mom's shoulders and gave them a squeeze. "Come on. I'll help you carry in your stuff."

"I didn't bring much." Her mom pulled a suitcase from the back seat.

Karli took it and motioned her into the house. When Mom stepped inside, she gasped and then bit her bottom lip.

"It's so pretty." Her gaze went to the archway and the kitchen with its white cupboards and oak floor. "Oh my!"

Dusty ran to the door to greet them. He eyed her mom with suspicion, then rubbed against Karli's ankles. He hadn't liked all the commotion when the medics came for Axel.

Mom smiled. "He looks like a feral cat to me."

Before Karli could answer, Ida and Sylvie came down the steps. They stopped and stared at their sister.

Sylvie's lips curved down as usual. "Hey, Donna, sounds like you've been livin' the good life."

Her mom eyed her warily. "I've been lucky. I married a wonderful man, and I have a good job and two great daughters."

"Ain't that nice?"

Mom's chin went up. "I bet you're happy for me."

As if . . . Karli didn't get it. What was with Sylvie? Her mom's happiness didn't cost her anything.

Ida waved a hand. "Your kid's spent a lot of her own, good money to fix this place up. Nice of her, isn't it? Did you teach her to be as wimpy as you were?"

What a bitch! Karli glared. Did Mom's siblings hate her? Resent her? Karli raised an eyebrow. "Screw you, Ida. What's the deal? Why are you picking on my mom?"

Sylvie snorted. "Because she's a weenie. She never stood up for herself."

"Why should she have to? Especially against her own sisters? Mom's only four years older than Ida. Was she mean to you or something?"

Ida flinched. "How would I know? I got out of here as fast as I could."

"You all did, but was Mom nice to you when you were little?"

"She was a kid. She couldn't make any difference."

"None of you could, so cut her some slack."

Sylvie raised a finger to point. "She doesn't need Dad's money. Why did she come?"

"Because I told her Axel was dying, and she wanted to see him before he was gone."

Ida looked genuinely confused. "Why?"

Mom answered. "Because he's our dad."

"So what?"

"A lot of time's passed. Things might be different now."

Sylvie barked a laugh. "You think the old goat turned nice? You haven't lived with him."

Kurt walked in from the back room to see what the commotion was. "Hey, Donna."

Ida sneered. "Donna cried when she saw how pretty the house is."

Mom locked gazes with her. "Maybe someone will buy the house that loves it."

Kurt looked out the windows at the fields that surrounded them. "More likely somebody will buy it for the property and let it fall apart."

Karli hadn't thought of that. Her stomach clenched. But Kurt was wrong. She shook her head. "Too many people came to help fix it, and there's a housing shortage around here. No one wants to see it turn back into rubble."

Sylvie walked to the refrigerator to get herself a beer. "You're just like your mama, too sentimental."

"Shut the hell up!"

They all turned to stare at her mom. Karli had never heard her mother curse before. Her jaw dropped.

Sylvie's eyes went round.

"That wasn't necessary," Ida hissed.

"Neither are you two." Mom squared her shoulders. "I'm not the girl you can push around anymore. Give me any more grief, and I'll tell Dad you're trying to have him put in a home."

"But we're not!" Kurt stared at her, upset.

Her mom shrugged. "Doesn't matter. Guess who he'll believe."

Sylvie threw back her head and laughed. "Little Donna grew a backbone! I think I like you better since you're a big girl."

"Who cares?" Her mom turned away from them and looked at Karli. "Where did you put me?"

Karli realized she'd made a mistake. Her mom wouldn't want to be near her siblings. "I cleaned a room upstairs, but I'm staying in the parlor."

"I bought a twin mattress when I heard how bad the house was. I'll put it in your room. I'm not sleeping anywhere close to them."

Karli glanced in their direction. "They blew it. I've been taking them in my stride. No more."

Kurt spread his hands by his sides. "I just said *hi.*"

True, but if push came to shove, he'd side with the evil twins. Karli narrowed her eyes at him. "You'd better be on your best behavior."

He grimaced. "What about supper?"

"You have lots of money. Eat out. No one touches the extras I bought for Axel, or so help me, you'll be at Art's grocery, buying your own food." Karli turned to show her mom to her room.

"Are they always like that?" Mom asked.

"They try to be pleasant if they think they can use you. They haven't given me too much grief." Karli showed her mom the parlor.

"Rose walls. They're beautiful." Mom sighed. "You've done a gorgeous job here."

"Thanks." Karli liked the way everything had turned out, too. They went to Mom's car, got the mattress, and placed it against the far wall. Then they shut the pocket doors and sat down to catch up with each other.

Chapter 40

On Sunday, since he wasn't going to his parents' house to eat and he couldn't take Karli to the forest and ravish her, Keagan went to his studio to finish as many orders as possible. If he kept busy, he wouldn't find himself wandering to Axel's place to see her. She'd said *I love you.* The words thrilled him and crushed him. Love might not be enough this time. How could he make her stay? But her mom was coming. He needed to leave her alone.

Shaping clay on his wheel took enough concentration, the time passed quickly. Then he moved to the glazing table, readying plates for the kiln. As usual, he ended up with splatters of clay and splotches of glaze on his old sweats, so he went home and changed into jeans and a sweater for his trip to Bloomington. Axel had called him, asking for something to read, so he stopped at Art's to grab a couple sports magazines and a *Field & Stream.* Tomorrow, he'd buy more at the cigar store in town. It had a huge selection of reading material.

Libby lived on the way out of town, so he decided to check on her, too. It was a gray, dreary day. The front of her Cape Cod was dark, but there was a light on in the back. He didn't think she went out much, so he was guessing she was home.

She opened the door on his third knock and blinked up at him. Pushing her glasses higher on her nose, she gave a shy smile. "I didn't really think you'd come."

"I told you I would, didn't I?"

Her cheeks turned scarlet and the blush spread to her hairline. "I thought you were just being nice."

"I don't want you to give up because you get discouraged, so I'm stopping every once in a while. Did you sign up for any classes?"

"They won't start until January." She opened the door a bit wider and motioned him inside. She was dressed in baggy jeans and an oversized sweater. Her thick, brown hair was in a messy knot. The sofa and coffee table were covered with sections of the Sunday paper.

"January's not that far away." He glanced to her well-lit kitchen. "Cooking?"

Her blush deepened. "I'm heating a frozen dinner." At his grimace, she asked, "Do you cook?"

"When I have to. I go out a lot, and my mom sends food home for me."

She wrinkled her nose. "My mom never cooked, didn't like to."

Keagan cocked his head to study her. "Your mom doesn't live in Mill Pond, does she?"

"No, she and my new step-father live in Bloomington."

He smiled. "So, if you sign up for classes there, you could stop to say *hi* to her sometimes."

"She's usually busy."

"I see." Keagan stopped to regroup. "But this is about you, not your mom. You need to sign up for a class before it fills up."

She pressed her lips together, unsure.

"Have you looked online to see what kind of photography classes are available?"

She looked away.

He leaned against the doorframe. "I'll let you off the hook this time, but I'll be back, so you'd better get busy."

"You don't have to coddle me, you know. I'm not your responsibility."

He shook his head. "I'm Mill Pond's mailman. I keep an eye on things, and now that you've caught my attention, I'll be watching out for you."

She raised her hand to salute him, then stopped herself. He chuckled. "That's good. You have a sense of humor. Get moving, though, or I'll tell Grams about you. She's Mill Pond's mover and shaker. If she takes you under her wing, you'll meet people whether you want to or not."

Libby looked horrified. She should be.

"You can do this. I like you. So will most everyone else." He walked to his SUV, then drove to the hospital in Bloomington.

When he got there, Sylvie and Ida were in the room with Axel. He hadn't expected them to come, but if Karli's mom drove all the way from Indy to see her dad, they probably felt like they had to. Karli had told him that she and Donna were planning on bringing Axel something for lunch. The old nuisance was already complaining about the hospital food. Keagan was guessing that Sylvie and Ida didn't want to be shown up.

It was cowardly, he knew, but he went down to the cafeteria to grab something to eat. He didn't want to see them. He was sitting at a table by himself when Kendall came to join him.

"Do you mind?" She had a plate full of nachos. They didn't look any more appealing than his sorry excuse for a burger. He couldn't blame Axel for complaining. Kendall smiled at the ketchup and mustard oozing from the sides of his bun. "No flavor, is there?"

"I didn't know food could be this boring."

"You've never eaten in a hospital before." She demolished a pile of chips. "Never got to stop for lunch today," she told him between bites.

He finished his burger and pushed his tray to the side.

She raised an eyebrow at him. "Can I ask you a personal question?"

Uh-oh. He braced himself. "Shoot."

"Is Brad seeing anyone?"

Relief! His roommate had claimed another girlie fan. "He's seeing lots of people."

"Anyone in particular?"

"Brad?" He couldn't hide his surprise.

Her expression brightened. "So he's not serious about any one woman?"

Keagan liked Kendall. He decided to give her fair warning. "Not Brad's style."

"Good, I'll have a clear playing field."

Keagan leaned forward to make his point. "As long as you're okay with just playing, you two will get along well. Brad doesn't believe in monogamy."

"We'll just have to test that out." She finished her food and stood. "I have to get back to my floor."

He stood, too. Hopefully, Sylvie and Ida would be gone by now. When he reached Axel's door, though, they were exiting his room. Sylvie cocked an eyebrow when she saw him.

"The white knight comes again. What's your angle?"

"Axel asked me to buy him some magazines and crossword puzzles to help him pass the time." He showed them to her.

Ida motioned to a book of devotions on Axel's rolling tray. "He should spend more time on those."

Yeah, right. Like that would happen.

Sylvie didn't give him time to answer. "Do you do everything Axel asks?"

She annoyed him, so he nodded. "Afraid so, that's why I became a serial killer. I dispose of anyone who aggravates him."

She stared, then her lips pulled back in a snarl. "You think you're clever, don't you? But I can see why Dad likes you. You're a good, little lapdog."

Keagan's humor took a hike. He gave her a hard look. "Not really, but I try to be a decent human being. You should try it sometime."

If looks could kill, he'd be dead. She stomped away. Exactly what he'd hoped for.

Chapter 41

The next day, after breakfast, Karli drove her mom to Bloomington again to see Axel. He was sitting up in bed, pillows propped behind him, and he looked pretty happy with himself.

"The doc says I can go home on Wednesday and have Thanksgiving with my family."

"He's happy with you?" Karli asked.

"As happy as he gets."

Karli nodded. He probably thought he'd done everything he could.

"Remember. You promised to make white bean chili and chocolate cake when I got back."

Karli raised an eyebrow. "Thursday's Thanksgiving. You're going to stuff yourself. Why not hold off on the cake?"

"I've earned it, girlie. I beat the Grim Reaper this round. I want my cake."

She looked at her mom and shrugged. "I said I'd make it, I will."

Axel grinned and leaned back with a sigh. "The nurses come in all night long, never let a body rest. I'm a little wiped out. Why don't you two go to town and buy the stuff to fix my homecoming meal?"

"Are you telling us to leave?" Her mom sounded amused.

Axel closed his eyes. "I'm an old man. I tire easily."

"What? There's no football on TV?" Karli knew his habits. He was probably just bored.

Mom laughed. "Good enough. Karli and I will go shopping today. It's time I see what Mill Pond is really like."

He opened one eye. "You could tell your sisters the doctor recommended no visitors tonight. I need to get strong enough to come home."

"You don't want to see them?"

"Do you?"

A fair question. "All you have to do is tell your nurse," Karli told him. "She won't let them in."

Mom shook her head. "I'll tell them. See you tomorrow, Dad."

"No need, just be here to pick me up on Wednesday."

Karli and her mom took the unsubtle hints and found themselves back in Mill Pond by lunchtime. They were both hungry.

"Want to try Joel's microbrewery?" Karli asked.

"Why not?"

After they got their food and sat down, people started stopping by to ask about Axel.

"It's been a long time since we've seen you," Buck Krieger said, taking a seat across from her mother.

Mom grinned at him. "You were ahead of me in school, but you were always nice to me."

"Someone had to be." He glanced at Karli's French fries and when she nodded, he took a few. "Your sister Sylvie was in a lot of my classes. Never met a more spiteful person. I thought your dad was the meanest man on earth, but Sylvie had a way of saying things that really hurt."

Her mom stole one of her fries, too. "She hasn't changed much."

Buck laughed. "Nice to know. I'll steer clear of her."

When Buck left, Iris Clinger stopped by, then Grams and Miguel sat and yakked for a while. When Karli finished her sausage sandwich and they started to leave, Mom got a faraway expression on her face, looking thoughtful. "I didn't believe you when you said how nice people are here, but you're right."

Her mom's compliment made Karli happy and proud. She'd grown to love Mill Pond and its people. She drove Mom to Main Street and found a place to park.

"You said people came for the national forest, but why are the shops so busy today?" Mom asked.

"People are picking up their holiday orders. Come on. I'll show you."

They stepped into Lefty's Jewelry Shop, and Karli showed her the polymer clay earrings and necklaces that Keagan's sister made. Mom had a thing about necklaces and bought one that had three painted leaves that fell at the base of her throat. They hit the Kitchen Goods shop next, and Mom bought a homemade white apron that tied around the waist and had a ruffled border of pumpkin pies and turkeys. Karli bought a table runner. Mom got three braided rugs at Cordelia's, and then they walked into Daphne's stained-glass shop.

Karli sighed. She was doomed. The line was so long at the counter, they had plenty of time to roam through each aisle. Plenty of time for her to find a stained-glass lamp that she loved, and a wall clock with deep greens edged against gold and bronze glass. She had to have them. They snagged two loaves of pumpkin bread at Maxwell's before they decided they'd better quit spending and go home.

"I didn't realize how many artists live in Mill Pond." Mom studied the scenery on the short drive to Axel's.

When they reached the farm, Karli popped her trunk and led Mom to the boxes pushed far to the back. Mom reached inside and lifted one of the plates wrapped in paper. When she peeled it back, her jaw dropped. She ran a finger over the snowflake pattern.

"Keagan's an artist," Karli explained.

"He made these?"

"He has some work on display at Art's Grocery. You love throwing dinner parties over the holidays. I thought you'd like these."

"They're beautiful." Mom's voice was reverent. Together, they moved the boxes to Mom's car.

They were hanging the wall clock in the parlor when Sylvie came downstairs. She stopped in the doorway to see it and laughed. "That's a lot of work for nothing, but whatever makes you happy."

They decided they wanted to stay in for supper, but they didn't want anything fancy.

They were cooking together, yakking away, when Kurt came to see what they were doing.

"Damn, that smells good."

Karli nodded toward five plates sitting on the worktable. "Hamburger gravy. It'll be ready in fifteen minutes. Mom just put the biscuits in the oven."

Sylvie and Ida came down, too.

"You're welcome to join us if you can be nice for half an hour while we eat."

"There are oranges and grapefruit in the refrigerator. Want me to make a fruit salad?" Ida asked.

"Sounds good." Ida could be tolerable when nothing was at stake.

"I can set the dining room table." Kurt went to the silverware drawer. Karli put a hand to her heart, shocked.

Sylvie got herself a beer and disappeared into the sun-room. Out of all of them, Sylvie was the hardest to work with.

During supper, Mom told them that Axel could come home on Wednesday.

"Whew! I was a little worried the doc would pressure him to go into a home," Ida said.

"I'm guessing Dad vetoed that." Mom reached for another biscuit.

After the meal, Mom shooed her siblings away. "Karli and I will clean up. It won't take much time."

All three of them started upstairs. Karli frowned at Kurt. "You're not watching TV tonight?"

"I bought myself a TV for my bedroom." He glanced sideways at Sylvie and Ida.

"Out of our money?" Sylvie demanded.

"Nope, it's all still in the tea canister."

Sylvie narrowed her eyes. "Where'd you get enough for a TV?"

"I had a little I was trying to hang on to. Figure I won't need it now."

With a nod, the sisters started up the steps. Kurt came to snag two more biscuits, then followed them.

Mom shook her head. "I brought some books to read. Do you have something?"

"I'm in the middle of an Agatha Christie. I'm set."

They finished work in the kitchen, then went to the parlor. Dusty jumped on the bed with Karli and her mom smiled. "That's one cute cat. It's going to come as a shock for him when he gets tossed in a barn."

Karli grimaced. "I'm taking him with me."

Mom laughed. "He looks like a keeper. Glad you found him."

While they read, Dusty's purrs filled the room.

Chapter 42

Mom looked at Axel's room and sighed. "Everything in here should be burned."

"I didn't dare do much when he was here."

Her mom smiled. "But he's not here now, is he?"

Karli stared. What had gotten into her mom? "What do you have in mind?"

Her mom grabbed the old, ratty drapes at the windows and gave a quick tug. They ripped apart. "These things are dead. Let's pitch them." Without the drapes, the room was almost cold. She yanked the blanket off Axel's bed and tossed it on the floor. The sheets and rubber-backed pad followed. "This room needs a redo.

Karli's heart squeezed in alarm, but Mom was right. She could imagine Axel's reaction, though, and cringed. Kurt, Ida, and Sylvie stayed out of their way while they stripped everything, cleaned the windows, and swept the indoor/outdoor carpet. Then they drove to the closest Target to buy everything new.

Once home again, they put the room back together. When they finished, her mom stood back and smiled. "It looks nice."

That was the problem. No more faded brown drapes. Instead, Mom had chosen white drapes with sage green leaves and little flowers. Not very manly. Karli was sure Axel would have plenty to say about them. "He's going to hate these," she told Mom.

Mom shrugged. "Then he should have paid for new ones."

At least the sheets and comforter were a solid color. Karli had insisted on sage green for those. She was afraid Axel would throw a flowered blanket at her. Mom had gotten her way and bought matching flowered cushions for the two rocking chairs on the porch.

When they were finished, the room looked and smelled nice. Everything was clean.

Karli had bought baby back ribs and put them in the oven while they worked. By the time she and Mom showered and changed, the ribs were fall apart tender. She slathered them with barbecue sauce and tested the baked potatoes she'd wrapped in foil. Ready to go. She'd bought a container of three-bean salad, and supper was complete.

Sylvie looked like she might burst with joy as they ate. "Dad's never goin' to forgive you, Donna. You've guaranteed that you'll be written out of the will."

"What will?" Mom scrunched her nose in disgust. "Dad's too lazy to make out a will."

Sylvie's lips pressed together in frustration. "He'll prob'ly scribble it on a piece of paper and have us sign it. You're doomed."

"Don't care." Mom licked her fingers. "It's been a long time since I've had ribs."

After supper, Mom stuck around to help Karli make the white bean chili soup for tomorrow.

"Why cook it tonight?" Ida asked. "You'll have plenty of time before Axel gets home."

"I promised him the soup and chocolate cake," Karli said.

Ida's eyes narrowed. "You're trying to win him over again."

"Don't be stupid," her mom snapped. "He asked her to make them. She didn't want to."

Ida thought a minute. "I'll make the cake. I love to bake."

Karli waved a hand. "Go for it. I stop at the bakery for my desserts."

Ida smiled and went to get her laptop. "I have a great recipe. Dad's going to love it."

Sylvie curled her fingers into fists. "What about me? All he does is grump about anythin' I do for him."

Karli went to the cupboard and tossed her two boxes of corn muffin mix. "I happen to know he loves cornbread."

They all got busy, and Kurt disappeared. A few minutes later, Axel's truck pulled out of the driveway. Maybe he was running to get Axel's favorite beer.

Later that night, the soup and cake were finished. The kitchen was clean, and Kurt returned with a new laptop.

This time, Sylvie's hands went to her hips. She went to the tea canister and counted the money inside it. All there. Then she stretched out her hand and said, "Show me your billfold."

"No." Kurt reached a hand to put over his back jeans pocket, but Ida beat him to it. She flipped the wallet open, pulled out a blue plastic card, and glared. "Dad had a credit card."

Kurt's face mottled with color. "I got here before either of you two showed up. I deserve more."

Sylvie leaned closer, and Karli worried she'd slap him, but instead, she hissed, "You've had your extra. Now give me the card."

"No." Mom's voice intervened. She went to a drawer, took out a pair of scissors, and held out her hand for the card.

Ida sighed, but handed it to her.

Mom cut it up. "There. That's done."

Kurt watched the pieces fall into the trash can, a forlorn look on his face.

"Well, might as well go to bed." Sylvie started up the steps and the others trailed behind.

Mom shook her head. "They haven't changed."

"You have." Karli gave her a quick hug. "You're stronger now."

Mom smiled, and while Karli fed Dusty, she went around the house, turning out lights. Once in their room, they sagged onto their mattresses and Mom laughed.

"We're the only ones without our own TVs," she said.

"I feel deprived." But Karli picked up her book, and Mom opened her laptop. They'd survive.

Chapter 43

After Keagan got off work on Wednesday, he brought Axel home. The women had obviously been cooking all day, getting things ready for Thanksgiving. Two pumpkin pies sat, cooling, on the wooden worktable. Karli was stuffing a turkey with quartered onions and oranges. Karli's mom was finishing a seven-layer salad. When Keagan wheeled Axel into the back room, his voice boomed, "What the hell happened in here?"

Sylvie's face crinkled in delight. She ran into the room. "Donna did it! She and Karli cleaned everything."

Donna and Karli came to stand in the doorway. Karli dried her hands on a kitchen towel and looked nervous.

Axel scowled at Donna. "This was *your* doing. What were you thinking?"

Donna raised her fingers. "First, this room smelled. No, it stank. I don't know how anyone could sit in here. Second, when was the last you cleaned it? The drapes fell apart when I was going to wash them. I'm surprised you could see out the windows. Third, if you're happy lying in urine, you need help. Fourth . . ."

Axel threw up his hands. "Never mind!"

Donna went on. "We put a new mattress topper on your bed that should make it more comfortable, and we bought new waterproof pads."

Keagan helped Axel onto his bed, and the old man blinked, surprised. Donna smiled. "Better?"

Axel breathed in the clean scent. "It's a good thing you didn't put some silly, flowered blanket on my bed."

"That's what Karli said, so we kept it plain."

He leaned back against fluffy, new pillows. "This isn't bad."

Donna shook her head. "Glad you're home. We've been cooking all day. Karli made your soup, Ida made a chocolate cake, and Sylvie made cornbread."

His eyes lit up. He looked at Keagan. "You staying for supper, boy?"

Keagan nodded. "Might as well." He looked at Karli. "Can you still make it to my family's for Thanksgiving?"

"She sure can." When Karli opened her mouth to protest, her mom shook her head. "We'll fix Dad a feast. The big stuff's already done. Karli's cooked enough." She looked at her daughter. "Get out of here tomorrow."

Karli smiled, and happiness flowed through Keagan. He'd been worried that things were so busy and muddled, he wouldn't get to see much of her before she left.

Karli nodded to Keagan. "Wheel the old coot into the dining room. Supper's ready."

She carried her Dutch oven to the table. Sylvie brought her cornbread, and Ida brought her cake. Keagan couldn't remember the last time he'd had a three-layered chocolate cake.

Axel let out a contented sigh. "If this was my last meal, I'd die happy."

Karli cringed. "Don't say that. You've got to stick around for Thanksgiving."

"Oh, I plan to. I love me a turkey, and Mom always made pumpkin pies."

They dug into their food, and supper was a success. Karli had made sure of that. What didn't Keagan like about her? Oh, yeah, the small matter of her moving away. That was a real downer.

Chapter 44

Karli and her mom got up early on Thanksgiving morning to put the turkey in the oven. Gray skies glowered outside, and tree branches whipped in the wind. The heat from the oven spread warmth that made its way to Axel's porch. They heard him give a small sigh and settle deeper into his pillows.

Ida came down, wrapped in her robe, to start cooking. Sylvie came, wearing a sweatshirt and a blanket wrapped around her waist. They meant to fill the dining room table for Axel. A feast. Karli played sous chef for anyone who needed her, since she was leaving to go to Keagan's.

When they heard Axel stirring in the back room, Karli took him a few slices of pumpkin bread.

She glanced at her mom. "You're going to be okay, aren't you? I feel bad leaving you with your family."

"We'll be fine today. We've called truce, and everyone's ready for a good meal."

Everyone did seem more jovial than usual, so when Keagan came and Karli ran to his SUV, she put her worries behind her to have fun. Keagan patted his stomach. "I didn't eat anything for breakfast to make room for gluttony."

He turned into his parents' driveway and parked near the front door. When he stepped in the house, Jenna and Jack attacked him. He smiled at Karli. "An uncle has to prove his worth."

Keagan's mom came to claim Karli. "Those kids are so wound up, Keagan's going to have his hands full. Come on out to the kitchen and have a glass of wine with Marcia and me."

Karli had brought wine and flowers. "Thanks for inviting me, Mrs. Monroe."

"None of that!" His mom tossed her hands. "You can call me Joyce. Someday . . ." She let it drop.

As they walked through the living room, Keagan's dad and Stuart looked up. "Hey, Karli!"

His mom took her hand and tugged her into the kitchen and offered her a glass of wine. "So, are you going to stay in Mill Pond a little longer to help Axel grow stronger?"

Marcia was putting the finishing touches on the turkey. "Mom, you couldn't be less subtle."

Joyce grimaced. "My son really likes you. I can tell. How do you feel about him?"

Marcia stared, but Karli didn't mind answering. "He's the most wonderful man I've ever met. I signed a contract in Indy, though. It starts the second week of December."

Joyce made a face. "Indy's not that far from here."

"Leave her alone, Mom. That's between her and Keagan." Marcia stuck two hot pads in front of her. "Grab a plate."

They each carried a dish to the table. The guys turned off the TV and Keagan led the kids into the dining room. They stood while Keagan's dad said the prayer, then they took their seats. Conversation flowed while they ate, and Karli found it easy to join in. She helped clear the table before dessert, and pressed a hand to her stomach. "I'm stuffed."

"You don't want to miss Mom's pumpkin roll," Keagan bragged.

His mom went to sit in the living room with his dad. "Let's take a little break first. Why don't you take her to the barn and show her the chickens? Let her work off a few calories and find a little space for dessert."

"I can do that." They bundled up, and Keagan took her hand to lead her past the garage to the back of the yard where the red barn sat. "Mom has a thing about specialty chickens," he told Karli. "She likes having different-sized eggs."

"Is that why some of the deviled eggs were big and some small?" Karli asked.

"Yeah, she gets a kick out of that." He cracked the big double doors and led her inside, then closed them against the wind. Leading her to a pen built on the side of the building, he gestured to a wide variety of chickens. Some gleamed a bright white and stood tall. Others had rusty-colored feathers, and a different breed's white feathers were laced with black. She gaped at a few with ruffled feet and a couple more with ruffled heads. There were all sizes from big to tiny.

"They can leave the barn and go into a large, fenced-in area outside to scratch in the dirt and grass. Mom throws them scraps, too," Keagan explained. "We close the door at night so no raccoons and foxes can get in, and they have plenty of perches to fly up to if they need them."

Karli had never thought about chicken safety before, but these hens looked happy to her. She motioned toward two big machines hunched in the barn's center. "Those things are huge."

Keagan smiled. "Dad has lots of acres to plow and care for."

The wind had blown his soft brown hair, mussing it on the walk over, and his cheeks were red. He looked as delicious as the food on his mom's table. Karli came to stand closer, and he wrapped his arms around her waist. She tilted her face up for a kiss. He immediately pulled her closer and lowered his head. His lips felt warm and inviting. She pressed harder, greedy for more.

A kid squealed close to the door and they separated. Soon, Jenna and Jack hurried inside.

Jenna's face fell. "Mom said you'd be kissing."

"Us? In a barn? It's too cold." Keagan laughed and dropped a kiss on Karli's cheek.

"Ugh." Jack turned his head.

Jenna was unimpressed. "That's not a real kiss."

Keagan raised an eyebrow. "Since when do you know about *real* kisses?"

"In the Disney movies, the prince always kisses the princess at the end."

Keagan sighed with relief. "All the chickens are in here today to stay out of the wind."

"We came to count them," Jack said.

Karli looked at the coop. "They keep moving round. It's going to be tricky."

"Help me." Jack took her hand.

The four of them had counted the chickens twice and gotten different numbers when someone clanged a bell. Keagan grinned. "Chow time. Let's get some dessert."

The wind had picked up when they rushed toward the house, their heads down and hands jammed in their pockets. Karli's curly hair sprang wildly, and she tried to pat it down. The table was ready, so they went to take their seats. A thick slice of pumpkin sponge cake, rolled around a creamy filling, lay on each plate. When Karli took a bite, she knew pumpkin nirvana. It was so rich and so lightweight, she wanted to lick her plate.

Keagan grinned. "Good, isn't it?"

"Delicious."

"It's easy," Joyce said. "I'll copy the recipe for you someday."

They sipped coffee before Keagan said, "The game's going to start soon. We're going to take off and let you guys do your thing."

His mom's eyes sparkled. "You always were a thoughtful boy."

His expression turned downright naughty. "Happy Thanksgiving, all. Everything was wonderful. Thanks."

"Get out of here." His dad teasingly waved him away.

Pulling out of the driveway, he gave the house one last glance. "My family's the best."

"They really are." Karli thought about her mom and dad. "Mine is, too, if you don't count the fringe."

He drove toward the national forest, and her body tensed with need. He glanced her way. "Is it still okay to stay out a while, or do you need to get back to your mom?"

"She doesn't expect me. She won't be happy if I cut my day short." That, and her libido would die of desperation if she didn't get laid.

"Good." He motioned to a blanket and a comforter on the back seat. "I thought we could do a little exploring."

"Great choice of words." She slid her hand to his thigh again. Taut. Muscular. She'd like to explore every centimeter of him.

He drove past massive oaks, young maple saplings, and beech trees before turning onto a small drive that wove to a rental cabin deep in the woods. This time of year, it sat empty, so he parked behind it where they'd be hidden from view. Then he flipped down the seats and spread the blanket over them. He turned to her. "I know what I'm thankful for this year."

Her breath caught. She'd had sex with a variety of men, but this was more than that. She'd had lust, fun, burning passion, and gentle friends with benefits, but no one had ever matched Keagan. She couldn't even imagine life without him, wouldn't let herself think about it. She stretched back and opened her arms. "Damn, you're special."

There was no rush this time. Their lovemaking was slow and tender, meaningful. She swore Keagan's hands touched every cell of her body, caressed every part of her. When they finished, she felt as if he'd claimed every inch of her, inside and out. She'd never felt so complete. She cradled next to him under the comforter, and it wouldn't have surprised her if her body had blended with his, they felt so much like one.

He took a deep breath. "I don't know if I'll ever find this again. It only happens with you."

She nodded, and he kissed the top of her head. She didn't want to lose him. "Would you wait for me?"

"How long?"

A fair question. "I signed up for thirteen weeks in Indy, then a hospital in Georgia said they'd sign me, but I don't have a contract yet."

He moved slightly, putting a little distance between them. "Are you going to sign?"

"I'd like to. It's great pay, and I'd be near the ocean. I've never spent time on the east coast before."

"You can't have it all, Karli. Everything's a choice."

And there it was. Her lifelong problem. She *wanted* it all.

"I'll wait for Indy, but not Georgia. After that, another job, another location will tempt you. I'd rather break it off when you leave, lick my wounds, and move on. That's what you'll be doing. You just won't admit it."

He didn't sugarcoat things. "I love you, Keagan."

He sighed. "I love you, too, but that doesn't mean we'll work." He sat up and moved to the front seat. He began pulling on clothes.

Karli squeezed her eyes shut. No matter what she chose, she was going to hurt when she finished caring for Axel. If she stayed, she'd wonder what adventures she'd miss. If she left . . . well, *if* she left, it would feel like her heart was ripped out of her. She started dressing, too.

Chapter 45

Keagan drove her home and dropped her at the door.

"Do you want to come in?" she asked.

"Not tonight."

They locked gazes. Finally, Keagan drove away. Pain settled inside her, a horrible ache. Would she see him again? When she entered the house, it was quiet. Dusty scampered to wind around her feet, and she bent to pet him. She glanced in the parlor. Mom was asleep with a fallen book on the floor. Turkey did that to you. If you sat down, you zonked out.

"Hey, girlie, I could use another slice of pumpkin pie!" Axel called from the back room.

She hung her coat on the coat rack and went to the kitchen to dish up his snack. When she carried it into him, he motioned for her to sit down.

"I thought Keagan would stop in a minute to say *hi* to me."

She shook her head. "He's had a busy week. He was ready to go home."

Axel's lips turned down. "You blew it, didn't you?"

She glared. "Did not."

"He left, didn't he? He likes you. Any fool can see that. What's the matter? Do you suck in bed?"

She gasped. "No one's ever complained."

"Then it's you. You just don't get it, do you? A Keagan only comes around once in a while. You either snag him, or someone else will."

"He's snagged, okay? So am I, but if I stay here, there's only one hospital close enough to work for, and it doesn't do any of the heavy-duty stuff I'm used to. Where's the challenge?"

"It's like that, is it?" He took a bite of pie, chewing it thoughtfully. "That's a tough call. No one can decide that for you. The good news is you've shaken the boy out of himself. He's over that silly filly Cecily. He's ready to move on."

"I'm glad I helped." *Not really.* If Keagan could have it all, why couldn't she?

Axel finished another bite and smiled. "You had good timing, too. One of the nurses who cared for me watched you two together, but was voting against you. He met a cute little bank teller friend of hers who ordered a special delivery just so she could flirt with Keagan."

Darkness spread inside her. What cute, little bank teller? Keagan hadn't mentioned her.

Axel finished his pie and handed her the empty plate. "Good job, girl! When you leave, you can both be happy. You'll have your job, and Keagan can help that shy, little teller until she catches him."

Karli raised an eyebrow. "Are you pushing my buttons?"

Axel reached for his remote and turned up the volume. "You've been fun to have around. There aren't many people I care about, but I'd like you and Keagan to be happy. Sounds like I don't need to worry about that." He turned to watch the TV.

Karli ground her teeth and stalked to the kitchen. Shows what the old man knew. She wasn't happy at all. She'd never been so confused.

She didn't want to wake her mom, so she grabbed her laptop and went into the living room to scroll through her e-mails and Facebook. She'd never spent any time in here, it was so close to Axel, but once she pulled her legs under her on the overstuffed sofa and turned on the table lamp, she basked in its golden glow. She looked around. This was a warm, inviting room. Dusty jumped up and coiled next to her. Pictures that Axel's mom must have picked out hung on the walls—landscapes and flowering gardens.

She kept herself distracted, so that she couldn't think about Keagan. She must have fallen asleep sometime because her neck ached in the early hours and she woke to rub it. Her laptop had gone into rest mode, so she switched it off and pushed it back farther on the cushions. Axel's TV was on, but he'd muted it. She tiptoed to the back room to check on him, and he was hunched up, as if cold. She tucked his blankets around him, and he stretched into a more comfortable position. Smiling, she quietly walked into the parlor and slipped into her own bed, Dusty curling next to her.

At 5:00 a.m., Dusty jerked up and stared at the doorway, his fur on end. Karli groggily glanced around the room, didn't see anything, and stroked his fur until he curled next to her again. At 9:00 a.m., Karli jerked awake, certain she'd overslept and it was late afternoon. Her night had been filled with strange dreams. She glanced at her mom's bed, and Mom was still asleep. Worrying about her dad and coming here must have drained her energy.

Karli slipped out of bed, but Mom's eyes opened and she smiled at her. "What time is it?" Mom asked.

"Nine fifteen."

Her mom shook her head. "After a snack for supper, I came in here to read, and that's the last thing I remember."

"All that turkey does a person in," Karli teased.

Mom pushed to her feet and they went to the kitchen together to start the coffee. Out of habit, Karli walked to the doorway to check on Axel. She frowned. Something was different, but she couldn't put her finger on it. She went to his bed and stared. Was he breathing? She reached for his wrist to check his pulse. *Oh shit.*

"Mom!"

Her mother came to the doorway.

Karli pressed her fingers to his neck. No carotid pulse either. "I think he's gone."

"What!" Her mother almost dropped her coffee cup.

Karli shook Axel's shoulder. "Axel! Wake up!"

Nothing.

She felt his forehead. Cold. Lifeless. She looked at her mom and shook her head.

Mom grabbed for the woodwork on the door to steady herself.

Karli tried to force herself to think. In the hospital, she'd push a code button or yell to her supervisor at the desk. What did you do at home? She reached for her cell phone and called Keagan.

"I'll call Sheriff Brickle. He'll send someone there soon. I'm in my mail truck, but I'll come as soon as I can."

Her shoulders relaxed. Keagan was coming. Everything would be all right.

Footsteps clattered on the stairs. The fab three came down in unison. Kurt held a hand to his head. "I'm feeling a little rough this morning."

"Who wouldn't after they finished a bottle of Jack Daniels?" Sylvie snarked.

Ida frowned at Karli. "You look a little rough, too. Need some aspirin?"

Karli blurted it out. "Axel's dead."

Kurt stared. "What do you mean? He ate two pieces of pie yesterday."

"He was awake when I got home," Karli said. "I talked to him for a while, and then I checked on him at two-thirty. The house was cold. He was fine then. He's gone now."

Sylvie raised her hands above her head and yelled, "Hallelujah! This place is ours!"

They rushed to the kitchen and took out bottles of beer and wine to celebrate. Mom's eyes filled with tears. Karli felt sick. Hands on her hips, she snapped, "Sheriff Brickle will be here soon. Who else comes when a person dies at home?"

They looked at each other, grinned, took their bottles, and headed upstairs. Karli had to rub her hands over her arms. They felt cold. How could anyone react like that to someone's death?

Mom started to the parlor. "We should get dressed before everyone gets here."

Karli nodded and tossed on clothes in record time. They'd both washed their faces and brushed their teeth before Brickle knocked on the door.

Karli went through her time frame again and Brickle stared at Axel's corpse. He sighed. "You gave him a great send-off. I hope you realize that. He'd gotten lonely and bitter, but Keagan said he sure enjoyed having you around."

Tears misted Karli's eyes, and she blinked them away. "That's all he'd let me do."

Brickle grinned. "Axel was one of Mill Pond's old-timers, a real character. You pushed him about as far as anyone could."

A hearse pulled into the driveway next. Two men with a gurney disappeared in the back room. Karli couldn't stay in the kitchen. She led the sheriff to the dining room.

Brickle took in his surroundings. "You've made the place look good."

What difference did it make now? Ida, Sylvie, and Kurt would sell it as fast as they could. She hoped the next people gave it the love it deserved.

Keagan, dressed in his uniform, came and pulled Karli straight into his arms. "Are you okay?"

She nodded. Burrowed against Keagan, she always felt better. He stayed with her until they'd carried Axel away and Brickle had left. They'd meet with the funeral director the next day and plan Axel's service and burial. After, there would be no more reason for Karli to stay in Mill Pond. Her job here was done.

Chapter 46

The next day, Karli woke to arguing. She pulled on a robe and stumbled into the kitchen.

The sun barely peeked above the horizon, and Sylvie, Ida, and Kurt were already wide awake, bickering with each other.

"I called for what's in the china cabinets first!" Ida claimed.

Sylvie pressed her hands on the wooden worktable, leaning forward. "Fine, you can have the china and silver if I get what's in the attic."

"What do want with antique bird cages and old mirrors and chairs?"

Karli frowned. "Have you two already gone through the attic?"

Sylvie ignored her. "Is it a deal?"

"Only if I get all the paintings in the house," Kurt said.

The arguing started all over again. Karli poured herself a cup of coffee and went to sit at the dining room table. She'd picked up a food magazine on their last shopping trip and was flipping through it when someone knocked on the door.

When she answered it, she recognized the man she'd seen leaving Axel's hospital room.

He smiled. "Good morning. I'm Everett Lansing from Bloomington. I'm Axel's lawyer. Brickle called me." He looked around. "Lovely home."

Karli couldn't hide her surprise. "Axel had a lawyer?"

Everett chuckled. "Axel and his wife came to me years ago to draw up a will. Didn't need one, but he was worried that if one of them died, their children would try to claim part of the property." He stopped to listen to the raised voices in the kitchen. "Now I can see why."

Karli nodded. Her mom walked out of the parlor, dressed, since she'd heard voices. Everett introduced himself to her.

Her mother smiled. "Would you care for some coffee? I could use a cup."

"I'd love some. Is everyone in the kitchen?"

"Yes." Karli led the way to Mom's siblings.

They hushed abruptly when they saw they had a visitor.

Everett accepted a mug of coffee and took a sip, then smiled. "Thank you. I drove here from Bloomington to make things simple and clear. No one is allowed to remove anything from the house until the will is read."

"When will that be?" Sylvie asked.

"After the graveside service. The funeral director's already informed me that Axel paid for a wooden box a few years ago and wants to be cremated. He insisted on no showings or readings. He just wants his ashes put in an urn and placed in the plot next to Eloise."

Karli smiled. She could see how that would please the old man. He didn't like being fussed over.

"Everything will be strictly private. Only family. Oh, and Keagan Monroe."

Sylvie's lips turned down. "He would invite Keagan."

Karli got sick of Sylvie sometimes! "Why wouldn't he? Keagan's helped him for years."

Kurt glanced at the calendar. "How soon can they burn him?"

The lawyer cleared his throat. "Amos, the funeral director, is seeing to that today."

"That fast?" Mom put a hand to her throat. "While he's alone with none of us there?"

"Axel specified that's what he'd like and to be buried next to Eloise as quickly as possible."

Karli blinked, slightly overwhelmed. Everything was happening so fast.

Everett paused, giving them a moment to catch up. "The director of the cemetery can bury the ashes tomorrow at one. After that, you can convene in my office." He handed them each a business card with his name and the address of his office in Bloomington.

Mom reached for Karli's hand, and Karli squeezed Mom's to comfort her.

"And we can't load nothin' in our cars ahead of time?" Sylvie asked.

"If you take so much as a salt shaker and I hear about it, you lose your inheritance."

Sylvie bit her bottom lip. Kurt and Ida nodded.

Everett gave a professional-looking smile. "Good. Now that you have all the information you need, there's really nothing more to do except to show up at the graveside tomorrow at one and then come to my office."

Karli hurried to ask, "Are we allowed to bring flowers?"

"What for?" Ida stared. "He'll be ashes by then, and no one will be there but us."

"Just a sign of remembrance," Karli said, defending herself.

Sylvie snorted. "Always wastin' your money."

But Everett looked pleased. "That would be nice." Then he gave a brief nod and left.

Karli had expected the bickering to stop, and it did. Each sibling grabbed for his laptop and started researching how much each thing in the house might be worth. She shook her head, and she and Mom got ready to drive to Neil and Sue-Ellen's florist shop to order flowers.

When they returned to the house, Keagan's mail truck was parked in the drive and he was carrying two casseroles to the door. Karli hurried to take one and Mom rushed to let him in.

Keagan motioned to the rectangular dish. "Mom sent a taco casserole. The deep, oval dish is from Tyne. Here." Keagan pulled a piece of paper from his pocket. "Salsa *verde* chicken with herbed cornmeal dumplings." He shook his head. "Fancy. I couldn't remember the name."

Karli smiled. "Thanks for both of them. They smell delicious. Do you want to stay for a quick lunch?"

He glanced to the kitchen where Sylvie, Ida, and Kurt were listing prices to each other. "No, I won't stay. I won't intrude on your grief."

Right. He couldn't stand the three grifters. She waved as he pulled away. She'd see him at Axel's service tomorrow.

Chapter 47

Karli and her mom woke and started packing. Karli had run to town yesterday to buy a cat carrier. She was taking Dusty with her. She hadn't seen a mouse since she got the cat, but Sylvie, Ida, and Kurt could figure out how to fight vermin on their own.

Karli hadn't brought a lot with her, so there wasn't a lot to tote to her car. She and her mom went through the motions. She felt numb. Couldn't concentrate. Keagan's dishes were already in her trunk, and she put her suitcases next to them. Mom helped her carry out the stained-glass lamp and wall clock. They even deflated their air mattresses and Karli stowed hers and the blankets she'd brought in the back seat of her Dodge. Once they left the lawyer's office, Mom planned to head back to Indy. Karli would grab Dusty and do the same.

She and Mom dressed in black slacks and sweaters, then decided to drive to Ralph's to eat. Karli was hungry, but had no desire to fix anything. It had been fun to cook meals for Axel, but she'd be damned if she'd cook for the fab three.

People nodded and offered sympathy when Jules led them to a table, but considerately left them alone. When they finished eating, they drove to the cemetery and arrived a few minutes before one. Keagan was already there, dressed in a charcoal-colored suit. Karli's mouth went dry. He looked good in a crisp, white shirt with its collar slightly open. Two big flower arrangements bordered the family headstone.

"One from my family," Keagan said, "and the other from you two."

* * * *

He glanced at her car, saw the bedding on the back seat, and his lips pressed in a tight line. "So as soon as the day's done, you're out of here?"

"I can't stay in that house with Sylvie, Ida, and Kurt. I just can't do it."

"I couldn't either. They'll be gloating and arguing over who gets what." She took his hand. "You could drive to Indy to see me."

"When do you start your new job?"

"Not for another week. If you come, you could stay at my apartment and I'd show you the sights."

"That would be nice. We could say our goodbyes." She could see the pain in his eyes.

She wanted to kick herself. She'd hurt the nicest man she'd ever met. "Are you all right?"

He took a deep breath. "This is why I swore off anything temporary. It always hurts when it ends. This is worse than losing Cecily."

Her heart clenched. She was suffering, too. She didn't want a goodbye. She wanted Keagan. She glanced away, trying to regain her composure. Her mom was studying her, her expression pinched.

A car door slammed, and Sylvie, Ida, and Kurt walked toward them, dressed in jeans and old shirts. Karli's fingers curled into her palms. "Couldn't you have dressed up a little?"

"What for?" Sylvie shrugged. "It's not like Dad's gonna see us."

A man in a dark suit walked toward them and nodded to an employee ready to lower Axel's ashes into the ground. "Are you ready? Does anyone want to say anything before he turns on the machine?"

Mom blew a kiss at the urn. "Farewell, Dad."

Karli took a deep breath and pressed her fingers to her throat. Keagan put his hand on her upper arm and gave it a gentle squeeze. The whole thing took less than fifteen minutes, and then Keagan invited Mom and Karli to ride with him to Bloomington.

Kurt loaded Sylvie and Ida into Axel's truck and left before them.

No one talked on the ride. Karli's thoughts were too jumbled. How could she have grown to like a mean old man? And how did she fall in love with Keagan?

The lawyer's office was in a three-story brick building on the top floor. Once they entered the vestibule, his secretary showed them into his office. "He's expecting you."

Directly in front of them, Everett Lansing sat behind a huge, mahogany desk. In front of it, six green leather chairs were lined in a semi-circle. A long sofa huddled in front of a floor to ceiling bookcase on one side of the room. A fireplace occupied the opposite side. The room was elegant and understated.

Everett motioned for them to take seats. Sylvie, Ida, and Kurt sat next to each other on one side. Keagan, Karli, and Mom sat on the other. Everett quirked a brow and smiled. "Axel's will is simple and to the point. He was of sound mind when he signed it, so there's no room to contest it. Axel cashed in his stocks and bonds, which he bought when he was a young man, and he's dividing the one hundred fifty thousand dollars equally between Sylvie Dalton, Kurt Crupe, and Ida Mendolls, since they came when he asked them to. From his savings, he's declared each of his twelve children will receive ten thousand dollars."

Karli couldn't believe it. The old man was rich and lived like a pauper.

"And the house and property?" Sylvie demanded.

Everett looked at Keagan. "Everything else goes to Keagan Monroe on the condition that he lives there for one year with Karli Redding."

Karli gasped. Had she heard right? She could feel her cheeks burn and glanced at Keagan. "Can Axel do that?"

Everett glanced at the papers on his desk. "He could and did." He looked at Keagan. "Axel said you're a stubborn, young man. Will you abide by his terms?"

Keagan's cobalt-blue eyes lingered on Karli, but his lips lifted in a smile. "If I have to, I have to, but what if she says *no*?"

"Then you lose it all."

Karli bit her bottom lip. Keagan loved that house as much as she did. She wouldn't take it away from him. What the hell was she was thinking? Why would she leave a house she loved and a man she was crazy about? She raised an eyebrow. "Axel only forced Keagan to stay with me one year?"

Everett chuckled. "Axel said if you couldn't catch him by then, you weren't half the girl he thought you were."

Karli looked smug. "It won't take that long."

The lawyer laughed and folded his papers. "In that case, Axel's will is settled."

"That's not fair!" Sylvie stood over Everett's desk, glaring at him.

The lawyer's voice turned soft, but menacing. "If you want to dispute this will, be warned, Axel said to make it iron-clad, and if the judge rules against you, any legal action of yours and my clients will come out of your pocket."

"The old bastard." She turned on her heels and stalked to the door. Kurt and Ida followed.

Kurt stopped and turned. "When will we get our money?"

"My secretary has a check for sixty thousand dollars for each of you, if you stop at her desk."

The three left the room, their expressions set and angry.

Karli's mom looked from Karli to Keagan and back again. "You two are going to share Dad's house?"

"We sure are." Keagan pulled Karli into his arms and kissed her thoroughly. "And that house is going to be filled with love again."

Her mom hugged herself, and Everett cleared his throat. "Go home and be happy."

Holding Karli's hand, Keagan led her out of the office. Her mom followed with a glow on her face.

Once the door closed behind them, Mom asked, "This is sort of sudden, isn't it?"

Karli shook her head. "I love him, Mom. I can't leave him."

The secretary smiled. "I'm so happy for them. Everyone's heard that Mill Pond has a way about it. Those two were meant for each other."

Mom gave a slow nod. "I believe you're right."

Chapter 48

When they reached the house, Kurt's old, rusted car sat near the barn and Axel's pickup was gone. Sylvie and Ida's cars were gone, too, along with all of the fine china and silverware, every picture on the wall, and anything else they could tote with them.

Keagan shrugged. "I don't care. Do you, Karli?"

She shook her head. "I want to make this house ours."

"Ours." He tasted the word and liked it. "Will this work for you? I know you didn't want me to lose the house, but what about your job in Indy? I don't want you to lose something you love because of me."

She went to wrap her arms around his waist. "Silly. Nothing's more important than you. Besides, I have an apartment in Indy. I'll stay there and work three-day shifts, then I'll come home to you and Dusty. Will that bother you?"

He raised his hand to touch her cheek. "Not as long as you're mine. Marry me, Karli."

"Yes!"

Tears streamed down her mom's cheeks. Karli turned to her, but Mom waved for her to stay with Keagan. "Tears of joy," Mom said. "I'm so happy for you!"

Karli glanced out the window across the field to Keagan's parents' house in the distance. "Do you have to take care of a hundred acres now?"

Keagan chuckled. "My dad and Stuart will farm them, if we can afford to keep them. We might have to sell part off to pay for the taxes, but we'll keep a big yard for ourselves and I'll make the barn into a studio."

"Which bedroom do you want upstairs?" she asked.

She'd caught him by surprise. "Um, I don't know. Why?"

"Because I'm sleeping wherever you are."

He liked the sound of that! "In that case, Brad and I will move my bed so that it's here tonight."

Her mom sighed. "You know, I dreaded coming here when Keagan called me about Dad, but look how well it worked out! I'm going home to tell your dad. Congratulations!" She wrapped them both in a quick hug and left.

Alone, Keagan looked around the house, then looked down at Karli. "Axel's made me a happy man."

"He's made us both happy. Now kiss me." She tilted her head toward his lips.

"Glad to oblige." There was no bed in this house he wanted to lie on, but there was a couch in the living room. And later, much later, he'd coerce Brad to help him bring his bed and clothing over. Brad could keep the furniture for the apartment, so it wouldn't take long for him to settle in here. With Karli. For keeps.

ABOUT THE AUTHOR

Judi Lynn received a master's degree from Indiana University as an elementary school teacher after attending the Fort Wayne campus. She taught 1st, 2nd, and 4th grades for six years before having her two daughters. She loves gardening, cooking, and trying new recipes. Readers can visit her website at www.judithpostswritingmusings.com and her blog, writingmusings.com.

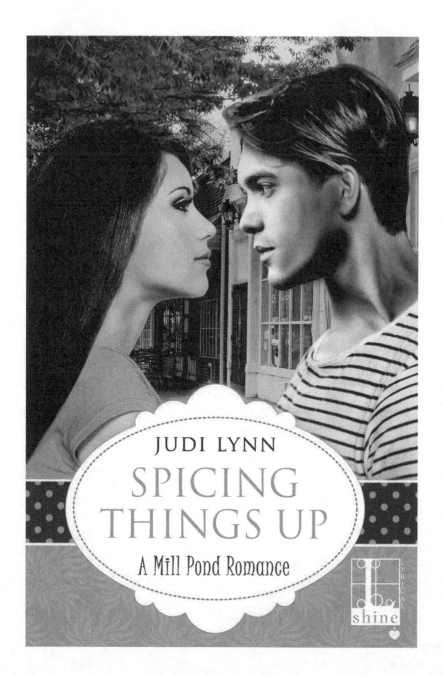

JUDI LYNN

SPICING
THINGS UP

A Mill Pond Romance

shine

JUDI LYNN

FIRST KISS,
ON THE HOUSE

A Mill Pond Romance

shine

Printed in the United States
by Baker & Taylor Publisher Services